ONE ENCHANTED EVENING

BY CRYSTAL INMAN

© INMAN BOOKS 2025

2ND (REVISED) EDITION

ALL RIGHTS RESERVED

INMAN BOOKS

INFINITE POSSIBILITIES

Dearest readers,

Fairy Tales are my jam. Well, those and Stephen King stories. Every year, I would receive a fairy tale book and a Stephen King hardback for Christmas.

Then I'd hole up in my room and wallow in the words.

Fairy tales are a special magic. An enchanting magic. And while not all fairy tales are happily-ever-after, full immersion still applies.

I've read fairy tales of different cultures. Myths and legends. The Brothers Grimm. World mythology. Aesop's Fables. Folk tales and legends. Anything I can absorb.

Our girl, Ivy? She has burnout, sibling fatigue, and is completely overwhelmed. But maybe, just maybe, this woefully unprepared witty woman is precisely what the fairy tale world needs.

The veil is thin, the stakes are high, and Ivy is so not prepared.

Happy reading!

Crystal*

10/4/25

Chapter 1

The gilded invitation slid through Ivy's mail slot soundlessly and billowed to the wood floor. She frowned and picked it up. Her fingers traced over her name in large gold letters on the front of the envelope, and she smiled. Someone had class at least. No advertiser she knew of would spend so much money trying to hook a client.

Ivy kicked her shoes off and padded to the kitchen in her socks. Work had been excessively long, and she needed a little break from the madness. The rest of the mail from the week lay on her wooden kitchen table, and she thumbed through it. Electric bill. Letter from her sister. A catalog. And two circulars. She would read the letter from Rose later. Her nerves couldn't take it right now.

Her sister probably dying from something or other. Ivy sighed. What a tacky thought. The simple fact was that Rose was a hypochondriac. Anything and everything could set her off in hysterics. The time they were children and their father found a tick on her. Afterwards, she was terrified for a week that she would die. Ivy rolled her eyes and tried to remain as far away as possible. And the condition seemed to worsen with age. It really went downhill when their parents died. Rose seemed scared of her own shadow.

Ivy tried at first. But then it seemed easier to let her sister spiral down into whatever state she was in. Rose was more than happy to stay in bed every day and watch television. Ivy would slit her wrists with the remote control. *Who could live like that?*

She turned her sister's letter over and over again in her hands. Today was Friday. If she waited until Sunday to call, she could make up an excuse about having to do something or be somewhere.

Rose wrote. Ivy called. It was another dynamic difference in their personalities.

Ivy dealt with people face-to-face all day long. Her job as a clerk at the police department meant she constantly typed, copied, and served the public. And she liked it. But she still didn't understand, even after eleven years, why Fridays were the days from hell. One would think the opposite would be true. Just a small slide into the weekend.

Like hell. Ivy grimaced.

The day began with the copier freaking out. Its beady little buttons told her there was a paper jam. She looked and looked. No paper jam. But the sorry piece of work still wouldn't function. Then the "add toner" light came on. Ivy gave it a swift kick when no one was looking. That light went off eventually, and the "service" light came on. She blew her wispy brown bangs back and took a defensive stance.

After looking at the four-inch-high stack of papers that needed copying, she promptly enlisted one of the secretarial aides to the chief of police to help her. Ivy sent the girl upstairs to do all the copying so they could pass out police reports and file everything. Then, the parade started.

People lined up at the window to ask for their police reports. Or to file a report. Or to talk to a police officer. Ivy needed to sort through the documents and put them in everybody's mailboxes. And still no break. Right in the middle of trying to figure out what in the hell a little old lady wanted, the phone rang.

The copier upstairs wasn't working either. Ivy pressed two fingers to her aching skull and ordered the assistant to take the papers to the courthouse to finish the copies. She then threatened to dismember the girl if even one piece of paper was left over there. Ivy was pretty sure she made her point.

The police officers switched shifts and meandered through her office. She glared at the first greeting, and the half a dozen men promptly snagged a couple of donuts and left. Missy, one of the female officers, stayed behind.

"Problems?"

Ivy turned and scowled. "Give me your damn gun. I need to put something out of its misery."

Missy bit her lip to keep from laughing. "I take it that all is not well?"

"Listen, woman." Ivy put her hands on her hips. "If you're going to laugh, you can take your happy ass to your police car and start your day. And if you don't have a bullet to spare for me, then we have nothing left to discuss."

The officer took a bite of the donut. "Copier again?"

"Hell yes!" Ivy kicked the offensive machine once more for good measure. She narrowed her brown eyes and peered down at it. "It's evil, I tell you. Pure, unadulterated evil."

"Um, yeah." Missy moved closer and pressed the buttons. She slid the trays open and shut. Her blonde ponytail swung side to side while she checked out the crevices of the copier.

"Here's your problem." She slid out the bottom tray and reached up under the machine. She pulled a piece of paper out the side of an index card. Missy stood and dropped the paper into Ivy's hand. When she saw the look on Ivy's face, she backed up quickly and headed for the door.

"No thanks is necessary!" she shouted over her shoulder.

Ivy recalled the day becoming a little more tolerable after the copier debacle. And Missy had been wise enough to not show her face in the office again. Ivy looked down at the envelope she held in her hand. Her fingers traced the letters of their own accord. *It really was beautiful.*

Ivy slid her fingers below the flap and opened it. A small smattering of fine gold powder spilled out onto the top of her table, and she touched it with the tip of her right index finger. She rubbed her thumb across it slowly. It was soft and fine as silk. Even more intrigued, Ivy pulled the card out and read it in mounting disbelief.

You are invited to join us for One Enchanted Evening. You are receiving this invitation because of your love of Fairy Tales, Magic, and the Unexplainable. There will be a dance and mixer for all attendees. The theme will be "A Taste of Magic."

Ivy flipped the invitation over and read the back.

Ivy, if you do not have anything to wear, don't worry. A little of this dust in the envelope will do the trick. Touch it and make a wish. Looking forward to your presence. The Charmed Committee.

She shook her head once to clear the cobwebs and then once again to reread the message. Someone was playing a joke on her, and she didn't care for it one little bit. So she loved fairy tales. *So what? Who knew that and would exploit it?* Ivy set her jaw as she wandered through her mental lists. Well, whoever it was would be in for a large disappointment. The whole idea ludicrous.

Ivy slid the invitation back into the envelope and tried not to think about the words or the feelings they inspired. She was too old for fairy tales now. Too old to believe in happily-ever-after. She hesitantly slid the invitation out again and turned it over. Her jaw dropped.

Ivy, please come. We would be most delighted to have you. A bit of gold dust, and you'll be ready. A carriage will arrive to pick you up at seven o'clock Saturday evening.

"Holy shit." Her nerveless fingers dropped the invitation, and it billowed gently down on the table. Her dark brown eyes huge in her face.

She slid the invitation back into the envelope again and then out. The words didn't change. Ivy blew out a shaky breath. It had been a long day. She was seeing things. Invitations didn't change. Words didn't move.

Ivy stood up and stepped back from the table. She pulled her shoulder-length chestnut hair up into a loose ponytail and looked for food. Someone's idea of a joke was not what she needed at the end of this interminable day. Those people could get their jollies by harassing other people. She wasn't playing.

She slammed a few cabinets before realizing she was low on the groceries. *Why did Friday have to be such a pain in the ass?* She should be relaxing right now. Planning her weekend.

Ivy's brown eyes skittered back to the mysterious invitation. *Interesting.* She picked it up again and slid the invitation out. The fine powder coated the tip of her index finger.

She was a realist. Pragmatic. So why was she rubbing gold glitter and pondering making a wish? Ivy stiffened her backbone and closed her eyes. *What the hell?* She brought one of her favorite fairy tales to mind and then opened her eyes. Nothing had changed.

"I'm so stupid," she muttered. Ivy reached down and started to tuck the invitation back into the envelope again when she paused in mid-reach.

A bright crimson cape covered her bare arm. She shrieked and brought her hand to her mouth. "Holy shit," she muttered. Ivy backed up slowly until her spine hit the wall. She flinched and tried not to scream. Her head dropped down to look at the outfit she wore.

Little Red Riding Hood's crimson cape billowed about her body. When Ivy stuck one leg out, she noticed a black boot encased her foot. She brought her left hand up and saw a brown, wicker basket hanging on her arm.

"I'm dreaming," she muttered. "I feel asleep on the couch, and I'm dreaming."

Ivy parted her red cape and looked down at what she wore. She sported a white peasant blouse covered with a black, leather, cinch corset. Her ample bosom was pushed up and framed perfectly with the device. The corset tapered off into a short miniskirt that matched her crimson cape.

"Whoa," she whispered. Ivy rubbed the fabric of her cape between her fingers. The velvet felt heavenly against her hand. She brought her hands up slowly and touched her chestnut hair. There were two short braids that fell on each side of her head. Ivy walked slowly into the hallway and stared at her reflection.

She was the mirror image of one of her favorite fairy tales. Little Red Riding Hood come to life. Ivy bit her lip and put the basket down. Gradually she reached out and touched the cool glass. It left a small smudge on the right corner.

"I'm not dreaming." The words sprang from her mouth before she could stop them. Ivy brought her hand back and pulled at the impossibly perfect braids that framed her face. Her dark brown eyes narrowed thoughtfully. If she wasn't dreaming, then what was happening? She was fairly mentally stable. This wasn't a delusion. Or hallucination. It was reality.

Ivy closed her eyes and blew out a slow breath. "Turn me back," she ordered. She counted to sixty and then opened her eyes. The mirror now reflected her normal appearance. Her hands shook slightly as she touched the cool glass again. Her fingers left a small smudge next to the first one.

"Oh shit." Ivy's legs weakened as she moved back into the kitchen. Her eyes didn't see anything but the invitation sitting in a small pool of gold powder. She sank into the chair and shook her head. *Magic. Fairy dust. Little Red Riding Hood. What in the hell was happening?*

She was an adult. No longer a child who believed in happy endings. Optimism waned as years mounted and her prince didn't show up to rescue her from painful relationships and substandard living arrangements. No fairy godmother whipped a wand around and let her go to the ball.

11

Ivy eyed the invitation distrustfully and stood up. She was hungry. She was going to the grocery store. A little space and perspective would do wonders for her. Or at least she hoped it would.

* * * *

Ivy drove to the grocery store with her mind a million miles away. As her fingers drummed on the steering wheel with the song on the radio, all she could see in her mind's eye was Little Red Riding Hood.

Ivy's practical mind dissected the problem. She was overtired. It was all a small misunderstanding with her brain. Or maybe the gold powder was a hallucinogenic. Absorbed through her fingers. Or perhaps the seal on the envelope.

But her dreamer's mind clung to the fact that she actually changed into Little Red Riding Hood. And it wouldn't let go. No matter how hard her practical mind tried to wrestle the notion away.

Ivy parked and walked purposefully toward the grocer's doors. Maybe she was overly hungry and feeling faint. That must have brought on the vision.

She pulled a cart out of the line and scowled. The store was packed with people buying food and drinks for the weekend. Several young adults packed the alcohol aisle and jostled each other to find the best buy on beer. The chips aisle was the same.

Ivy frowned and thought about the date. It wasn't a Super Bowl weekend. No Final Four. Nothing special at all. How odd. She

12

pushed her cart through the crowds with her apologies and caught a small snippet of a conversation.

"…going to be the coolest thing you've ever seen."

"We're having the whole gang over. And Mark promised to cook his famous ribs."

"The watch party is going to be huge!"

Ivy sighed but couldn't help herself. She tapped one of the young men's arms. "Excuse me."

"Yeah?" He turned and smiled down at her.

"What are you talking about?"

His blue eyes widened in his face. "Lady. You're kidding. You don't know what's happening tomorrow night?"

"Sorry." Ivy shrugged her shoulders. "What's happening?"

"A meteor shower. And a lunar eclipse." His grin exploded. "All in one night!" The young man's fist pumped in the air. "Let the party begin."

"Thanks." Ivy turned around wandered back down the aisle. She shook her head. Apparently, most of the young people were gathering to watch the sky. It ought to be quite a show.

Ivy sighed and picked up a bag of sour cream and onion chips. She looked down at her ample curves and grimaced. Maybe she ought to buy the baked ones. It seriously couldn't hurt matters. She popped the baked bag of chips into her cart and walked toward the lunch meat.

When she finished shopping, Ivy loaded the groceries into her car and glanced up at the sky. It should be a spectacular show tomorrow night. *The night of the party*. She groaned and parked the cart. Couldn't even get away from the thought for half an hour. It haunted her.

She hopped into her car and drove home quickly. After unloading the groceries, she looked down at her kitchen table again and swore. Ivy bit her lip and swept the gold powder back into the envelope and left it there. She would eat first and deal with the supernatural later.

Ivy made a turkey sandwich and popped some baked chips on her plate. She walked back into the living room and sat down on her worn brown couch. It was threadbare in places, but she couldn't bear to part with it. She and the couch had been through two bad boyfriends and three places to live. They were attached.

The light from the almost full moon filtered through her back patio and lit part of her living room. Ivy turned on the television and idly thumbed through several channels. Even with close to two hundred choices, she didn't ever find much to watch. She took a bite of her sandwich and cocked her head to the side.

Who would have sent her an invitation? *A magical invitation*, her inner voice reminded her.

"Shut up," she snapped. That part bothered her beyond belief. When she was a young girl, she often imagined such things occurring. But now that it seemingly had, she questioned all of it.

14

The bloom was off the rose, so to speak. *And who in their right mind would accept any of this at face value?*

Ivy ate her sandwich and didn't taste a bite. She grimaced and turned off the television. She stiffened her backbone and marched back into the kitchen. There were only a couple ways to deal with this. Accept it or reject it. Her fingers traced over her name one more time, and she allowed herself a small smile. Maybe she should just go. And if it was someone's idea of a practical joke, she could leave.

But what if it wasn't?

* * * *

Cybele glanced into the looking glass and noted the acceptances. As soon as the mortals made their decision, the notification appeared in her mirror. She frowned darkly at the next note that appeared. Ivy Daniels was pondering not going. That was an impossibility. They waited for years for the perfect time to invite her. *The mortal had to come!*

Freya looked up from her computer at Cybele. "What's wrong?"

"This!" Cybele brought the glass over and pointed at it. Her crimson nail poked accusingly at the notation. "Ivy Daniels might not come."

"What?" Freya shot up and snatched the mirror away. "Damn it! This is not acceptable. We've waited so long to get her. What is she thinking?" Her blonde hair billowed about her shoulders while she paced. "We have to fix this."

15

Isis carried a big brown box into the room and set it down carefully. "The fairies finally decided to help out. I swear, I don't know what they were thinking. Last minute drives me insane."

"We've got problems." Cybele held out the mirror and watched as Isis scanned the words.

"Hell in a handbasket, women!" Isis shoved her long black hair out of her face and read further down. "Did you handle the invitation correctly?"

"I've been doing this for years." Cybele narrowed her eyes. "And I don't care for the insinuation."

"Simmer." Freya stood between them. "We're not losing this woman." She tilted her head to the side. "We'll simply have to be more persuasive."

Cybele frowned. "You're not sending Adonis, are you? That's hardly fair." She adjusted her ebony hair and sighed. Her almond-shaped eyes narrowed. "Besides, last time we couldn't get the mortal to leave him alone at the party. He's not going to be pleased."

"He owes me one." Freya tossed her blonde hair and grinned wickedly. "Details not provided."

"Oh hell." Isis thumped her hand on the box. "You best watch what you're doing."

"What could go wrong?" Freya's blue eyes danced. "No mortal stands a chance against him. Few Goddesses do."

"You would know," Cybele snickered.

"Children." Isis sighed. "We have a party to put on in less than twenty-four hours. Now get back to work."

* * * *

Ivy went to bed Friday evening with so many things on her mind, it was a small wonder she could sleep. And it all stemmed from the beautiful invitation that could change her into Little Red Riding Hood. She tossed and turned for an hour before she slid into slumber.

Saturday morning was no better. Ivy stumbled out of bed around nine o'clock and pulled her brown hair back into a ponytail. She slid on some kitty slippers and shuffled to the kitchen. Her brown eyes blinked owlishly in the light, and she grimaced. Mornings sucked. And that hadn't changed since she was a child.

Ivy took down a white cereal bowl and flipped through her cereal boxes until she found the one with the most sugar content. She poured the cereal to the top and pillaged the fridge for the milk. It was, of course, in the very back.

Her hands shook slightly as she poured the milk onto her sugary breakfast. Ivy sank into a chair and propped her head up with her right hand while her left spooned the cereal into her mouth.

The day stretched out before her with endless possibilities. Unfortunately for her, she couldn't think of one right this minute. Ivy finished her cereal and put the bowl in the sink. She yawned hugely and walked into the living room. She'd read the paper first and then go run errands or something.

The engraved invitation called to her from the table by the couch. She ignored it. Too early to think. Too early to face the magic this morning.

When the knock sounded, Ivy was a foot away from the front door. She stumbled back a step and held her hand to her chest. Her heart beat frantically. She never had visitors. And certainly not this early.

She moved closer and looked for something to defend herself with. Working at the police station taught her to be careful at all times. Her hand closed around an umbrella, and she pasted a smile on her face.

Ivy swung the door open, and the smile slid off her face. Her hand loosened on the umbrella, and it dropped with a thump on the wood floor.

The bronze man stood there with an easy smile and inquiring blue eyes. His face was perfection. Every curve. Every line. Chiseled. And then Ivy's eyes traveled lower and felt her heart began to race in an entirely different way. The man's muscles were clearly outlined in the white T-shirt and jeans he sported. She looked up again and tried to form a thought.

"Ivy Daniels?" The man's voice washed over her skin, and she bit her lip to keep from sighing. No man's voice should evoke wanton thoughts like the ones she entertained right this moment.

"Yes?" Her voice rasped, and she cleared her throat. "May I help you?"

"Did you receive an invitation?" He held up an invitation like the one she had on her living room table. A. Donis was clearly engraved on the front.

Ivy frowned. "How did you know?"

He flipped the invitation over, and Ivy saw her address. "I thought maybe you would know something about this."

"I don't know a thing." Ivy bit her lip. "Did you touch the gold powder?"

"No." The man's blue eyes twinkled. "Something I should know about?"

"Be careful what you wish for," Ivy said cryptically. She held out her hand and cringed as she realized she was still in her faded, fairy pajamas. Hundreds of fairies with wands out zipped along the fabric of her clothes, and Ivy blushed.

The man placed the invitation in her hand, brushing against her. Ivy fought the urge to orgasm and steadied herself.

"You have no idea where this came from?" Ivy's brown eyes studied his invitation.

He shrugged. "Strange things happen sometimes." He studied her. "Are you going?"

"I don't know." Ivy sighed. "It's rather disconcerting. I gave up fairy tales long ago."

"Did you?" The man reached out and skimmed the arm of her pajamas with his finger. "You appear to be covered in fairies."

"Oh hell," Ivy muttered. She handed the invitation back.

19

"Are you going to go?" The man's voice softened. "It would be nice to see you there." His blue eyes moved over her face.

"Maybe," Ivy conceded. "Just maybe." She shook her head. "It's been pleasant. But I have errands to run. Nice to meet you."

The man winked at her. "My pleasure." He turned and walked down the sidewalk.

Ivy shamelessly watched his muscles flex with every step. Mostly his ass. *Oh my.* She fanned herself. *He was perfection.* She shut the door as soon as he faded from sight. Now what was she going to do?

* * * *

Adonis strolled into the party central room and grinned at Freya. Cybele rolled her eyes, and Isis strode over and planted herself directly between him and Freya.

"Did you get her?"

"Good grief!" Adonis held up his hands and shook his head. "She's a tough nut. Are you sure she's meant to be here?"

Isis plucked a scroll out of thin air and unrolled it. "We should have had her here ten years ago." Her finger tapped the parchment. "But things happened. Timing problems. It's been a cluster."

He blew out a breath. "Listen. I did my best. Other than throwing her on the floor and having my way with her. And even then, who knows?"

"Hardheaded." Isis scowled down at the name. "I knew we waited too long."

"Maybe not." Cybele brought out her looking glass and scrolled until she reached Ivy's name. "She's considering it. And right now, that's all we can hope."

* * * *

Ivy scowled as she dusted. Her mind was cluttered with thoughts of hot men, fairy dust, and engraved invitations. It was driving her mad. *It was only a damn party. And it might be fun.* And what else was she doing this evening? *Not a damn thing.*

She glanced at the clock on the wall. It was almost six. She had to decide whether she was going or not. And not a lot of time was left.

Ivy walked around to the back of the couch and picked up the invitation again. She had nothing to lose. Nothing at all. And she might catch a glimpse of her visitor.

"Oh hell." Ivy ran her fingers underneath the flap again. She took the invitation out and let the powder spill onto her fingertips. Her hands shook slightly. She set the invitation back down and closed her eyes.

Ivy rubbed the powder between her fingers and opened her eyes. She walked slowly into the hall and stopped in front of the mirror.

Her brown hair was now a shining red that cascaded in slight curls down her shoulders. A pink, shimmery gown hugged her curves from shoulder to floor. The dress fell low on her shoulders and dipped down between her breasts.

A pale circlet adorned her head with tiny drops of crystals hanging from it. The crystals were repeated on the thin, gold rope encircling her waist.

Ivy's jaw dropped. And her waist was at least four sizes smaller. She moved her hands down to her waist and let her fingers span the smaller area. Her hands moved up and cupped her breasts that were at least a size smaller. Ivy peeked down the front of her pale bodice and laughed. Her breasts even looked perkier.

She moved her hands back down the smooth silk that flared at her hips and lifted the hem of the gown. Petite, pearlescent slippers hugged her feet. They boasted more crystals that draped over the toe of the shoe.

Ivy moved closer and looked at her pale blue eyes, slim nose, and rosebud mouth. "Good God," she murmured. "I really am Beauty." Her hand came up to trace the perfect features. She opened her mouth and found two rows of shining white teeth. Not even her most expensive white strips could do that.

She ran her fingers through her hair and sighed. It was pure silk. Ivy moved her hair off of her ear and looked in disbelief at the perfect gold earring with two crystal droplets. "Holy hell." The comment was entirely too humorous coming out of a mouth that looked like hers.

Ivy clutched her stomach and laughed until tears streamed from her eyes. "Too funny." She snickered. "Oh geez." Ivy stood up straight and looked at herself in the mirror again. She would have to get rid of the tear streaks if she were to look halfway decent for the party.

But there were no lines on her face. Her make-up was perfect. Flawless. "Incredible," she murmured. "I could have used a touch of this when Hot Guy came by." Ivy reached out and touched her reflection. "I'm ready."

* * * *

Ivy lurked in her doorway from six forty-five on. She was scared to death she was going to miss her carriage. *A carriage, for cripes sake!* Her hand shook slightly as she picked up her matching bag and stood there.

At seven on the dot, a gold-filigreed coach rolled up to her doorstep. A uniformed coachman stepped down smartly from his perch and bowed low.

"M'lady."

Ivy shut her door behind her and walked leisurely to the carriage. Her knees were knocking, and she tried to steady herself.

When she approached the door, the coachman stood and opened it for her. He held out his hand, and she slipped hers inside. Ivy climbed inside and sank down on a plush, violet seat. The door shut behind her, and she sat back.

The carriage was beyond luxurious. There were gold handles and trim for the windows. Every inch of the surface was either covered in the plush velvet or gilded. Gold tassels hung from the ceiling, and she reached out to touch one.

23

Ivy's nerves jumped in her stomach, and she tried a slow breathing method. *Easy in. Easy out. Simple.* Until she felt the carriage slide to a stop. She pressed her hand to her stomach and put a smile on her face.

What lay beyond her carriage door was unknown. But the possibilities were endless. Ivy heard the coachman hop down and open her door. His hand moved inside, and she slid hers into his once again.

When she stepped out of the carriage, her old world fell away. Ivy would have stumbled a bit if the coachman hadn't steadied her.

"Easy, Miss." The coachman winked at her.

Ivy thanked him and moved forward one small step at a time. She couldn't take everything in at once. It was too much. And then she saw a stunning woman who couldn't possibly be step forward.

"Welcome, child. We're so glad you could be here."

The words washed over Ivy, and she didn't understand one of them. What she did know was that Snow White seemed glad to see her.

Chapter 2

Ivy extended her hand, and Snow White took it with a smile. A feeling of peace descended on Ivy immediately, and she exhaled.

"You're Snow White." The words were certain, even if spoken quietly.

"Yes, child." Her black hair was pulled back in a stylish chignon that accented her slim neck. Her blue eyes sparkled with humor. And her pale skin shone in a cobalt sheath that hugged her slim figure. "You can call me Snow."

"Um. Of course." Ivy tried her smile back on and was relieved to see it still fit. "I don't suppose this is a regular party." She glanced around at the outside of the sparkling building. Small lights appeared to float above the door and windows. Gold carriages lined a parking lot along with ivory horses that grazed on dark, green grass.

Snow threw her head back and laughed throatily. "Oh, child. You could say that." She chuckled once more and nodded toward the front door. "I am the door greeter. A familiar face, if you will. It's my job to make sure the guests are comfortable. Soothe the frazzled nerves." Her blue eyes studied Ivy's. "How are you?"

"Great." Ivy clutched her bag until her knuckles whitened. "I suppose there are other fairy tale people in there?" She motioned to the open door where music and laughter filtered out.

"Don't fret, Ivy. You are a guest here." Snow leaned forward. "Actually, we've been looking forward to seeing you for quite some time."

Ivy puzzled over those words as Snow patted her hand. "Go inside. Enjoy your evening. And thank you."

She smiled at Snow and stepped around her to walk through the doorway. Ivy moved to the right side of the door and tried to acclimate herself. Because the picture in front of her defied explanation.

To her right, Hansel and Gretel spun songs at a deejay booth. Something instrumental seemingly poured out of every inch of the dance floor. Ivy watched in disbelief as Little Miss Muffet and Robin Hood danced. Jack and Jill joined them. Ivy rubbed her eyes quickly and looked again. They were still there.

Directly in front of her was a long table weighed down with mounds of food from one end to the other. Creamy confections, masses of meat, and food of every description vied for attention. Little Boy Blue led the line. At least a dozen people were behind him. She could make out Peter Rabbit and Cinderella.

And to her left, there were tables with cards set in front of each chair.

Gold and silver streamers draped over every inch of the tables and walls. A rainbow of balloons framed all the doorways and all sides. All the colors were jewel tones. The bold and dramatic hues enhanced the entire ambiance.

26

Flowers adorned each table and threaded through streamers. Vase after vase of roses decorated every table as far as the eye could see. It was overwhelming. But it was perfect.

"You really are Beauty."

Ivy whipped around at the voice and tried to breathe. The thought of inhaling air completely left her when she gazed at the man in front of her.

"Prince Charming." Her lips felt numb as she uttered the words. *Who knew he would be so hot off the pages?*

The golden man in front of her winked. His blue eyes moved over her body slowly, and he smiled. "Adam Stott, actually."

Ivy's lips parted. "You're not Prince Charming?"

"Just for tonight." His eyes moved around the room. "I take it you're a mortal, too?"

"Yes." Ivy exhaled and shook her head. "Are you as overwhelmed as I am?"

"More."

She chuckled and patted his arm. "So. I'm assuming the invitation freaked you out a bit?"

"Are you kidding?" Adam rolled his eyes. "I was being a smartass and wished to be the Big Bad Wolf first. It's a wonder I didn't die of a heart attack in my living room."

Ivy's laughter pealed out of her. At least she wasn't alone. "I tried Little Red Riding Hood first. It was freaky enough."

Adam held out his hand. "Shall we go find where we're sitting?"

Ivy put her hand in his and smiled. "Delighted."

* * * *

Luckily, they were sitting at the same table. Ivy moved around the chairs and read each placard.

"We're sitting with Rapunzel, The Pied Piper, and Jack." Ivy tapped her cheek. "I wonder which Jack that will be."

"I take it you loved fairy tales as a child?" Adam looked at Ivy.

"Yes. My head was always in the clouds. Dreaming of a different world. A world where problems seemed to disappear at the end of the book, and everything worked out."

"I had severe asthma as a child," Adam explained. "I could go anywhere and be anything in the books. You wouldn't believe what an expert swordsman I was." He wriggled his eyebrows.

Ivy laughed. "Tell me all about it." She smiled as Adam pulled out her chair and then sat down.

The next half an hour went by quickly. More characters filtered into the party, and Ivy tried not to let them sidetrack her. But it was difficult. She had sensory overload. The dance floor filled, and she had to bite her lip from laughing when Humpty-Dumpty cut a rug with Little Bo Peep.

Their table filled up quickly, and Ivy smiled as Jack from *Jack and the Beanstalk* sat down. It was the outfit which gave him away.

The five of them began an earnest discussion about their love of fairy tales and their experience with the gold powder.

"Let's just keep our fairy tale names," Adam suggested. "It'll be too confusing to keep track of two sets of names."

"I agree." Ivy grinned. "Though I really like being called Beauty." The whole table laughed.

Five minutes later they heard a bell, and the whole room silenced.

Three stunning women moved to stand in front of the food table. The first was a slender, tall Egyptian with dark skin and jewelry that adorned her bare arms and head. The next was a shorter blonde with silken tresses that flowed about her. The third was an Asian woman who was a bit taller than the middle woman. And they were absolutely breathtaking.

Each wore a sarong style dress with bare feet. *Well.* The feet weren't exactly bare. Ivy squinted her eyes and looked at each woman in turn. Jewels were placed on the topsides of the feet and wound to the women's ankles. The first woman had blue. The second had red. The third had green.

"Welcome honored guests." The Egyptian woman spoke first. "I am Isis. This is Freya." She motioned to the blonde. "And Cybele. We are pleased you could join us this evening." Her eyes moved over the crowd. "You wonder why we have invited you."

There was a small murmuring, and she held up her hands.

"We would be nothing without your love. Without your trust. Mortals don't know the power of their thoughts." The crowd was spellbound. "For every thought you give us, we grow. Develop. We live."

"This is our thank you," Freya continued. "Our gift to you as supporters. A wonderful night as the character of your dreams. A magical party where anything can happen. And special guests you will never forget."

Cybele swung her arms open wide, and the roof disappeared above the room. The crowd *ahhed* as one, and she smiled. Stars twinkled and glittered in the sky. "I give you two guests each of you will recognize. They wanted to thank you personally."

Each person looked up and waited expectantly.

Ivy's breath caught in her throat as the moon darkened to an incredible red shade. The eclipse fascinated her. But that was nothing compared to what happened next.

A bright beam of light began as a white speck in the sky. Ivy strained to see it. But she noticed it moved closer and closer.

The meteors. We're all going to be toasted. She shifted in her seat and felt a hand touch her shoulder.

"Just watch," the male voice advised. "You're in no danger, Beauty."

She tried to turn her head, but the crowd made another sound. She swung back to the sky and saw the white circle flare closer and closer. It grew in size until it covered half the room. But then it

30

shrank down into a single strand and landed in the middle of the dance floor.

White mist swirled higher and higher, spinning like a small tornado. And then Ivy's breath caught in her throat as the form emerged.

Applause broke out loudly across the room as Mother Goose waved and bowed low. Everyone stood and clapped louder and louder until her cheeks reddened in her face.

"Please," she murmured. She patted her white hair tucked beneath her robin's egg blue bonnet. "You flatter me." Her hands moved and smoothed down the light blue dress. The applause continued, and she patted her hands down.

"Thank you. Thank you so much." Her blue eyes twinkled behind her circular wire frames. "But we have one more guest for your enjoyment." She reached up behind her and waved.

Once again, a small white speck appeared in the sky. Ivy watched expectantly as it neared their room. It hovered for a bit above the area and then dropped down gracefully on the floor beside Mother Goose.

The white ball unfurled as if petals from a flower until a beautiful woman in a silver dress stood there. She held a wand in her right hand and bowed low before the crowd.

The crowd, still on its feet, clapped until their hands were sore.

The fairy godmother bowed low and then stood and winked. Her wand glittered. Her blonde hair threaded with sparkling diamonds and sapphires. She wore a silver gown that folded about her body and moved as if a slight wind stroked it.

"Hello, my lovelies." The fairy godmother nodded her head to each section of the crowd and smiled. "We are honored to make your acquaintance. To be here. And we've brought gifts."

Both women touched hands and looked toward the sky. Hundreds of balls of light showered down through the sky and hurled toward the room with all the guests. Each ball landed on the table in front of a guest and opened before them. A lifelike miniature lay on the table. It was an exact replica of the guest it landed in front of.

Ivy picked up the small Beauty and felt a tear slide down her cheek. It was so beautiful. And it was a memento from this magical night she could always cherish.

"Please feel free to enjoy your evening. It ends only when you wish it." Both women bowed low again, and the music played.

Ivy turned to find the man who whispered in her ear. But no one was there. She tapped Adam on his arm. "Did you see anyone behind me a minute ago?"

"Are you kidding?" Adam picked up the figurine and traced every curve with his finger. "I was a little preoccupied. Why?"

"No reason." Ivy shrugged. She stood and walked toward the food table. The three women and two special guests laughed together. Several people circled around them but didn't approach.

Ivy walked up, stood there, and completed the circle.

32

All the women turned to her and smiled.

"Is that the eclipse and meteor shower everyone else watched?"

"Yes, child." Mother Goose put her arm around Ivy. "I'm so pleased to see you. We've been wondering where you've been." She winked at Isis. "It's about time you made it."

"I'm sorry, Mother." Isis sighed. "I've already apologized twice."

"I know." Mother Goose kissed Ivy lightly on the cheek. "Mingle. Enjoy. And never forget."

Ivy nodded her head and beamed. "Thank you. Excuse me, please." She moved to make a plate. Her hand picked up an ivory dish with floral designs on it, and she smiled. Eating in the presence of fairy tale greatness was a new and different experience.

She looked down at her newly slender figure and snickered. Not to mention the fact she looked halfway decent this evening. And all the food was so tempting.

Ivy plucked thin pieces of meat and placed them on her plate. Next came the vegetables. She tilted her head to the right and studied the various pastries on the last third of the table. There were creamy confections with pink and white swirls. Tiny pieces of cake with detailed pictures on top. Mini-castles filled with crème. A platter of sugared sticks in every color imaginable.

"What's your preference?" The husky male voice over her right shoulder startled her.

Ivy looked up and smiled. The beautiful males in the room no longer intimidated her. They were the same as her, it seemed. This one was at least six four with straight shoulder-length brown hair. He wore a crimson silk shirt with gold lacings on it. The shirt fell to almost his knees. He wore black pants and black, shiny boots.

But it was his face that held her attention. Bright green eyes stared down at her. Impossibly high cheekbones accented his beautiful face, and his full lips smiled. Every inch of his skin was bronze and flawless.

"You're lovely." Ivy winked and then laughed.

The man chuckled. "You're not so bad yourself."

"This old thing?" Ivy pulled the dress out to the side and let it fall back against her. She leaned in and whispered. "I don't really look like this."

"You're a beauty." The man blinked slowly, and Ivy could have sworn his eyes changed color for a sliver of a second. "Yes. A beauty. I knew it."

She shook her head and picked up a cookie with a mound of icing on it. "A hungry beauty."

The man stepped back and bowed low. "My name is Duncan, my lady."

"Duncan, you can call me Ivy."

He stood and picked up her hand. He placed his lips to the back of it and kissed it soundly.

Ivy saw the three hostesses walk toward her, and she waved at them. Duncan looked up and frowned. He walked toward them quickly. They made an odd little movement, and Duncan shook his head and jerked it lightly toward her.

The whole tableau puzzled her. Ivy strode toward the quartet with plate in hand and stopped a couple of feet away. Duncan turned and held out his hand. "Let me carry your plate for you, love."

Ivy placed her plate in his hand and chuckled. "I'm sitting over here. Would you care to join me?" She waved toward the table she shared with the others.

"I'd be delighted."

Ivy led him over to the table and sat down. Another chair magically appeared next to her. Duncan sank into it with a sigh.

"These shindigs are a great lot of fun." He popped a small cake into his mouth. His eyes roved around the room.

"Help yourself." Ivy laughed and cut her meat. She forked a bite and turned back to him. "So. What do you do when you're not a handsome prince?"

"I manage things."

"That's suitably vague." Ivy chewed the meat slowly and savored the flavor. She swallowed and motioned with her fork. "You seem to know your way around."

"I have a knack with people." Duncan's dark green eyes met hers, and she blushed.

"You're a flirt."

35

"That, too." He took the fork from her hand and fed her a bite of potato. "Good?"

Ivy nodded her head and told herself not to choke. It certainly wasn't every day a handsome man fed her.

They talked of inconsequential matters while she finished the food on her plate. When she was through, the plate disappeared. Duncan stood and extended his hand.

"A dance, milady?"

Ivy stood and curtsied. "I'd be delighted."

Duncan pulled her into his arms, and Ivy closed her eyes. His strong body pressed to hers inspired all sorts of naughty thoughts. She felt safe. Protected. It was a feeling she could grow used to.

When the song ended, Ivy pulled back and looked around. At least half the partygoers left. The others scattered about the room and talked or danced.

"I should really be going soon." Ivy sighed.

"Your life is complicated, isn't it?" Duncan's eyes probed hers. "You want things a certain way, but you don't think it will come about."

Ivy turned her head. "I didn't think I'd be here tonight, but here I am. I'll take what comes my way and do my best. It's all I know."

Duncan took her chin in his hand and brought her head back around. "Some things are meant to be, Ivy. No matter how long it takes. No matter how rough the road seems. Remember that."

Ivy stood stock-still as Duncan moved closer. She shut her eyes for a brief second and felt his warm lips touch hers. Her insides melted, and her arms came up to close around Duncan's neck. Liquid heat rushed through her body.

He never deepened the kiss. But it was enough to leave Ivy shaking in her slippers. She opened her eyes and stared at the man in front of her. When she opened her mouth to speak, he placed his finger to her lips.

"We'll meet again, Ivy. I look forward to it." He bowed low and strode from the room.

She watched him go with mixed emotions. His lips against hers sparked feelings she didn't know she had. They left her both uncomfortable and excited.

Mother Goose walked over and guided Ivy into a chair. "You look faint, child." Her blue eyes sparkled with laughter. "A kiss from a man like that would do it, I imagine."

Ivy sank into the chair and sighed. "He's beautiful."

"Ah, my love. But you are Beauty. And you should never forget that."

Ivy shook her head and patted her dress. "This is only a costume. I'm rather plain out of it. A little on the heavy side. Prone to fits and cursing. Hardly a character worth emulating."

Mother Goose laughed roundly. "You'll do, child. You'll do just fine." She stood and bent low to kiss Ivy's forehead. "I look forward to seeing you again."

Before Ivy could say another word, Mother Goose spun into a single strand of white light and disappeared.

"Unbelievable," Ivy murmured. She glanced around the room again and decided to call it a night. Adam was talking at length with Rapunzel. But she didn't want to leave before saying goodbye. She tucked her miniature in her bag and walked over to the couple.

Adam looked up and smiled at her approach. "Hello, Beauty."

"Hello." Ivy smiled broadly. "And goodbye. I think I'm readying to leave. But I didn't want to miss the opportunity to tell you how much I've enjoyed your company this evening."

Adam bowed low and stood up with a grin. "The pleasure is distinctly mine."

Ivy moved closer and gave him a peck on the cheek. "Goodnight, Prince Charming."

"Goodnight, Beauty."

She turned and walked toward the front door. The music played behind her. The stars sparkled above her. And Ivy reveled in the moment.

"Carriage, Miss?" Her coachman swung the golden coach to a stop in front of her, and she nodded.

"Thank you."

He held the door open, and Ivy climbed inside. Her fingers plucked on the velvet seat while she remembered every second of her enchanted evening.

The coach came to a stop sometime later, and the coachman opened the door again. He reached in and helped Ivy out to the sidewalk.

She watched him turn from her, and she touched his arm gently. "Thank you," she said.

"My pleasure, Miss." The coachman's cheeks turned a fiery red. "An evening I'll never forget." He tipped his hat and climbed back on top the carriage.

Ivy watched until she couldn't see him anymore and then turned to walk to her doorway. She touched her silky hair one last time and smoothed down her pink, shimmery dress. Her hands traced the circlet placed on her head, and she smiled.

She opened her front door and shut it quietly behind her. Ivy slipped off her shoes and stood in her living room barefoot. The clock read almost midnight, and she chuckled. Somehow, she knew it would. Her invitation no longer sat on the table behind the couch. It had long since disappeared.

Ivy reached into her bag and pulled out the miniature and stroked it lightly. Some fairy tales did come true. And she was honored to be a part of it. She set the figurine down on the living room table behind the couch and looked around.

Weariness washed over her, but she fought it. Who wanted to go to sleep after the evening she experienced?

Ivy walked into her bedroom and flopped back on the bed. Her gown rustled around her, and she chuckled. It beat the hell out of her fairy pajamas.

* * * *

Ivy stretched and groaned as her back popped. She moved around a little but still didn't open her eyes. She was utterly comfortable right now. Except for the overwhelming urge to go to the bathroom. Her body shifted once again, and she grimaced. Apparently, there was no time to wait. She stood and walked into the bathroom.

When she finished, she walked back into her bedroom and looked around. Everything looked the same. But it wasn't. Nor would it ever be again. Ivy slipped on her kitty slippers and walked into the living room. She strode immediately to the living room table and scooped the figurine into her hand.

"That was me," she murmured.

The miniature even more beautiful in the daylight. It was a work of art, and Ivy glanced around for a safe place to keep it. She opted for the highest shelf in the living room where the sun shone through the shades. It was perfect.

Ivy yawned hugely and shuffled into the kitchen. She slammed two pieces of toast into her toaster and took the cream cheese out of the fridge. With her head still a bit groggy, she replayed last evening over and over again in her mind until it became clear.

The bread popped up, and she slathered the cream cheese on it and ate it standing up. Her mind was a million miles away. On fairy tale characters and kisses that affected her equilibrium.

How was everyone else faring this morning? Were they shell-shocked? Pleased? Ivy snickered. *There should be a morning-after support meeting somewhere.*

"Oh well," she murmured. She poured some milk into a cup and drank it. Today was for reality. And calling sisters she didn't really want to talk to.

Ivy picked up the phone and winced. What excuse could she use to get off the phone? It was quite sad that she had to resort to that, but she didn't want to spend the day listening to the lengthy list of ailments Rose embraced.

She could tell her sister she had to wash her clothes. Rose didn't know that Ivy bought a washer and dryer about three months ago. It was a handy excuse when she needed it. And Rose would understand the need to keep the sheets and whatnot clean. Her room was spotless.

Ivy took a deep breath and dialed the number.

"Hello?" The voice was whisper thin.

"Hi, Rose." Ivy rolled her eyes and told herself not to launch into hatefulness the first five seconds of the call. "How are you feeling?"

"Oh, Ivy. I'm so glad you called." The voice became a little stronger. But not much. "I have the most dreadful cold right now.

41

And I think the medicine is making it worse. My head hurts terribly. And my ears don't feel right."

Ivy let Rose ramble on for about five minutes before she cleared her throat. "Do you need anything?"

"No." Rose sighed. "I don't suppose so. Unless you'd like to come over." She waited expectantly.

"I can't, Rose. I'm sorry." Ivy kicked the wall. Her guilt was only overridden by the memory of her last visit. She had sat on Rose's bed the entire time while Rose complained some more about her health and well-being. She vaguely remembered picking up beer on the way home.

Her sister's pale countenance drove her up the wall. All the curtains were always drawn. And it's not like Rose needed to work. Their parents' will had provided them both with financial independence. And so Rose lay in bed like a sickly princess. And it was more than Ivy could stand. Her sister belonged back in Victorian England when women got the vapors and all that nonsense.

"I didn't think so." Sadness welled up in Rose's voice, and Ivy clenched her teeth. She wouldn't fall prey to the guilt. Not this time.

"I'll talk to you next week, Rose. Goodbye."

"Goodbye." The phone clicked loudly in Ivy's ear.

"Shit," she murmured. She felt like scum of the earth. Why couldn't her sister have been a little more active? A little less sickly?

Ivy blew out a breath and marched into her bedroom. She pulled on a pair of blue shorts and a blue tank. There was nothing like talking to her sister that was a kick in the ass to go outside. She picked up some bulbs last week and hadn't planted them yet. Today would be perfect.

She lugged the bag outside and took her small trowel and dug up the dirt in a few areas. Ivy's backyard wasn't big by any means. She didn't need any major equipment. All the little handheld tools would do.

When her rows were as perfect as they were going to get, Ivy dropped the bulbs down one at a time and covered them up. She kissed her hand after each bulb and laid it on the dirt over it. "Grow," she whispered.

There was a small flash of light that rocked Ivy back on her heels. She fell on her ass.

"What in the hell was that?" Her eyes shot around the garden but didn't see a thing. She shakily stood up and wiped her hands off. The sun was in the middle of the sky, and she needed to eat lunch.

Ivy walked into her kitchen and washed her hands. She picked through the fridge until she found some lettuce and lunchmeat. She threw together a salad and sat at the table. Her life was beginning to become a tad bit peculiar. Maybe she only imagined the flash of light. But what if she hadn't? Was there something she wasn't seeing? Should be seeing?

She finished her sandwich and washed it down with tea. Her hands shook slightly as she stood and walked back outside.

"Hello?" she called softly. "Is anyone out here?"

Ivy waited for a couple of minutes before she shook her head and groaned. She was losing her mind. How many times did she need to make a fool of herself before she got it? Just because she went to a magical party last night didn't mean a thing. It was a one-shot affair.

She turned back toward the screen door when she heard a small, high-pitched buzzing noise.

Ivy turned back toward the garden again, and her jaw dropped. Hundreds of tiny lights zipped around her garden. They would land in one area and then move around some more.

She closed her eyes and opened them slowly. The lights remained.

"Hello?" she whispered.

A tiny light flew straight toward her and stopped inches from her face. A beautiful fairy with silver wings and hair smiled at her. Her dress shimmered in the sunlight, and her wand glowed a bright blue. Bright crystal blue eyes smiled at Ivy.

"Hello," the fairy squeaked.

"Am I dreaming?" Ivy muttered.

"No, silly." The fairy laughed. It sounded like tiny wind chimes brushing against each other. "You're awake."

"Why are you here?"

44

The fairy tilted her head. "Because you planted your garden. We come every year. You simply didn't see us before."

"And I see you now because…"

"It's your wish." The fairy bowed low. When she straightened, she motioned toward the other lights. "My family and I will make sure your flowers survive and thrive. We are thrilled to be your fairies."

Ivy accepted the explanation because at the moment she couldn't think of anything else to say. She nodded her head and tried to smile. "I'm honored to have you."

The small fairy pressed her hand to her heart, and a tear seeped out of her eye. "You honor us, Miss." She dabbed at her eye with the hem of her dress. "I must get back to work." She bowed again and promptly zipped off toward the other lights.

Ivy walked backwards through her screen door and shut it behind her. The lights still whizzed about, and she turned around toward the couch.

"I have fairies in my garden." Ivy blinked twice and sank down slowly on her threadbare couch. "I have fairies." She paused. "In my garden." It still didn't quite sink in.

Ivy walked into her bedroom and gathered her dirty clothes up. She ambled into the laundry room and dumped the clothes into the washer. She set the controls and made her way back to the bedroom.

She looked around the room, but she didn't notice anything different. Ivy crawled onto her bed and lay on her back. She picked

45

up the remote and turned on the television. Maybe life would go back to normal tomorrow.

* * * *

Ivy woke up early Monday. She opened one eye and peered at her alarm clock. It wasn't even six-thirty yet. She still had half an hour. But try as she might, she couldn't go back to sleep.

"Damn it." Ivy stood and walked into the bathroom. She stripped her pajamas and took a quick shower. Her spirit perked up a bit under the hot water. She wrapped a towel around herself and made her way to her closet.

A nice pair of tan slacks and a button-up crème shirt. Ivy wound the towel around her dark brown hair and dressed for the day. As soon as she was dressed, she put her head down and towel-dried her hair. Then she pulled it up into a loose bun. She put on her socks and padded into the kitchen.

Ivy glanced around and noted nothing had moved or changed. She nodded briskly to herself and made a sandwich for her lunch and one for breakfast. She packed her lunch and went to the living room to watch television until she had to leave.

Her garden was still in the early morning. Ivy glanced up to the tallest shelf and noted her figurine. And then she looked back at the garden. Rays of sun filtered through her fence and lit softly on the dirt.

She watched in fascination as the rays shattered into tiny bits. And then the garden seemed to explode. Hundreds of balls of light moved through the air and lit upon every surface.

Ivy sat forward on her couch and watched the spectacle with slack jaw and wide eyes. It seemed like fairy visits were turning out to be an everyday thing.

* * * *

Ivy drove to work and told herself to focus on the day ahead. Mondays weren't as bad as Fridays. Nothing was. But they came in a close second. All the reports over the weekend would have to be entered, filed, and distributed. That meant she had the ability to bring in one of the assistants to help her. And she would, if the copier gave her fits again.

She pulled into her parking space and turned the engine off. *Back to normal. Back to chaos.* Back to her workday.

Ivy locked her car and strode into her office. She put her purse up and glanced around. There were still stacks of papers on her desk that needed filed. She set the donuts on the large, round table on the far side of the room and waited for her police friends. They would filter in over the next hour or so.

She looked at the stack of papers and then at the copier. Nothing accomplished by standing there.

Ivy stiffened her backbone and opened the lid of the copier. She put the first paper in and pushed the copy button. Nothing happened.

"Son of a bitch." She kicked the bottom of the copier, and the "service copier" light came on.

"That is it!" Ivy bent down and yanked open the same tray where Missy found the paper jam before.

She rocked back on her heels and stifled a scream.

The leprechaun looked up and tipped his hat to her. "Morning, Miss. Would you mind not kicking the copier? It upsets the gremlin."

Chapter 3

Ivy looked in disbelief at the leprechaun propped in the tray. He wore emerald green pants and an ivory shirt with a fitted green vest. Tiny gold buttons adorned the vest. And his small shoes curled prettily at the toe.

"Gremlin?" Ivy repeated. Never mind she was talking with a leprechaun. *No. Never mind that.*

"Yes, Miss." The leprechaun tilted his head to the side. "The gremlin asks that you not kick his house. It knocks his belongings about."

"There are gremlin belongings in my copier." Ivy repeated the facts as best she knew them. "And what are you doing in there?"

"I'm the mediator, Miss." He grinned up at her and winked. "No one better than a leprechaun to sort out situations such as these."

"Of course." Ivy glanced around her office and noted it was normal. And then she looked back down. She opened her mouth to ask another question when she heard footsteps in the hallway. She didn't think about it. Her foot automatically connected with the tray and slammed it shut.

Ivy winced at the muffled oath and stood up straight. Four officers walked in and ambled over to the donut table.

"How's your morning, Ivy?" Bret took two maple donuts and put them on a napkin.

"Great." She smiled briefly. "Just great. You guys help yourself."

She waited impatiently while they made small talk and loitered around the snack table. Ivy glanced at her watch and cleared her throat. "Don't you guys have a meeting or something this morning?"

"Yeah." Bret grimaced. "See you later."

Ivy watched them leave and sighed. She bent down and opened the tray again. The leprechaun rubbed his bald pate.

"You might want to warn a man, Miss."

She winced. "I'm so sorry. But my co-workers walked in." Her eyebrows arched. "I don't think they would quite understand this." She paused. "Hell. I don't understand this."

"It's quite simple." The leprechaun whipped out a pipe and lit it. Miniscule smoke rings billowed up and disappeared. "I'm here to broker a solution between you and the gremlin."

"What does he want?"

"Well, Miss." The leprechaun stroked his beard. "Kicking the copier is nonnegotiable."

"Done." She nodded briskly.

"This next bit might take a little give on your part."

Ivy frowned. "What else does he want?"

"Well, Miss." The leprechaun blew a few more smoke rings. "The smell of those donuts is quite tempting. Perhaps you could put a bite or two in this slot each morning."

"That's it?" Ivy blinked. "No kicking and donuts in the copier?"

"Yes, Miss."

"Oh, good grief!" Ivy laughed. "No problem. I can do that." She glanced back down. "And he'll quit sabotaging my copier?"

"Yes, Miss."

"It's a deal." Ivy blew out a breath. "Thank you."

"Pleasure, Miss." A smile wreathed the leprechaun's face. He winked and disappeared.

Ivy walked over to the table and pinched off a large piece of glazed donut and placed it in the tray. She slid the tray gently shut and waited a minute. The "service copier" light disappeared.

"Holy shit," Ivy murmured. She divided the papers and put them on the glass. She shut the lid and hit the "copy" button. It went off without a hitch.

"Hey!"

Ivy jumped and spun around. Missy stood there with a grin on her face. "I see you've got the copier working."

"Yeah." Ivy took the papers and set them on the table. She smiled grimly. "Just a little gremlin in the works."

Missy chuckled and picked up a donut. "Glad you've got it working now. Because I wasn't loaning you my gun."

"Spoilsport."

Ivy made copies while Missy ate a donut and washed it down with two cups of coffee. Ivy finished and input the data. People came to her window and asked for various reports and documents. The day slid by seamlessly after that. Ivy clocked out at five and drove home.

She refused to think about her morning until she had dinner on the table, and she could relax. Fairies, gremlins, and leprechauns were a tad bit much to handle all in one day.

Ivy parked her car and walked slowly to her front door. A bouquet of white roses lay on her doormat. She bent to pick them up and cradled them close. The fragrant petals made her smile.

How many more surprises would she have? Or could she take?

Ivy unlocked her front door and stepped inside. She shut the door behind her and put her keys on the table. The bouquet's scent filled the room, and she smiled. She felt around and tried to find a card. But there was none. She frowned and put them down.

Her fingers worked through the stems again. But she didn't find anything. Ivy's brows knit together. If ever anyone had a day that made no sense, it was her. *Today.*

Ivy walked into the kitchen and opened the fridge. She took out two pork chops and set them on the cabinet. Then she threw together a salad and put it in the fridge. She cooked the meat and slid it onto her dinner plate.

It was almost six o'clock. Time to watch the news. Ivy made her way into the living room and sat on her couch. She didn't glance outside at the garden. She didn't look up to her figurine. Ivy mentally shut down while she ate. Just a bit of news on the television to wind down the night. But it wasn't meant to be.

"We're not going away, you know."

Ivy shrieked and almost knocked the plate off her lap. She scrambled to her feet and blinked rapidly.

The seven dwarfs spread out in her living room on pieces of furniture and shelves.

She stumbled back until her spine hit the wall. "This absolutely tops it." Ivy picked her plate up and pressed the palms of her hands to her eyes. When she moved her hands, the dwarfs were still there.

A dwarf with glasses moved forward and grasped Ivy's hand. "Come sit down, Ivy. You look as if you're about to break."

The dwarf led her back to the couch. She sank down to the cushion and looked around. Her hands shook a little when she put them in her lap.

"Listen." Ivy's eyes sought out each and every small face. "I've had a long day. There are things happening in my life that I can't explain. Beings in my life I can't explain. You shouldn't be here!" Her brown eyes were wide, close to panic.

"Calm yourself, Ivy." The dwarf patted her leg comfortingly. "We mean you no harm. We are your friends."

"I don't understand." She shook her head back and forth.

"We were there for you in your childhood." The dwarf's eyes were kind. "We helped you through the bad days. The long days. We showed you worlds you never could have dared dream."

Ivy relaxed a little at the dwarf's words. Everything he said was true. "What do you want?"

"We need help."

"And what am I going to do for you?" Ivy stood up and paced in front of the television. "You're magical beings. I'm a mortal. I don't have anything to offer." She spread her hands out, as if pleading. "I'm not who you need."

"You're exactly who we need." The other dwarfs nodded their heads in assent.

Ivy rubbed her temple with her fingers. "Can I have a day or two to think about it?"

The dwarf smiled sadly. "Time dwindles, child. But no one can force you to do something you are uncomfortable doing. And we are certainly not going to try." He picked up Ivy's hand and kissed the top of it. All the other dwarfs fell in line and did the same.

"Until we meet again." The dwarfs disappeared in the blink of an eye.

* * * *

Ivy left the roses on the living room table and walked into her bedroom. There was no one on the earth she could possibly tell what was happening to her. Her closest relative would promptly book her an extended stay at an asylum. And how could she honestly expect Rose to listen to her when she didn't reciprocate?

Ivy flopped back on the bed and crossed her hands on her stomach. She studied the designs on her ceiling for half an hour before she finally gave up and walked into the kitchen. It was almost eight o'clock. Rose was probably already asleep for the night. But Ivy was dying to share at least a part of her day with someone.

She dialed Rose's number and held her breath while it rang.

"Hello?" The voice was puzzled.

"Hello, Rose." Ivy clutched the receiver tightly. "What are you doing?"

"I'm watching television." Rose's voice was worried. "Are you all right, Ivy? You never call this late. And never on a weekday."

"I'm having a hard day." Her voice trembled even as she struggled to steady it. "Would it be okay if I came over?"

"Sure." Ivy could hear Rose shuffling around. "I'll be waiting in the kitchen. Knock on the back door."

"Thanks, Rose." Ivy hung up the phone and rested her head against the wall. Maybe if she talked it all out, it would make more sense.

Ivy put her shoes on and swept her keys off the table. She shut the door behind her and walked briskly toward her car. Maybe her younger sister could shed a little light on recent happenings. And maybe she would simply listen and let her older sister clear her mind.

* * * *

Ivy pulled into Rose's driveway and killed the engine. She stepped out and strode straight up the rock path to the kitchen. Her knuckles rapped loudly on the door. Not even a minute later, Rose opened the door and swept Ivy inside.

Even after all these years, Rose's appearance still surprised her. Rose was ethereal. Her skin was almost translucent, and her long blonde hair trailed down her slender body then curled at her waist. Her pale blue eyes so clear Ivy swore they went on forever. Even her lips were nearly colorless. The satin ivory robe she wrapped around herself only added to the delicate picture. How they came out of the same parents constantly amazed Ivy.

"What's wrong?" Rose shut the door and locked it. Her voice was soft and melodic.

Ivy blew out a breath to steady herself. "You have to promise to listen to what I'm saying."

"Okay." Rose sat down at the white kitchen table, and Ivy did the same.

"I received an invitation Saturday night to a special party."

Rose nodded.

Ivy twisted her hands together. "I don't think I realized how special it was going to be." Her brown eyes searched her sister's pale blue ones. "It was a magical evening." She paused.

Rose leaned forward. "Okay."

"No." Ivy stood. "It was a magical evening."

"I don't understand."

"I met Mother Goose and The Fairy Godmother."

Rose blinked once. Twice. Three times. She stood and put her hands on the table. "I have some medication I think you should take."

"Rose." Ivy grasped her sister's hand before she could leave the table. "I'm not losing my mind. I'm not imagining things. I've visited the magical world. And now it won't leave me alone." She sighed. "They said they need me."

Rose sank back down into her chair. "Ivy. I think you're working too hard."

Ivy laughed aloud. "It's not the working that's shaking me up. It's the playing."

Her sister studied her silently for another minute. "Start at the beginning."

Ivy nodded and told Rose about the special invitation and the party. She told her sister about the fairies in the garden and the gremlin in her copier. And she ended with the dwarfs pleading for her help.

Rose stood and walked to her refrigerator. She took out the milk and poured a glass for herself and one for Ivy. She sat back down in her chair and sipped it slowly.

"Do you see them now?" Rose motioned around her kitchen.

Ivy looked at the ivory and gold room. Her eyes searched out every corner. She traced each cabinet visually. But she couldn't see a thing.

"No." Her voice was both disappointed and relieved.

Rose sighed. "You realize how this sounds, don't you?"

"I know." Ivy took a drink of her milk and shook her head. "I'm sorry to bother you, Rose. Maybe I'm simply overtired." She stood

57

and put her glass in the sink. Her eyes looked at the window behind the sink, and she whirled around quickly.

A small, brown bear sat on the floor in the doorway between the kitchen and the living room. He smiled kindly at Ivy and winked. She shook her head slowly and walked over to Rose.

"What's your favorite fairy tale, Rose?"

"Don't be silly." Rose looked at her. "You know it's *Little Brown Bear*. That little devil could get into nine kinds of trouble." Her blue eyes softened in remembrance. "Daddy bought me one when I was four. I slept with it for years. Now it's upstairs in my hope chest."

"What would you say if I told you that Little Brown Bear was sitting on your carpet right inside the living room doorway?"

Rose started to turn when Ivy touched her hand. "I'm simply asking, Rose. What would you say?"

"I don't know." She frowned. "I don't know what I'd say." Rose held a hand up to her mouth. "Do you see him?"

"Yes."

Rose turned around, and Ivy was both shocked and thankful at her sister's swift intake of breath.

"I see him," she whispered. Rose stood and bent down low. She reached out and sighed when her hand touched soft, brown fur. "You're real."

"Yes, Rose." The voice from the bear was young and excited. "And I'm pleased to finally meet you."

"Oh my God."

Ivy moved quickly and stood behind her sister. She was scared to death Rose would faint, and the bear would disappear. But her sister was made of sterner stuff.

Rose turned with bright blue eyes and color in her cheeks. "Little Brown Bear is in my living room."

"I know!" Ivy and Rose collapsed in each other's arms with laughter. After a couple of minutes, they dabbed their eyes and simply looked at each other.

"How does this stuff happen to you?" Rose shook her head. "You were serious about the party, the gremlin, and the dwarfs, weren't you?"

"Yes."

Rose bent down. "May I pick you up?"

The bear lifted his arms, and Rose swung him up. She settled him on her hip. Her hand moved to stroke his velvety fur again. She pinned Ivy with her eyes. "Why are they here?"

Ivy shrugged. "I don't know." They both looked at the bear.

"I'm just a small bear, Miss. No matters of great importance are passed down to me." He held out both hands. "I'm here because the lady wished it."

"The lady?" Ivy repeated. "You mean me?"

"Of course!" The bear wriggled excitedly in Rose's arms. "You were wishing to prove to your sister that you weren't insane." At

Ivy's quick intake of breath, he stuttered. "I'm sorry, my lady. That may have come out wrong." His button eyes drooped sadly.

"That's exactly what I was thinking." Ivy patted his head. "No need to apologize for the truth."

"And here I am!" The bear threw his arms open wide and beamed. "I've never been to the mortal world." He glanced around the kitchen. "It's awfully jagged. Not a lot of foliage. But the colors are lovely."

Rose laughed. "I'm sure it pales in comparison to where you live." She frowned suddenly. "Is someone going to miss you? A parent? Sibling?"

"I'm on my own, Miss Rose. I always have been."

Ivy shot a look to Rose. She shook her head slightly. *Don't even think about it*, she mouthed.

Rose scowled. "Mr. Bear…" she began.

"Oh!" The bear sat upright suddenly and blinked rapidly. "I must go! Pardon me!" And in a blink, he was gone.

"Well that was odd," Ivy commented. "Even for my kind of day."

"It's rather sad to be alone." Rose sniffed a little as she turned.

"Honey." Ivy stood up and hugged her sister. "I'm sorry I haven't come around more. I'm so sorry. I don't have any excuses to offer."

"You think I'm a hypochondriac. Always complaining. Always whining." Rose's voice was muffled behind her hands.

Ivy winced. "I think perhaps you stretch the truth a bit. A little exaggeration, maybe."

Rose turned. Her blue eyes watered, and her nose turned red. "I know I may not be much help, but I want to try." She sniffed again. "Do you want my help?"

She looked at her sister kindly. "Rose. You let me sit at your table and tell you fantastic things that anybody else would have construed as madness. I welcome any help you'd like to give me." Ivy moved forward and hugged her little sister.

"Well that's all well and good," a masculine voice said behind them. "Because it's probably going to take both of you."

The sisters separated and spun around. Duncan stood there and looked at the both of them. Ivy frowned. "You still have the gold dust? Because mine disappeared."

Duncan winced. "About that…" he began.

"Wait." Ivy frowned and held up her hand. She moved closer and studied all the markings on his gold shirt. There were emblems and insignia she didn't understand. But she knew enough to see he was royalty. "You lied to me." The words tumbled out of her mouth, and she fought to keep from crying.

Here she stood, in all her glory. No make-up. Her usual size. And the devious bastard from the party looked like he stepped off the pages of a magazine. She stiffened her backbone. Her pride lay in tatters at her feet.

"Ivy." Duncan held out his hands. "Don't be angry. I'm still the same person you met."

"What do you want?" Her voice was harsh, even to her own ears.

He sighed. "My kingdom needs your help."

"Your kingdom?" she sneered. "How nice. And how perfectly trite."

"Ivy." Rose's voice was soft. "Give him a chance."

Ivy bit down on her humiliation and nodded. "Say what you have to say."

"I'd rather show you." Duncan held out his hands.

The women looked at each other and then to him. Rose shrugged and slipped her hand into his. Ivy scowled but did the same.

"Close your eyes, ladies. It's only a short trip."

Ivy did as he asked and felt a small breeze ripple against her skin.

"Open your eyes."

At the soft command, both women opened their eyes.

A wondrous world appeared before them. Every illustration in every fairy tale book they ever read paled in comparison to the real thing.

They stood on a dirt road while three narrow paths spread out before them. To their right was a thick forest with trees filled with emerald leaves and dark chocolate bark. Silver dots decorated each leaf. And when the wind blew, a silvery tune played. A thick hedge with copper-colored flowers circled the forest. Ivy strained her eyes and could see the copper flowers were actually bells. They shifted positions with the wind and echoed through the street.

Directly in front of them, a road led to a castle in the distance. Ivy could barely make out the jutting towers and flags. And between the forest and the castle on her right side were cottages.

Each cottage sported a small wooden fence and mailbox. The roofs had dark brown shingles that sloped down and tipped up at the ends. A silver chimney rose from the top of them. The cottages were all the same. Yet they were all different.

The first cottage was blue. Blue flowers. Blue curtains. Everything matched. The next cottage was green. The colors were vibrant and dynamic. They almost seemed to dance in the slight breeze. And the size of the houses grew and dwindled down the row.

Ivy watched as three kittens walked out of the first cottage with mittens in their hands. They stood on their hind feet and walked to the clothesline on the side of the house. When they caught sight of Duncan, they bowed low.

"Highness," they purred.

"Kittens." Duncan bowed back. "Washing day?"

"Yes." They nodded together. The black and white kitten grinned. "Mama warned us not to lose them again. She's running out of yarn."

"Your mother is wise." Duncan winked at the felines and turned to the women. "Kittens, meet Ivy and Rose. They are guests here in our kingdom."

The kitten's eyes widened. "Are they…"

"They are visitors, Kitten." Duncan's green eyes narrowed.

The kittens bowed low. "Have a pleasant day, ladies." They waved with their paws, and the trio waved back.

Duncan led the woman a little further down the road. The sun shone directly above them and on the right. But it seemed cloudy on the left side. Dark clouds drifted by and then seemed to dissipate as they moved to the right.

They walked for perhaps a quarter of a mile before Duncan stopped. A black bridge extended over blue water to their left.

"I have someone I have to see. Would you mind coming along?" He looked at Ivy and then Rose.

Ivy frowned. "Why is your kingdom divided?"

Duncan sighed. "Some wounds take longer to heal." He looked up at the sky. "It grows late. But I need to stop and see someone."

"Over there?" Rose pointed toward the dark side of the bridge. Silver swirls of mist moved over the ground. She shivered. "It's ominous. Foreboding."

"No harm will come to you, fair Rose." Duncan touched his chest. "I swear."

"Rose, you don't have to come." Ivy smiled at her sister and turned to Duncan. "She's had a cold. She probably shouldn't be traipsing off into chill."

"Nonsense." Rose blew out a breath that wasn't quite steady. "If you two are going, then so am I." She brushed her blonde hair back determinedly.

"You don't have to." Ivy moved closer and searched her sister's eyes. "I don't want you ill."

"I'll be fine." Rose nodded. "Just fine."

Ivy scowled as she turned to Duncan. "Couldn't wait, could you?" She set her jaw. "You best hope nothing happens to my sister. Not even the Fairy Godmother will be able to save you then."

Duncan bowed. "On my life, ladies. Nothing will harm you this evening." He turned and walked over the black bridge. Ivy let Rose follow, and she trailed. Small blue bubbles oozed up from the liquid beneath them.

Ivy frowned. There was something not quite right here. They made it to the other side, and she looked around. Not only did the sun not shine over on this side, it was cool. Clammy almost. She looked down and couldn't see her feet.

Duncan swept his arm out. "I'll lead. You two stay close."

Rose took his advice to heart and almost pressed up against him. Ivy shook her head. She'd be damned if she'd crawl into his pants just because of a little spookiness. She was still pissed off he was a prince. Her new crazy filled with layers.

Duncan moved down the path and glanced back occasionally. They passed cottages here, too. But these were all dark and depressing. The browns and blacks melded together with spinach green. No flowers grew. Just thorny bushes with jagged black flowers. The gates to the cottages all hung off their hinges. And shingles swayed in the breeze. No windows open. Everything and everybody closed off and separate.

More than once, Ivy felt as though eyes watched her. She glanced at her sister and saw the same concern. Rose stumbled a bit on the road and Duncan reached out to steady her.

Jealousy, hard and cruel, balled in her belly. Ivy clenched her fists and told herself she was being stupid. Rose didn't need gold dust. She was perfect as she was. And if Duncan liked her, then so be it. Ivy pushed the thought of his lips against hers far, far away.

The smell hit them first. Ivy blinked rapidly as her eyes watered. Rose made a gagging sound. The aroma of raw sewage and road kill permeated the air. Duncan stopped for a minute and looked at them apologetically.

"Here." He waved his hand over their noses, and the smell dimmed somewhat.

Ivy tried not to gag and dug in her pocket for a handkerchief she sometimes kept in it. She thanked all that was good it was still there. Her hand closed around it and brought it out. She tapped Rose and handed it to her.

Rose's blue eyes were thankful as she took it. She nodded and smiled briefly before she pressed it to her face.

Duncan looked around. "Just a little farther." His green eyes searched the dimness around them.

They walked a little further and then Duncan stepped off the main road and onto a side path. The brambles grew closer together and tore at them if they walked side by side. It was hard enough to walk single file.

Ivy cursed under her breath as the thorns scratched her arms. They better have a damn good reason for walking through this hell. A mere social call wasn't going to do it.

Duncan stopped abruptly and pointed.

The two women looked ahead of them, and Ivy tried not to gape.

A large black house rose among the brambles. It towered above them, unfriendly. All the windows painted black. Two towers on each side rose forbiddingly into the sky. A black rock path led them straight to the front door.

Ivy thought she was going to throw up. The smell was so strong, she was afraid to breathe too deeply.

Duncan rapped his knuckles on the door and waited. No one approached. He scowled and knocked again.

Someone yanked the door open and growled down at them.

"What in the hell do you want?"

Ivy looked up and couldn't believe her eyes. In the doorway a man towered with a sneer. He was at least as tall as Duncan. His ebony hair hung to his waist in wild knots. His dark eyes narrowed, and Ivy saw Rose shudder. A long, jagged scar raced down the right side of his face from his ear to his jawbone. It emphasized the paleness of his skin.

The man wore a black tunic and black pants. Both were stained terribly. And Ivy was quite sure she didn't want to know what made the stains.

"Rupert." Duncan wrinkled his nose. "I need to speak to you."

Rupert glowered. "I don't know why you think you have the right to just show up on my doorstep and demand an audience."

"I am your prince." Duncan's voice hardened perceptibly. "You will let me in."

The man narrowed his eyes. "Then by all means." His voice was silky. "Come in, Highness." He moved back and swept his arm open wide.

Rose shot a terrified look back to Ivy. Ivy smiled reassuringly and tilted her head toward the open door.

Duncan patted Rose's arm. "It's okay, Rose. All bark and all that."

Ivy wasn't too sure about that, but she did feel mildly reassured the man wouldn't kill them. Mildly.

They stepped into the house, and Duncan moved forward. He motioned to the bubbling cauldron in the corner. "What are you cooking, Rupert?"

"None of your business." The man's voice was rough, as though he hasn't used it in a while. "But it's not a potion for making the Prospat plants disappear. Or the healing fish." His sly eyes met the prince's. "If that's what you're worried about."

"Don't trifle with me." Duncan's green eyes flashed. "It's no joking matter."

"Obviously." Rupert sneered. He motioned to the two women. "I see you've brought the token mortals along. Worthless lot, though they are."

Ivy moved forward. "Don't speak about what you don't know."

Rupert's eyebrows shot up. "I see the heavy one has a mouth on her." He glanced back at Duncan. "I hope you can handle her." His mouth stretched into a parody of a grin. His eyes met Ivy's. "And yes, woman. I know what I'm talking about."

"My name is Ivy." She studied him with cool, brown eyes. "This is my sister, Rose."

"It doesn't matter your name." Rupert cocked his head to the side. "What matters here is that the prince thinks you can do something for him. Don't you, Duncan?"

Ivy watched Rupert's eyes. Not once did they focus on Rose. It was an interesting tidbit. Rose, for her part, studied the interior of the house.

It was decorated in early medieval torture chamber. Chains and weapons hung on each wall. Axes. Swords. Armor. A shelf of bottles took up an entire side of the house. There was something that

69

looked like a torture device propped up against the back wall. The floor had various skins placed on it.

Ivy could make out a bear and deer head. The effect wasn't the least bit soothing.

Rupert looked at the trio. "And the prince here thinks I can do something for him. Don't you?"

"The first thing you can do is stem the aroma of whatever the hell you're cooking." Duncan pointed at the caldron. "We're already here. No need to pretend you rolled out the welcome wagon for us."

Rupert almost smiled. He waved his hand above the caldron, and the air cleared immediately.

Rose lowered the handkerchief with a shaky breath. "Thank you," she whispered. Ivy took a deep breath.

"State your business." Rupert's deep voice rumbled through the room. "You're not welcome here for long. And it grows late."

"What do you know about the missing plants and fish?" Duncan studied the man in front of him with an unwavering gaze. "Because I believe you know more than you're telling."

"Believe what you want." Rupert shrugged his massive shoulders. "Your conjectures do nothing but waste your breath. How is King Cedric?"

Duncan moved forward and growled. "Don't bait me. You know what I can do to you."

"Ah, yes. Lock me up and throw away the key." Rupert's eyes darkened even farther. "But you won't, will you? Because our

70

wonderful king wastes away day by day. And you have no idea what ails him. It must be hard to watch someone you love die."

"Please." Rose stepped forward with tears on her lashes. She put her hand on Rupert's arm. "Please help if you can."

The man's face changed for a minute, before he picked up Rose's hand and moved it. "Save your tears for someone who will appreciate them." His voice gruff. "You're the weak one. Always sickly. Puny." His eyes bored into her face. "Maybe you should look for a cure for yourself."

Ivy moved forward quickly and planted herself squarely in front of the giant of a man. "And you best keep a civil tongue in your head when you speak to my sister." She glared up at him.

Rupert looked at the prince blandly. "You can move her. Or I can."

Duncan moved forward and grabbed Ivy's arm. "We're done here for now." He glanced at Rupert. "But we're not done with this discussion."

"Of course." He sneered. "You know where I live."

The trio left and started down the path again. Ivy put her arms around Rose's shoulders. "He's quite an asshole, isn't he?"

Rose's laugh was shaky. "Blunt to say the least."

Duncan left them to their own thoughts as they moved to the main path. The hair on Ivy's neck stood on end a split second before a low growl split the air. A moment later, a wolf stepped out of the brambles with deep black eyes and a muzzle filled with sharp teeth.

His fur matted to his body. And sharp, ragged nails at the end of his paws. He looked quickly to the left and right. Rose's eyes widened in fear, and Ivy braced her feet for a fight.

Chapter 4

Both women watched in amazement as Duncan moved forward and embraced the creature.

"Wolf," he whispered. "I hoped to see you."

"Come, Prince." His black eyes glanced at the mortal women. "And assure your friends I won't eat them."

"It's okay." Duncan jerked his head toward the wolf. "He's a friend. A rarity in this part of the kingdom."

Rose's hand shook as she extended it. The wolf smiled widely. A smile which showed all his pointy teeth. "My lady." He closed her small hand in his paw.

Ivy waited until he dropped Rose's hand before offering hers. He looked deeply into her face when he took her hand. And then he dropped into a low bow. "My lady." When he stood, he looked around again.

"Follow me."

Duncan motioned for the women to follow them through the hole in the thorny foliage.

Ivy made sure Rose was right behind Duncan before she stepped in behind her sister. The darkness seemed to seep through her bones as she kept sight of the back of her sister's robe. And then the whole situation struck her as funny.

Rose was in her robe. *Geez.* She had to make sure her sister dressed accordingly next time.

They hurried through the maze and finally popped into a clearing about five minutes later. Rose's breath hitched in her chest, and Ivy patted her sister's back. She glared at Duncan.

"Could you possibly slow the hell down for a minute?"

Duncan glanced behind him and noted the fury in Ivy's eyes. He moved back and took Rose by the shoulders. "Breathe easy, Rose."

Ivy watched her sister's breath slow. She glanced up gratefully at Duncan, and Ivy bit her tongue. She wouldn't be hateful. Not right now. Perhaps if she were on her own turf.

"Hurry." The wolf glanced around again. He ducked into the house and left the door open.

Duncan ushered Rose inside and looked back at Ivy. "I swear I will explain everything in just a little while." She didn't budge. "Please, Ivy. Just a little longer."

"If you let anything happen to my sister, I'll make sure you won't have any heirs." Ivy's brown eyes were hard. "Do I make myself clear?"

"Crystal."

Ivy nodded and ducked inside the wolf's house.

The interior of the wolf's house was alarmingly pleasant. Cozy and warm. Ivy frowned as she noted the house plants in the kitchen windowsill. She glanced at the wolf. "Aren't you on the wrong side of town?"

The wolf moved into the kitchen and poured everyone a drink. "I live here because it suits a purpose, lady."

He brought a tray into the living room and handed out wooden cups. "Please sit. Be at ease."

Ivy sat Rose down at the table and sank beside her. The wolf waited on his guests before he settled in a large, blue recliner. He propped his feet up on a footstool and sipped his drink.

"What do you know, Wolf?"

"More things are disappearing, my Prince."

"Dammit!" Duncan shot up from his chair and paced the living room. "I thought I had more time." He stopped and looked at the wolf. "What has Rupert been doing?"

"He collects herbs on a daily basis. Always at night. He is careful. I do not know what he is doing. I'm afraid to watch too closely. He has an uncanny knack for knowing things."

"That he does." Duncan stroked his chin thoughtfully. "And he's far too secretive."

"Will you go to the castle now?" The wolf sat forward and steepled his furry fingers. "Your brother seems most anxious for your return."

Rose sat up. "You have a brother?"

"Yes." Duncan smiled at her. "My younger brother Eric. I told him I had business to attend to out of our realm."

"Why is your father ill?" Ivy set her cup down and stood. "Why are we here? And why are we sitting in a wolf's house while a highly

75

unpleasant man plots to do unspeakable things?" Her brown eyes pinned Duncan. "You have a lot of explaining to do."

"Ivy." Duncan held out his hands, and Ivy looked at him coldly.

"My sister is out in her robe. Can you at least find her something suitable to wear?"

The wolf stood. "I have spare clothes. Maybe something will fit your sister." He smiled kindly at her. "Will you join me, fair Rose?"

Rose smiled and stood. "I'd be delighted."

Ivy watched her sister follow the wolf out of the room. She turned and opened her mouth when Duncan spoke.

"You have no reason to fear Wolf. He is a good soul. And a vegetarian, in case you were worried."

"A vegetarian?" Ivy looked toward the door her sister left through. "Well, doesn't that beat all?"

"There is so much to say." Duncan's dark green eyes pleaded with her. "I only ask for time, Ivy. I realize it's a lot to take in."

Ivy's eyebrows shot up. "You think?" She narrowed her eyes. "Nothing has been quite right since the invitation." She put her hands on her hips. "You've plotted the entire time, haven't you?" Ivy glared at him. "You pompous, arrogant ass!" She held up her hand. "I want to go home. I want my sister home. And whatever bullshit your kingdom is dealing with, you just go right ahead and deal."

Duncan moved forward and took Ivy's hands in his. "Please, Ivy."

She steeled herself against the immediate attraction. Her body longed to sway against him. To be held tightly. Protected. But she kept herself still.

He bent his head down, and Ivy's body shuddered in need. "Please," he murmured.

"Quit trying to seduce me." She withdrew her hands and stepped back. "You would have a better chance with the not-heavy sister."

Duncan growled low in his throat. "Must you make everything so difficult?"

"It's a gift." Her eyes flashed.

"What do you think?" Rose twirled in the doorway, a smile on her face.

Ivy turned to her sister and applauded loudly. Rose bowed. She wore a silky blue dress with fitted sleeves that flared out at the hip and settled to the ground. Her hair was tied back in a bow with a blue ribbon. And she looked lovely.

"Can you believe how pretty this is?" Rose picked up the side and showed Ivy her blue satin slippers.

"You're beautiful, Rose. Absolutely breathtaking." Ivy beamed proudly at her sister.

Wolf appeared in the doorway, and Ivy smiled. "Thank you, Mr. Wolf. You're a wonderful host."

"My pleasure, lady." His dark eyes were pleased.

"But we must be going home now."

77

At her words, Wolf frowned, and Rose cried out. Duncan set his jaw.

Ivy looked at the three in front of her. "I don't quite understand what's going on. And I really don't think it matters much. This has been a nice ride. But my sister and I are getting off."

"Ivy, please." Rose moved forward and took her sister to the other side of the room. Her blue eyes were soft. "This is beyond anything I could imagine. I want to see more."

"Rose." Ivy shot a glance toward Duncan and the wolf. "We are up against things here which could harm us. We have no idea what we're doing. We don't know what they have planned. And the prince here," she jerked her head toward Duncan, "he's full of surprises."

"I know you're mad at him." Rose looked at Ivy sympathetically. "But his father is sick. Don't you want to help?"

"You have far too soft of a heart, sister." Ivy sighed. "We'll spend the night. And that's it. Do we have a deal?"

"Yes." Rose smiled and patted Ivy's cheek. "Quit worrying so much."

"Easy for you to say," Ivy murmured.

They turned back around.

"When can we see your father?" Ivy asked.

"Now." Duncan moved forward quickly and picked up Ivy's hand. He placed a kiss on the back of it. "You honor me."

Ivy fought the blush that crept into her cheeks. "Quit," she snapped. "Kiss Rose. She's the voice of insanity around here."

The wolf chuckled. "You have your hands full, Prince."

"Indeed I do." He turned to the wolf. "Your loyalty will not be forgotten, dear friend." Duncan moved to open the door and ushered the women through. He shut it behind him and led them back down a different path. The full moon shone down through the clouds. He moved surely through the woods and glanced back to make sure the women followed him closely.

They came upon a clearing a few yards downstream from the bridge they crossed earlier. Duncan turned and studied the females behind him. "A carriage will arrive momentarily to take us to the castle." He led them to the black bridge, and they walked across it.

"Where are the special fish?" Ivy motioned down to the stream where the bubbles rose six inches above the water and popped.

Duncan's shoulders slumped. "I don't know. And that is one of the reasons I need your help."

"Your kingdom is going to hell in a handbasket, isn't it?" Ivy glanced around. "But I still don't understand why my sister and I are here."

A crimson carriage rolled down the main path and stopped a few feet from the group. The coachman hopped down and opened the door.

Duncan looked at the women and glanced longingly at his home. He pushed his hair back. "Please. I'll explain everything when I arrive home. Just a couple more minutes."

Rose moved to the carriage, and Ivy followed her. She stopped and looked closely at the coachman. "I know you. You came to pick me up."

The coachman lowered his eyes. "Yes, lady."

"I'm glad." Ivy patted his arm. "You were so nice to me." She stepped behind Rose into the carriage.

She heard a murmur of voices and poked her head back out. "Are you coming?"

Duncan's lips twitched. "Yes, woman. I'm coming."

* * * *

The ride to the castle was smooth and quiet. Ivy and Rose both looked out windows and tried to take in the sights and sounds of the new world. Characters of every sort played on lawns and hung out clothes. The full moon they saw on the far side of the bridge had faded into daylight on the other side of town.

When Ivy asked, Duncan shrugged. "It is how it has always been. Some prefer the dark."

They approached the castle and pulled up to the front gate. When Ivy noted Rose's hands shook in her lap, she stilled them with her own. "Are you okay?" she asked.

Rose's blue eyes welled up. "I'm dressed as a princess. About to enter a castle. And I've seen things I've read about in books all my life. I'm a little off-kilter."

"It's okay. We'll let Duncan rattle on. And then we'll go home." Ivy hugged Rose tightly. "Try and stay calm."

Duncan opened the door, stepped out, and extended his hand. Rose took it and moved out of the carriage. Ivy scowled. "I've got it myself, thanks."

He stood there and looked at her blandly. "I've got all day, you know."

Ivy ran her tongue over her teeth and snarled. "Fine. You be the prince." She put her hand in his and fought the thrill of the mere touch of his skin against hers. It didn't bear thinking what else she'd like to have pressed against her. She stepped quickly outside of the carriage and looked around. Her breath caught in her throat.

Magnificent was too tame a word. Her eyes traveled up the rock walls to towers where jewel tone flags billowed in the breeze. Sentries posted at every corner. The castle's size was overwhelming. It rose majestically into the sky and spanned at least a mile.

Ivy touched the wall in front of her and traced the blue rock. And then a brown one. The cool stones brought her back to reality. She was standing in front of a fairy tale castle. With her sister. And a prince. She turned and looked at her sister.

Rose's jaw hung open, and she stared straight up to the heavens. Her hand pressed to her breast as if to slow down her frantically beating heart.

Ivy reached out and took Rose's hand in her own. Everything up to this point was worth it. Her sister deserved to enjoy the day. Ivy would simply try to calm down and let things unfold. Then she would politely decline to help and toddle off back to the real world. The small pang in her heart would go away.

"Oh my." Rose struggled to capture the right words.

"Don't worry, sis. I believe Duncan knew what affect the castle would have on us." Her brown eyes narrowed on his green ones. "Didn't you?"

"Come, ladies." Duncan's face seemed to grow longer. His eyes deepened a bit, and he tried to smile. "I need to see my father. And I'm sure he wants to see the both of you."

The trio moved forward a couple of steps when a young man strode purposefully forward. Ivy bit her tongue. Hard. Apparently plain people need not live here. Because this man was beautiful.

His blonde hair curled haphazardly along his ears. It was so light it seemed to absorb the sun's rays. His baby blue tunic and gold pants shone brightly. Neither hid the ease and gracefulness the man carried in every step. And his blue boots dazzled the eyes. The man's body was lithe and graceful. His whole being seemed to bounce with energy.

As he approached, Ivy watched Rose. And she could see that the kingdom had more perks than she originally thought. Her sister was overwhelmed, and who could blame her? As the man came closer, Ivy could make out his aristocratic features and baby blue eyes. He was a perfect specimen of fairy tale royalty.

"Eric!" Duncan rushed forward, and the men embraced. They looked like night and day standing there. One so dark and handsome

82

while the other was light and beautiful. It was almost too much for a poor mortal's heart to take.

Ivy moved over to Rose and whispered in her ear, "Easy, woman. Let's not give the eye candy too much power."

Rose snickered and shot Ivy a glance. "The eye candy is really persuasive."

Ivy coughed to cover her laugh as the two men approached.

"Ladies." Eric bowed low and then stood straight. He moved forward and brought Rose's hand to his lips. "My pleasure to make your acquaintance."

She blushed. "The pleasure is mine, Prince Eric." Her eyes seemed to take in his entire being.

"Just call me Eric." He winked and turned. "And you must be Ivy."

"I am." Ivy studied him objectively. She watched him take her hand and press a kiss to the back of it. It did absolutely nothing for her. Obviously, she needed professional help.

Eric stood and smiled sadly. "I hoped you would be back soon. Father wants to see you."

Duncan jerked his head in acknowledgement. "Let me settle our guests. And then I will go see him."

"He wants to see them, too." Eric looked at Rose and then Ivy.

"We'd be honored." Rose smiled prettily.

"Come." Duncan moved everyone forward. "We'll show you the castle and serve refreshments. Then you can meet our father."

Ivy pinched herself only once as they entered the main hallway. Because nothing she had ever read prepared her for the magnitude or the majesty of the castle. The furnishings gleamed while the floor and stairs boasted polished marble. Oil paintings hung on some of the walls, and Ivy moved forward to study the portraits. One, in particular, moved her.

It was a family portrait. A tall, dark-skinned man stood proudly above a woman with two small boys.

Ivy studied the man and saw Duncan in every line. It had to be the king. His emerald eyes seemed to penetrate every inch of the room and missed nothing. The gold tunic he wore fit to perfection. Rock-hard muscles perfectly outlined. Crimson pants fit muscular thighs. Ivy shot a glance to Duncan and noted he received quite a bit from his father's gene pool. There had to be something morally wrong about lusting after a fairy tale prince. At least for a mortal. Ivy had a snowball's chance. She shot him another look. But she could at least look her fill.

Her eyes moved back to the portrait. The older boy looked to be about ten. And the younger boy, six. It was obviously the royal brothers. Duncan dressed exactly like his father. Eric wore the same blue as his mother. Ivy leaned in and looked closely at their mother.

She was exquisite. Her blonde hair curled around her face in soft tendrils that looked like silk. Her cornflower blue eyes held a hint of laughter, and her mouth smiled generously. The woman's petite frame sat elegantly with a boy on each side. Her light blue silk gown fell in graceful folds.

Ivy felt someone walk up behind her. She jumped a little when Duncan's warm breath fanned the back of her neck.

"Mother passed a year after it was made."

She turned, and her eyes burned a little. "I'm so sorry." Ivy touched Duncan's arm in sympathy. "I know how hard it is to lose a parent."

"Thank you." Duncan's green eyes moved back to the portrait. He looked at his father, and Ivy saw pain. "He doesn't look like that much anymore. His health has declined rapidly in the last couple of months. And we don't know what's wrong."

Ivy winced but asked anyway. "What happened to your mother?"

Duncan shook his head. "No one knows. She came down with a fever and went to bed. She only lasted for a week. Our physician couldn't do a thing but make her comfortable." He looked back at his brother. "Eric was inconsolable for almost a year."

Ivy glanced behind her. Her sister and the prince had their heads together.

"And then we lost our stepmother."

The words startled Ivy. "You had a stepmother?"

"For a short while." Duncan frowned. "Father married Ellen about three years after mother died." His eyes dimmed in remembrance. "Ellen was always laughing. So lively. Blonde hair like mother's. But green eyes. She went out on a hunting trip not long after they were married. She never came back. Our guards searched and searched. All they ever found was her shoes. It was as if she disappeared off the face of the earth."

"One family should not have to endure so much tragedy."

"I agree." Duncan took Ivy's hand and put it on his arm. "However we're not here to discuss tragedy but hope."

"What do you want from us?" Ivy's brown eyes searched his. "You've told us nothing about why we're here. And why is it going to take both of us?"

Duncan shook his head. "I'll tell you everything. But first a bite to eat and then a visit with Father."

Eric walked over, smiling. "Rose is famished. Let's go into the dining room and be social for a bit. And then we'll take you to see Father."

"Excellent idea." Duncan clapped Eric on the back. "And perhaps you can show the ladies your latest hobbies. I think they would enjoy it."

Rose's blue eyes lit. "A prince and his hobbies. Sounds fascinating."

Eric held up his hands with a smile. "Just something to while the time, Rose. Hardly worth showing you."

"Come on, Eric," Duncan chided. "I'm sure the ladies will be fascinated."

Eric's blue eyes flashed for a minute before he conceded with a smile. "Okay, brother. A tour it will be."

Rose glanced down at Ivy's hand on Duncan's arm, and she grinned. Ivy scowled and snatched her hand back quickly. "Are we ready to eat?"

"Of course." Duncan moved to touch her hand again when she arched her eyebrow. "You don't have to make nice with the lowbrow guests. And I can follow you just fine." She watched Ivy place her hand on Eric's arm and gaze up at him with adoration.

"Oh geez," she muttered. "I knew I should have left her at home."

"Pardon me?"

Ivy turned to Duncan and touched his long, dark locks. His eyes darkened considerably. "You and your brother are too pretty by half. One dark. The other light. And both so gorgeous it hurts my eyes."

Duncan chuckled. "I have a feeling that wasn't a compliment."

"You're astute."

"Why are you so angry?"

Ivy watched her sister and Eric disappear into another room. She sighed and turned to Duncan. "I'm not angry so much as realistic." She put her hands on her hips. "Doesn't your kingdom overflow with beautiful women? Women-in-waiting to be your betrothed or something of the sort?"

Duncan lifted Ivy's chin and chuckled. "Beauty comes in many forms." His eyes dropped to her mouth.

"Don't." Ivy's voice was firm. "You don't know me. And I won't be some piece on the side for you." She removed his warm hand from her skin. "Even if I won't ever look like that." She motioned to the room her sister was in.

"I'm disappointed."

"Yeah, well. So am I." Ivy turned to go when Duncan took her arm again. She spun around.

Duncan placed his right hand over her heart. His fingers fanned out and warmed her skin through her thin shirt. Ivy's heart sped up, and she struggled to even her breathing. Duncan's hand against her breast was something she could get used to. In fact, she would probably be just fine if he never moved it from her skin. Ever.

Her body tightened, and her nipple peaked. The palm of his hand a mere inch from where she truly wanted it.

"Ivy." Duncan's husky voice washed over her skin. "A heart is a separate entity. It feels what it feels. And nothing can change that." He lips twitched. "And your heart feels perfectly lovely."

Ivy's eyes traced over Duncan's flawless features. Her heart needed to mind its own business. And the rest of her body just better fall in line. "Find someone else to cop a feel from." She plucked his hand from her chest and let it fall. "I'm hungry."

She could have sworn she heard him murmur, "So am I."

* * * *

Cook prepared quail, chicken, and beef. Several servants brought out corn, potatoes, and broccoli. And just when Ivy thought

88

she would pop, a server brought out apple pie. She groaned and pushed back from the table.

Eric and Rose had their heads together again at the foot of the table, and Ivy knew it would be an uphill battle to get her sister to leave this world and its problems behind. That was one of Rose's traits. She had this obsessive need to mother everyone. Ivy was the only person she had given up on with the mothering. But every now and then, Rose would still try.

"It's not all bad." Duncan cut a wedge of pie and slid it onto a plate for Ivy. "He's reasonably well-behaved. House trained."

"Quit making light of it." Ivy glared down at the piece of pie. "It would have to be apple, wouldn't it?" she muttered. She picked up her fork and took a bite.

"Ivy." Duncan's voice was soft. "Quit worrying." He glanced at his brother and Rose. "They're just talking. Getting to know one another." He looked at her hopefully. "We could try that."

Ivy put the fork down and looked Duncan full in the face. "What about me fascinates you?"

"Everything." He leaned forward farther, his face inches from her. His eyes traced every feature of her face.

"Quit," she snapped. "There is never something for nothing. So tell me what you want."

"Your life is harsh."

"My life is fine, thanks." Ivy's brown eyes glared at him. "So quit looking so damn understanding. You don't understand anything at all."

Duncan sat back in his chair. Ivy watched his tunic stretch across his chest and looked down quickly at the pie. It wouldn't keep her up at night. He simply sat there.

Ivy shot a look up at him and sighed. She opened her mouth to be hateful again, when her sister's voice broke in.

"Are you two finished?"

Ivy's head jerked up. "Yes." She stood up quickly. "Let's go visit the king."

Eric started to say something when Rose laid her hand on his arm. He shut his mouth with a snap. Ivy thought it highly unfair she couldn't do the same with Duncan.

Duncan stood and took Ivy by the arm. "Father is fragile right now. Please don't say anything to upset him."

"Understood." Ivy smoothed down her brown hair and wished for the thousandth time she could look halfway decent with no effort whatsoever. She looked over at Rose and smiled. At least her sister could properly represent the mortals.

Duncan and Ivy led Eric and Rose up the marble steps toward the second floor. Tapestries representing different fairy tales hung with care by huge windows. Ivy let her fingers play along the gold tassels at the bottom. They were utterly gorgeous renderings of some of the best-loved stories of all times. There were tables between the windows with vases full of exotic flowers. They spilled out in every direction and gave the hall a pleasant floral aroma.

They stopped outside a massive wooden door, and Ivy watched Duncan gather himself quickly. He motioned Eric and Rose to go in first. Eric knocked and waited. He put his arm around Rose's waist and guided her inside as soon as the door opened. Duncan and Ivy followed.

The room was dim but not dark. The largest bed Ivy ever laid eyes on sat in the middle of the room. The hand-carved oak headboard was pushed flush against the wall. There were massive windows on either side with heavy crimson curtains. The king's crimson and gold bedspread tucked against him to ward off the chill or more sickness, Ivy couldn't tell. But she felt her heart give a little at the sight before her.

The king appeared to have aged decades. His once dark hair now thin and gray. The young face marred with lines and age. All his strength drained away. He looked like a mere shadow of his former self. Ivy found it hard to believe it was Duncan's father in the bed. It looked like his great-grandfather.

Eric and Rose moved to the king's right side, and Rose curtsied. The king chuckled low.

"I see you have a beauty there, Eric. See that her every wish is granted."

"Yes, Father." Eric put his hand over his father's and squeezed lightly.

Duncan escorted Ivy forward to the king's left. "I also have a guest, Father."

Ivy looked down into the king's face and smiled. "It's a pleasure, Your Highness." She also curtsied.

"You brought me two beautiful ladies?" The king's voice was weak but amused. "What have I done to deserve this?"

Ivy looked down into his face and noted the lively green eyes behind the aged skin. She bit her lip to fight the tears behind her eyelids.

The king looked from one woman to the other. His eyes glinted, and Ivy swore they changed colors briefly. "Ah," he breathed. "Sisters. The resemblance is unmistakable."

Ivy frowned and started to say something when Duncan touched her hand. She bit down the remark and sat on the side of the bed. Eric moved forward but Duncan motioned him back. She took the king's ancient hand in her own and stroked it lightly.

"Thank you for letting us visit, Your Highness. Your lands are beautiful. Precious. And they give hope to so many."

"Child. You touch an old man's heart." The king smiled and studied her face. "You have too many shadows for one so young." He glanced back at Duncan. "But there may be something here for you besides fairy tales."

"Now I see where your son gets it," Ivy murmured. "Attractive flirts, such as yourself. shouldn't be let loose on the female population."

92

The king chuckled and then coughed. The female servant by the door rushed over and helped him sit up. She gave him a glass of an amber liquid out of a gold goblet.

Eric frowned. "We've bothered you too long, Father. Duncan and I will show the ladies around the castle. You rest."

"I want to see these two again." The king looked from his older son to the younger. And Ivy could see the strength even in his frail face.

"Yes, Father." Duncan walked over and hugged his father tightly. Eric did the same.

They filed out of the room, and Eric shut it behind him. He blew out a shaky breath and glanced at Duncan.

Ivy read the look and quickly turned away. She didn't want to feel anything. She looked at Rose and mentally sighed. Her sister had large tears wavering in her eyelashes. Rose blinked and one slid down her right cheek slowly. She brushed it away and turned her head.

Eric patted her shoulder, and she turned into him. Ivy raised her eyebrows at the show of affection on both parts. Things were moving far too fast in this land of make-believe.

"You were going to give us a tour?" Ivy stepped forward.

Rose lifted her head and looked at her sister. "Don't you feel anything?" She pleaded with her soft, blue eyes. "He's hurting. Can you not see that?"

Ivy set her jaw. "I saw everything. And now I'd like a tour of the castle."

Eric nodded and bowed. "As you wish." He tucked Rose's arm into his and led them down the hall. Rose looked back with a frown on her face, but Ivy ignored her.

Ivy felt Duncan's eyes on her but refused to give him the satisfaction of meeting his gaze. She held tight to her belief that she didn't belong here. Helping Prince Duncan. Dealing with something this important. It didn't hold with her.

"So." Duncan's voice broke into her thoughts. "Have you always been this stubborn?"

Ivy shot him a glance that could have dried a waterfall. "Yes. And you?"

He sighed. "I'm afraid so."

"I'm not giving in." Ivy stopped and dared him with her eyes.

"I'm not giving up." Duncan stopped also and set himself firmly in front of her. "Not only is the fate of my kingdom at stake. But my father's life." His green eyes looked deeply into hers. "You can't tell me you don't care."

Ivy looked down the hall at Eric and Rose. She allowed herself to touch Duncan's smooth cheek. "And if I'm not enough? If my sister somehow gets hurt? Or I fail?" She lowered her gaze. "How could I live with it?"

Duncan kept her hand on his face with his own. "Ivy." He lowered his mouth to hers slowly. "You're enough," he whispered softly against her parted lips.

Her eyes dilated in arousal. And time stood still. All she wanted was Duncan. His mouth against hers. His hands stroking her skin. His body pressed to hers.

Someone cleared his or her throat loudly. Duncan and Ivy both turned their heads to see Eric motion from the far end of the hall.

Ivy straightened abruptly and smoothed her hair back. "Our tour guide is impatient."

"I have something I have to show you later." Duncan took her hand in his. "Will you let me?" His fingers stroked her palm.

Ivy licked her lips and tried not to think too hard about his finger. "Yes."

"Ah, progress." Duncan's green eyes twinkled. He peered closely. "And you don't appear to have been harmed. Amazing."

"Smartass."

He chuckled. "Mortals are fascinating."

"You really are pushing it." Ivy rolled her eyes.

Chapter 5

Eric led the group down a wooden staircase near the end of the hallway. The steps spiraled down further and further into the darkness. A small lamp attached to the wall lit the space every twenty steps or so.

Ivy tried not to look down any more than she needed. Heights petrified her. She watched the back of Rose's head and little else. After what felt like a small eternity, she saw the end of the stairs.

The quartet stopped and paused outside a heavy oak door. Eric removed a key from his pocket and held it up.

"I like my privacy."

Rose's laughter pealed out. "I believe we all realize that now." She looked up toward the staircase. "How many stairs?"

"Two hundred and twenty." Eric chuckled. "Give or take." He bent and fit the key in the keyhole. He turned it quickly to the left and pushed the door open.

Rose walked in first. Ivy and Duncan followed.

It was one of the largest rooms Ivy had ever seen. It used to be an old wine cellar. The mahogany wood gleamed even in the dim light of the room. There were shelving units along the far wall with built-in storage. Multicolored bottles with corks nested side by side in the squares. There were also large circles that held a variety of dried herbs and flowers.

To her right, stood a large mahogany table with a scale and various knives placed on top. There was a small burner, which, even now, held a yellow bubbling liquid. A piece of glass the size of the top of her stove took up a quarter of it. Small flasks and vials stood at the ready.

Straight ahead, stacked shelves held more bottles with ancient, peeling labels. Daddy longlegs spiders crawled leisurely along the wood. To her left, the space went on for another two or three rooms.

Ivy walked toward the empty space when Eric grasped her arm. "Would you like to hear what I'm working on now?"

She blinked and looked up at him. "Of course." She glanced back at the other rooms. "I'm sorry. Curiosity, you know."

Duncan chuckled. "Eric has become quite the alchemist. He took to it like a duck to water several years ago."

"Thanks." Eric motioned to the table. "I'm trying to find a way to simplify fertilizer." He picked up the yellow liquid with a towel and swirled it. "Plant food in one easy liquid. One drop, and no more worries. No weeds. And all the nutrition it will ever need."

Rose stepped closer. "That's amazing." Her delicate skin glowed in the shadow of the liquid.

Eric cleared his throat and smiled. "I'm glad you like it." He walked to the built-in shelves and pulled an amethyst bottle out. The cork slid out of the bottle, and Eric held it up to Rose's nose. "What do you think?"

She inhaled deeply, and her eyes softened. "It smells like my mother."

Ivy frowned. "How did you do that?"

Eric walked over and held it up. "Your turn."

She looked at him distrustfully but dutifully leaned forward and inhaled. A light powdery scent filled her senses. *Mom.* Ivy blinked back the strong emotions the aroma brought. Duncan touched her back softly.

"It's a memory fragrance." Eric corked the bottle again and slid it back. "Scent triggers memory. It's one of our strongest senses."

"It's certainly powerful enough." Ivy fought the tears and turned her back to the rest of them. She pointed toward the open doorway that led into at least two more areas. "Can we see what's in there?"

Eric frowned. "It's quite a mess right now. We can reschedule if you like. I promise I'll show it to you another time."

Rose nodded. "That's fine." She yawned hugely. "I feel like I've been through the wringer today."

"Of course." Duncan moved forward and held up his hands apologetically. "I forgot how overwhelming our world could be." He looked at his brother. "Is the lift still in order?"

"Yes." Eric led them back through the doorway and locked the door behind him. He flipped open a panel on the wood door and pressed a black button.

Ivy heard a quiet clanging that became louder by the second. And then Duncan slid a large panel open to reveal a box held up by cables.

"Please." Duncan motioned them in.

They stepped inside, and Eric shut the panel. The box lifted higher and higher. Duncan turned and studied the two women. "Ladies, why don't you settle in for the night and let me instruct Cook to prepare dinner for you. We can have trays delivered to your rooms."

The lift stopped, and Eric stepped out first and held the door open.

Rose walked out next with Ivy close behind her. They exchanged quick looks.

"No problem." Ivy smiled briefly. "Where will we be staying?"

"This way." Duncan pointed down the hallway and up another flight of stairs. "The west wing is available. And I think you'll like the accommodations."

The women followed Duncan while Eric went downstairs to talk to Cook. Ivy touched the banners they passed and studied every inch of artwork. Sculptures of fauns and fairies stood in the moonlight of the windows. The castle was magnificent inside and out.

They stopped at the top of the stairs, and Duncan pointed to the first two doors on the right.

"These two are yours. They are adjoining." He bowed low. "I'll go and see if Eric needs any help."

The sisters watched the brothers leave. Ivy waited a couple of minutes and glanced at her sister. "How are you feeling?"

"Besides overwhelmed, freaked out, and excited?" Rose's color was high in her cheeks. "Not bad." Her blue eyes searched Ivy's face. "And you?"

"The same. More or less." Ivy cocked her head to the side. "Do you like Eric?"

Rose snorted. "I have a pulse, sis. So yeah. I like him." She pulled the blue ribbon out of her hair and let her blonde hair hang loosely. She ran her fingers through it and sighed. "What did you and tall, dark, and dreamy have to talk about?"

Ivy rolled her eyes. "You're killing me. You know that, right?"

Rose laughed. "And loving every minute of it." She sighed. "Not many of us get past the prickly exterior."

"He says he has something to show me."

Rose's eyes widened considerably. "That has possibilities."

"Shut up." Ivy shook her finger at her sister. "Right now."

"Maybe." Rose looked around and frowned. "This place should be the happiest on earth. Or whatever." She motioned around. "But it has this huge, gray cloud hovering over it." She shuddered suddenly. "Do you feel it?"

"Yes." Ivy opened the nearest door and motioned to her sister. "C'mon."

Rose stepped inside with Ivy right behind. Then they both simply stood there in awe.

It was a princess' room. Or maybe a genie. Strips of silky fabric hung from corner to corner and down the walls. Large, overstuffed pillows lay on the floor and across the massive bed against the far wall. Everything was crimson, cobalt, or an emerald color. Two large mirrors took up the walls on either side of the bed. And two immense windows filtered in moonlight through vibrant netting.

"They don't do anything halfway, do they?" Rose ran her fingers through the red silk piece closest to her. "I wonder what *my* room looks like?"

They turned as one, and Ivy watched Rose open the adjoining door. Instead of bold colors, the room was decorated in pastels.

Rose walked slowly inside and then her arms opened wide and she spun around. "Look at this!" She ran over and brushed her hand across her silken sheets. She flopped back on them and made a sheet angel.

Ivy watched from the doorway with a grin. Her sister acting carefree was something she didn't get to see every day. It was a rare and welcome sight.

Rose's blonde hair moved back and forth across the bed with her arms and legs. She slid off and stood up. Her hair held the static and floated about her head like a halo.

"I want a bedroom like this at home."

"Well sure." Ivy snickered. "In a perfect world."

101

They heard a knock, and Rose walked to the door and opened it. Duncan stood in the doorway with a massive tray in his hands. It was covered with a silver lid.

"I hope you two are hungry."

Rose frowned and stepped out to look behind him. "Where's Eric?"

"Back in his lab." Duncan moved inside and put the tray on a large, wooden table. He bit his lip when he looked at Rose. "Um. You have…" He motioned to her hair. He looked over at Ivy with a pleading look.

Ivy laughed and patted her sister's arm. "I think you've alarmed the prince."

Rose smoothed down her hair and grinned. "Sorry about that."

Duncan removed the lid from the tray, and Ivy's mouth watered. There was a large chicken dish in the center of the tray surrounded by vegetables and salads. And there were three plates.

Ivy arched her eyebrow and looked at Duncan. "You joining us?"

"If you'll allow me."

Ivy opened her mouth, and Rose interrupted. "Of course you can join us. We'd be delighted."

"Delighted," Ivy repeated.

Duncan pulled the chairs back and slid the women to the table. He set the plates in front of them and served the food. When they had everything they needed, he sat down.

He poured scarlet wine into three goblets and lifted his for a toast. "To destiny."

Rose shot Ivy a look and smiled. "To destiny."

"Destiny," Ivy muttered and clinked glasses with both of them. She cut her meat apart and looked over at Duncan. "What did you want to show me?"

Rose choked on her drink of wine.

Duncan patted her on the back and looked at Ivy. "A poem I think you'll find interesting. It's been passed down for generations."

"Okay." Ivy waited. "Do you have it on you?"

Her sister glared at her. Ivy looked blandly back.

Duncan shook his head. "No need to go see it. I have it memorized." He closed his eyes and spoke.

"A woman comes into a man's life
To save the kingdom, to be his wife
A beauty uncommon, a power rare
Her soul kept hidden, now laid bare
Hopes and dreams filter through
The kingdom old, now becomes new."

Rose's eyes widened in her face. "That's absolutely beautiful."

Ivy drank some more wine and looked at Duncan. "Now tell me what you think it means."

"It's fairly self-explanatory." Duncan's dark green eyes studied Ivy's face. "Just because you choose not to see it." He shrugged.

"Listen." Ivy sat forward. "We're not staying. Rose isn't hooking up with anyone. I sure as hell am not. So, there has to be another way to save your father." She cocked her head to the side. "Have Eric work on something."

"I would." Duncan set his jaw. "But that would require the Prospat plants and/or the healing fish. And unfortunately, those seem to have disappeared."

"I'm sorry." Ivy put her hand on top of Duncan's. "I really am. But there has to be a way to have Rupert give them back."

"He may not have them." Rose looked at Duncan and then Ivy.

"Have you lost your mind?" Ivy's eyebrows shot up. "You saw him. He threatened violence. He's insubordinate. Good God, Rose! All he needed was a red arrow pointing directly at him saying 'guilty'."

"He knows something," Duncan agreed. "And there is too much bad blood between us for me to get an answer from him."

Ivy opened her mouth to ask when Duncan held up his hand. "Now is not the time to rehash that."

"Fine." Ivy looked around. "We appreciate the accommodations. But I have work tomorrow. And I'm sure Rose needs to get back to bed and rest. When are we leaving?"

"In the morning." Duncan's eyes saddened. "You won't stay?"

"No." The word short and cruel.

He pushed back from the table and bowed. "Ladies. I leave you to your meal." Duncan walked out the front door and shut it behind him.

"Ivy!" Rose stood up and stared furiously at her sister. "You didn't have to be so damn mean. How would you feel if it were you?"

"I'm sorry!" Ivy threw up her hands. "I'm doing the best I can with what I have to work with. Do you honestly think that either of us is going to save this place?" She opened her arms wide. "Rupert was right. We're the token mortals. Useless in a magical world. Geez, Rose! Can't you see that?"

"You're afraid to fail." Rose studied her older sister. "You've never been afraid to fight."

Ivy set her jaw. "I'm going to bed. I suggest you do the same." She turned toward her room. "I'll see you in the morning."

Rose's voice softened. "The poem is beautiful."

"Yes." Ivy agreed. "It was. But I won't sacrifice my sister." She shut the door soundly.

* * * *

Rose looked at the door for a long time before she sank onto her bed. "I may not be the one to make the sacrifice."

* * * *

Ivy readied herself for bed. There were clothes stacked in the wardrobe in her size. A fact which both amazed and horrified her. Her world spun out of control faster by the second. It seemed like a

105

week ago she was at work dealing with a gremlin in her copier. Compared to what they faced now, she'd take the gremlin and make him donuts herself.

She walked over to one of the large mirrors and looked hard at herself. Ivy could have been any one of thousands of women. Average looks. Average size. Nothing remarkable. But just for a second, she imagined herself the heroine of Duncan's poem. Until the "beauty uncommon" part.

Duncan couldn't ask her to take part in something which could risk her sister. Rose was frail. She deserved a good life. A good husband. Not some half-assed shot at saving a magical kingdom and king. She needed someone to take care of her. Not the other way around.

A light tap at her door interrupted her thoughts.

Ivy pulled a sapphire robe down and wrapped herself in it. She opened the door and saw Duncan.

"I expected you." She swept her arm inside. "Come in."

Duncan walked in and waited for Ivy to shut the door. "Please listen to me."

She allowed herself a smile. "That's all I've done today. Listen to you." Ivy's eyes hardened. "Now listen to me." Her gaze swept over him, and he didn't flinch. "This whole tag team flirting thing?" She barked out a laugh. "Clever. But not going to work."

He waited while she vented.

"You and your brother wooing my sister and me. Did you draw the short straw?" Ivy's brown eyes flashed. "You don't know which one of us you need. So you want us both on a string." She paused. "And this is dangerous, is it not?"

"Incredibly."

"But anything for the greater good, right?" Ivy crossed her arms and glowered.

"Do you think so little of yourself? Or your sister?" Duncan shook his head. "I don't understand mortals." He moved closer to her and cupped her chin in his hand. "What I feel has nothing to do with the poem. Nothing at all."

Ivy's heart raced. Duncan's warm fingers on her skin made every other thought leave her. As he moved to cover her mouth with his, her lips parted gently.

The first touch shook her. Her body trembled under his gentle ministrations. Then she sighed. Duncan wrapped his arms around her and brought her closer to him, fitting her body tightly to his.

His mouth moved against hers. His tongue traced the soft sweetness of her mouth and flicked playfully against her own.

Ivy's hands clutched his long hair as she brought him closer. She needed to feel. To touch. To have him as close as humanly possible. Her body ached. Need balled inside her with such force she felt faint.

Heat rushed through every nerve ending, and she struggled with it. Sanity left her. All she knew was Duncan.

His hands moved gently down her shoulders and to her waist. He undid her robe and let it fall open. And then those hands moved up her stomach, past her rib cage, and cupped her breasts gently in his hand.

"Duncan." Ivy murmured the name against his lips. "Please."

He moved his fingers gently against her nipples, and she arched against him. Duncan moved his right hand to her shoulder and pushed the strap of her nightgown down. He let it fall over her breast and to her waist.

Ivy trembled as his mouth left hers and moved across her collarbone down to her breast. And when his mouth closed hotly on her skin, she cried out softly. Her hand clutched his hair tightly as desire burned inside her.

Duncan sucked the nipple gently and brought his left hand to her shoulder. He slid the other strap down and sighed in satisfaction as both of Ivy's breasts were bared to him. His hands moved to her lower back as he brought her closer.

Need poured through Ivy's body, and she trembled on shaking knees. "Duncan," she murmured.

He lifted his head and looked deeply into her eyes. His emerald eyes so dark, she felt herself falling somewhere she'd never been.

"We need to quit." Ivy lifted the straps up and tried to put them back on her shoulders.

Duncan sighed and helped her.

He ran his thumb over her swollen lips and shook his head. "This isn't about a poem. It's about two people who want each other."

Ivy fought to keep control of her body and her emotions. It was the hardest thing she'd ever done. She lifted her head and stared at Duncan. "We're not staying." Her eyes searched his. "And if you truly want to be with me, you'll come to me in my world."

Duncan shook his head and walked to the bedroom door. "Goodnight, Ivy." His gaze never wavered from hers.

She heard the door shut with a finality that broke her heart into pieces. She was no fool. When she asked him to come to her, it was as if she asked him to give up everything he was. It was the only way she could think of to sever any kind of relationship.

All the feelings of inadequacy welled up inside Ivy and choked her. Silent tears slid down her face and dropped onto the plush crimson carpet.

Duncan would find his princess. His rare beauty. The woman who would fit in this world and help him rule it. But that wasn't her. And it never would be.

* * * *

Ivy woke up early the next morning and opened her curtains. The sun broke across the horizon and beamed its rays along the land. The orange yellow globe grew as she watched it, and she marveled at it.

The loud knock at her door startled her. Ivy opened it and smiled at the maid on the other side.

The woman bowed politely then brought a tray inside and set it down. "Morning, lady."

"Good morning."

"Prince Duncan asked me to give you this." She produced a parchment from her pocket and handed it to her.

"Thank you." Ivy smiled and let the maid out.

As soon as the door shut, she unrolled the paper and read it.

Dearest Ivy,

Our coachmen will take you and your sister back to your homes. I have business to attend at the other side of the kingdom. Please reconsider what we discussed. And know that I will think of you often.

Duncan

Ivy rolled the parchment back up and set it on the table. Of course he had business to attend to somewhere else. That was fine. It was about what she expected. She walked over to the adjoining door and tapped on it.

Rose opened the door and smiled. "Morning, sis."

"Morning, hon." Ivy motioned back to her room. "The maid brought lots of food. Come on over."

Rose glanced around. "Where's Duncan?"

Ivy looked back at her quickly. "Have you lost your mind?"

"You let him leave?" Rose frowned. "What good is that?"

"Listen very carefully." Ivy led her sister to a chair. "Duncan is a prince in the land of make-believe. I'm a mortal. I have a job. Responsibilities. This foray into madness is done."

Rose opened her mouth again, and Ivy shook her finger at her. "Not another word. We'll leave. And this will all be over."

"I'm worried about the king." The words soft but firm.

The admission touched Ivy's heart. So was she. And that's why she was convinced Duncan was mistaken. There had to be another woman who could actually help.

Ivy stroked her sister's hair softly. "Rose. We've done what we could. We can't produce the fish or plants. We can't help because we don't know what the hell we're doing."

She made Rose a plate and passed it to her. "Not to mention that it's dangerous here. That Rupert fellow looks like he eats mortals who piss him off. And I'm pretty sure that if I stayed, I'd be on the menu."

"He's sad."

Ivy rolled her eyes at her sister. "Rose, he's homicidal. I'm sorry you've mistaken that for sad."

Rose shook her head. "Not everything is black and white. Just because you see criminals and the baser element all the time does not mean they're all like that." She buttered her toast and took a bite.

"I don't want to fight." Ivy made her plate and watched her sister. "I'm sorry you have to leave Eric."

Color rose in her sister's cheeks. "He is rather pretty."

"Rather," Ivy said dryly.

"Do you think we'll see them again?" Rose's blue eyes were soft as she looked at her sister.

"I don't know." Ivy's answer was painfully honest.

Rose pushed her plate back. "I'm going to dress, and we can leave."

Ivy watched her sister shuffle back into her room and shut the door. She pushed herself back from the table and walked to the large mirror nearest to her.

"What do you say?" Ivy looked at her reflection curiously. "Will Duncan find his Beauty?"

The mirror wavered at the words and misted over. Ivy watched in shock as images filtered through the glass.

Duncan. And then a picture of him kneeling at the feet of a beautiful woman with black hair. The woman almost looked like Snow White. Fair skin. Rose-red lips. Duncan smiled, and she smiled back.

Ivy's stomach rolled painfully at the sight. She turned her back to the mirror and walked on trembling legs to her bed.

"I was right," she whispered. *Then why does it hurt so badly?*

* * * *

The coach dropped Rose off first. Then it rolled up to Ivy's house. When the coachman came to help her out, she leaned forward and kissed his cheek.

His eyes grew wide.

Ivy smiled and stepped down the stairs. "Take care."

"Same to you, Miss." He tipped his hat and climbed back on the coach.

Ivy waited for him to leave. But instead, he took a small box out of his pocket and handed it down to her.

"Something for you, Miss. In case you need a ride sometime."

Ivy took the box with a smile and watched until the carriage disappeared. She opened the box and saw a big, black button. She smiled and shut the lid. Her own carriage on call.

Then she turned and walked slowly up her sidewalk. It was still Monday in the real world. Not even an hour after she got off work. And Ivy had a lot on her mind.

She unlocked her front door and stepped inside. Home looked the same. No unicorns or giants lounging about. No witches or warlocks menaced her. Maybe her venture into wonderland was truly over.

Ivy kicked her shoes off and shuffled into the kitchen. She grabbed a soda out of the fridge and pulled her hair back out of her face. The flowers she received earlier lay on her kitchen counter, and she frowned. She never asked Duncan if he sent them. But it didn't matter now, did it?

She picked them up and threw them in the nearest trash. Fat lot of good they did her now. Only a reminder of her insecurities and wishes that didn't come true.

"Room for another at your pity party?"

Ivy shrieked and dropped her soda on the kitchen floor. She looked up in disbelief at the mermaid sitting on her counter.

The redhead flipped her glittery tail around and brushed back her glossy hair. Her blue eyes studied Ivy with curiosity. The kitchen light accented the mermaid's sparkling scales.

"There is not a revolving door on my house, damn it!" Ivy grabbed the cloth off the sink, wetted it, and wiped up her sticky mess. "And you creatures," she pointed, "need to get the memo on that."

"Ivy." The mermaid's eyes shined brightly. "You opened the door yourself." She picked up the toaster and studied her reflection in the silvery surface.

"Bullshit." Ivy slammed the sticky cloth into the sink and took the toaster from the mermaid. "Get out of my house." She looked at the mermaid closely. "Aren't you supposed to be in water or something?" And then curiosity got the better of her. "And how do you keep those shells in place?" She motioned to the mermaid's chest.

The mermaid leaned forward. "A new invention allows us to spray our fins and be out of water for hours at a time. And these," she pointed at her breasts, "I'm not quite sure." She laughed. "Isn't it marvelous, though?"

"Peachy," Ivy sniped. "Absolutely damn fantastic."

The mermaid pouted. "No need to be hateful. I am here to help." She threw her arms open wide.

Ivy shook her head. "What in the hell are you talking about?"

"You're a little rough around the edges..." she began.

"Out." Ivy's voice shook with anger. "Now. And don't bother showing your fins in this neck of the woods again." Her eyes flattened dangerously. "And tell everybody else they are not welcome here."

The mermaid frowned and waved as she disappeared.

"Good heavens!" Ivy reached into the fridge for another soda. She popped the top and drained half of it down. "Totally unacceptable," she murmured.

And then the flowers exploded.

"Shit!" she screamed.

Petals fluttered down from the ceiling and littered her kitchen floor. Ivy walked over to the metal trashcan and grimaced. The container was toast. Several dents marred all sides of it. And the bottom still smoked ominously.

Ivy turned and snatched the fire extinguisher from beneath the kitchen sink. She sprayed it into the can and leaned against the kitchen cabinet.

"Well that was a fine ending to a lovely day."

115

* * * *

Ivy went to work Tuesday and put two large pieces of doughnuts into the copier. She did her job. She was the picture of professionalism. And if she thought of a dying king and the prince of a fairy tale kingdom, no one ever knew.

If a pixie wanted to sit on the top of her monitor while she typed, fine. If a gnome sat on her bookshelves in the office, fine. Apparently, she was the only one to see the unusual visitors. And Ivy was becoming really good at ignoring them.

She clocked out at the end of her day and drove over to Rose's house. Her sister was a bit frailer than she was. And she worried about Rose all day. Calling seemed rather impersonal at this stage in the game.

Ivy pulled into the driveway and walked directly to the kitchen door. She tapped on it twice and moved back when it opened. Her mouth dropped open at the sight before her.

Rose set the kitchen table for tea. And she had guests. Little Brown Bear sipped contentedly from his cup while his stuffed animal counterpart sat across the table.

But it was the sight of her sister which affected her most. Rose wore make-up. She brushed her hair and plaited it. And she wore jeans and a pink T-shirt.

"Am I at the right house?" Ivy swallowed convulsively and looked around.

Rose ushered her in and shut the door behind her. She winked at Ivy. "I have guests."

"I see that."

"Hello!" Little Brown Bear squeaked.

"Hi." Ivy waved and then pulled her sister to the side. "I can't get rid of them, and you're inviting them over for tea," she whispered.

"I couldn't just leave him there by himself." Rose shook her head. "He's all alone. At least here I can take care of him."

"You care too much," Ivy accused.

"You don't care enough." Rose's blue eyes were hard and unyielding.

Ivy ran her tongue over her teeth at the pain of the words. "You decide to get a backbone while you were in wonderland?"

"Quit being such a bitch."

Ivy's jaw dropped. She could count the number of times she'd heard her sister curse on one hand.

Rose glared at her sister. "Just because you feel like proving how tough you are at the expense of an important man, doesn't mean I agree with you."

"Okay." Ivy fought back the pain and nodded. "I see. So your solution is to go back and possibly get us killed for the cause. How perfectly stupid."

Rose shook. "I have spent far too long locked up in my own, safe, little world. Watching television. Ignoring life." Her blue eyes

117

flashed. "And now I realize we both did that. I was obvious. But you had your own cave, didn't you?"

Ivy turned on her heel and walked to the door. "When you come to your senses, you know where I'll be." She stopped in her tracks when Rose touched her arm.

"They need us, Ivy. They need us. How can you say no?"

Ivy shook her head and walked back to her car. She started it and sat in the driveway. "Son of a bitch!" She slammed her hand on her steering wheel. Her hand throbbed painfully. Ivy killed the engine and walked back to the kitchen door. She knocked and waited for Rose to answer.

"Yes?" Rose smiled at her sister.

"If we're going to save the entire fairy tale kingdom, we need a game plan."

Chapter 6

Ivy sat at Rose's kitchen table and drank tea with Little Brown Bear and her sister. Her mind raced over the possibilities of what they were going to embark on. And fear for her sister was forefront in her mind.

She set her cup down and studied Rose. Her sister looked like their father. Blonde hair and blue eyes. Fair complexion. Their dad was a handsome man. Ivy pushed the accident that took their parents' lives into the far corners of her mind. Ever since her parents passed, she had taken on the parental role for her sister. She wouldn't dwell on what she couldn't change. Her main concern was Rose.

"I think we need to be careful." Ivy looked into Rose's eyes. "We don't know what we're doing. And I won't sacrifice you for anyone. King or not."

Rose steepled her fingers. "And if I'm not the beauty the poem refers to?"

Ivy thought of the dark-haired woman in her bedroom mirror. *Who was she?* She shook her a head slightly, as if to clear it. She smiled at her sister. "How could anyone look at you and not think you're a beauty?"

"Please." Rose rolled her eyes. "We need to be objective. It could be either of us. Or someone else entirely."

"I'm worried the price of this little caper will be too high." Ivy tapped her fingernails on the table. "I keep getting visits from creatures trying to help persuade me. It's annoying."

Rose's eyes lit up. "Who else came by?"

"Oh gee." Ivy shook her head. "Just a mermaid. And a pixie and a gnome kept me company at work."

"Really?" Rose's blue eyes sparkled.

"Quit finding this so exciting! That's what I'm worried about. We'll go off half-cocked and end up in a world of hurt."

"What did the characters say?" Rose leaned forward and waited.

"The pixie and gnome were quiet. They simply kept me company. And the mermaid," Ivy groaned, "wanted to give me a makeover."

Rose laughed so hard she snorted.

Ivy glared at her sister. "You're not right."

"A seaweed mask?" Rose had tears streaming down her face. "A kelp facial?"

Little Brown Bear looked from one sister to the other. He grinned broadly.

"Shut up," Ivy snapped, even though her lips twitched.

The bear stood in his seat. "I like you two."

Rose scooped the bear up and hugged him. "Good. Because you're family now." She kissed his head and put him back down. She put her hand on her Ivy's. "And family sticks together."

* * * *

Ivy drove home and felt better about her decision. At least she would be assured she and Rose could keep an eye on each other. The last thing she needed was to worry about her sister meddling in otherworldly affairs by herself.

She parked and walked up to her front door. Just as she slid the key in the lock, she heard someone walk up behind her. Ivy spun and held out her keys as a weapon.

"Easy!" The slender man backed up with his hands held in the air. "I didn't mean to startle you."

"Well you did." Ivy scowled and glanced around. It grew dark quickly. The last thing she needed was to be at the mercy of some unknown assailant. She studied the man. He didn't look like he was particularly strong, but one never knew. His face was almost delicate. She took a mental picture for the police report later.

"I'm going to reach into my pocket."

Ivy shook her head. "I don't think so, big boy." She dug into her purse as if to pull something out. "I have mace."

"Please." His brown eyes pleaded behind his silver-framed glasses. "I have something to show you. And if you still want me to leave afterwards, you'll never see me again."

"Keep your hands above your waist," Ivy threatened. "Or you'll be a writhing mass of pain."

The man leisurely reached into his pocket and delicately pulled something out. He opened his hand slowly and showed Ivy what he held.

A miniature of Prince Charming looked back at her.

"Holy shit," she muttered and then looked up into the man's brown eyes. "Adam?"

"Yes, Beauty." He bowed low and grinned.

She pushed her keys back into her purse and launched herself at him. "Oh my God! How did you find me?"

Adam hugged her tightly and laughed. "Simple process of elimination."

"You almost had your ass tied in a knot," Ivy admonished and stepped back. "You shouldn't sneak up on women like that."

"Writhing mass of pain," Adam repeated and smirked. "You crack me up."

"You're an ass." Ivy took her keys back out and opened her front door. "Come in. Tell me what's going on."

Adam stepped inside and looked around. "You have a nice house."

"Thanks. But I don't think you came all this way to admire my living arrangements."

"You're right." Adam took a deep breath. "The other night was magical. Literally. And I had a great time." His eyes studied her. "But I have this feeling it's not over yet."

Ivy was cautious. "What do you mean?" She put her purse down and pulled her hair back in a ponytail.

He sighed. "This is going to sound crazy. But I thought you might understand." He raked his hand through his short, brown hair. "Old King Cole has set up residence in my living room."

Ivy bit her lip. "Are you sure?"

"Um…yeah. Considering he brought his bowl, pipe, and fiddlers three." He blew out a breath. "That was a lot harder to say than I thought it would be." Adam rubbed his hands together. "So, are you going to call the men in white coats, or what?"

"We can have adjoining rooms." Ivy took Adam's hand and led him out to her garden. "Because I see fairies." She motioned to the hundreds of lights sparkling on the plants before them. "Oh. Not to mention mermaids, pixies, and gnomes."

"Shit." Adam's voice was faint. He clutched Ivy's hand tightly. "We're not insane, are we?"

"No." Ivy patted his thin shoulder. "We're not. We're soldiers of a sort."

"But who recruited us?" Adam turned, and his brown eyes searched hers.

"A kingdom with a dying king. A couple of princes. And every mythical creature under the sun."

He laughed shakily. "I always wanted to be in the stories I read. I thought being a part of a fairy tale story would be the height of excitement."

123

Ivy glanced at her garden and then her guest. "You excited yet?"

* * * *

Ivy led Adam back into the kitchen. She poured him a soda and one for herself.

"Are you willing to become part of this?"

He looked up, both scared and excited. "Yes. Being an accountant has its perks. But nothing compared to this."

"It could be dangerous." Ivy sipped her drink and studied Adam. He was slender. Almost to the point of being frail. She recalled what he said about childhood illnesses. And she was scared for him. His brown hair hung shaggily over his forehead. But his brown eyes shone with intelligence. He would be a handy ally.

"I know." Adam blew out a breath. "But I have to do something."

"You sound like my sister." Ivy's tone was wry.

"You have a sister?"

She rolled her eyes. "Let's just call and invite her to join this meeting of the mortals, shall we?" Ivy punched in Rose's number and had a brief conversation. She hung up the phone afterwards and looked at the clock. "Rose should arrive in the next ten minutes or so. And she's bringing company."

Adam looked at Ivy closely. "You're not telling me something. Or several somethings."

"We'll wait for Rose and her guest. Then we'll plot and gnash our teeth to our heart's content." She chuckled. "What's Old King Cole doing now that you've left him to his own devices?"

"I haven't the faintest." Adam shrugged. "He's really quite pleasant, though."

They made small talk until they heard a knock.

Ivy rose and walked to the front door. She opened it and laughed aloud at the picture she saw.

Rose stood there with Little Brown Bear on her hip. She leaned forward and kissed Ivy's cheek. "Hi, sis." She walked inside and looked around. "No more otherworldly visitors?"

"Nah. Just a nice mortal man sitting in the kitchen. He also attended the 'One Enchanted Evening' party." Ivy chuckled. "And he has Old King Cole as a boarder now."

Little Brown Bear smiled. "I heard he moved."

"C'mon." Ivy took Rose's hand. "We're having a meeting to see how much sanity we have left between us."

They entered the kitchen, and Adam stood up. He frowned suddenly. "How did you get more gold dust? My invitation disappeared as soon as I came back from the party."

"No gold dust." Ivy looked into Adam's eyes.

He blushed furiously and cleared his throat. "Oh."

"She naturally looks like that." Ivy rolled her eyes. "It's her cross to bear."

Rose walked forward and extended her hand. "Pleased to meet you, Adam." She held up her bear. "And this is Little Brown Bear."

Adam shook her hand and pulled out a chair for her. "The pleasure is mine."

Ivy sat down and waited for Adam to do the same. "I've gathered you here today…" she began.

Rose snickered.

"I've always wanted to say that." Ivy sighed. "Anyway. We're in a shitload of trouble. And we need to decide what the hell we're doing." She held up her hand and ticked off her fingers one at a time. "Here are the options. One, do nothing. Two, do something." She looked at the other people at the table. "Anything I missed?"

"We've got to help." Rose patted Little Brown Bear's head absently.

"I agree." Adam nodded.

Rose smiled at him, and he blushed again.

Ivy snapped her fingers. "Okay. Here's the deal. We do this together. All right? I say we wait until the end of the week. Gather our forces. And storm the castle, so to speak."

"Why the end of the week?" Rose looked worried. "We may not have that much time."

Ivy put her hand on her sister's. "We have time. And I'm sure Prince Light and Prince Dark will be just as happy to see us."

Rose looked disgusted. "Sarcasm isn't a sword you can hack at people with."

126

"Listen." Ivy cocked her head to the side. "It's served me well. So I'm going to hone it and wield it at my leisure."

Adam threw back his head and laughed. "You two ought to take your show on the road."

Ivy smiled. "We will. This weekend. And you're coming along for the ride."

* * * *

Ivy woke the next morning at six-thirty again and groaned loudly. She heard a small rustling and sat bolt upright. Six mice and six small birds perched on her windowsill by her bed. They looked at her curiously.

She held up her hand. "If you all think you're going to break out in song and try to dress me, I'd advise against it."

The biggest mouse looked horrified. "We wouldn't dare, Miss!"

Ivy rolled her eyes and bit back a chuckle. "Yeah. Okay. To what do I owe the pleasure of this morning visit?"

A bluebird with a red polka dot handkerchief on her head spoke up. "It was our turn."

"What?" Ivy rubbed her brown eyes and yawned. "You're not making any sense."

Another bird bumped wings with the one who spoke. "Nothing, Miss. We're only keeping you company."

"Great," Ivy muttered. "Anyone know who else is on the schedule today?"

Not one creature uttered a sound.

Ivy ran her tongue over her teeth. "I think I would prefer the twittering and singing to the silence." She ran her hands through her hair and reached for a ponytail holder. She pulled her hair up and studied her guests.

"How is King Cedric?"

Everyone's shoulders drooped perceptibly.

"Not good, Miss." The smallest mouse sighed. "His health still declines at a rapid rate."

Ivy winced. "How is Prince Duncan?"

"He travels, Miss." The mouse bobbed his head. "He hopes that someone in our kingdom can help." His whiskers twitched. "He hasn't been home since you left."

She grabbed jeans and a T-shirt out of her closet and turned around. "Will you be staying here today? Or are you joining me at work?"

"Here, Miss," the bluebirds said as one.

"Ah." Ivy smiled. "Okay, then. I'll make toast for the lot of you. And then I'm going to work."

* * * *

Work kept Ivy hopping the entire time. There were a rash of burglaries in the city, and many people filed reports and came by to give statements. Her fingers ached by the end of the day, and she groaned.

"We can help you, lady." The pixie on the top of her computer peered down at her. "You don't have to do this all yourself."

128

"Somehow I've managed all these years without you," Ivy said dryly. "But thanks for the offer."

"She's a proud one," the gnome grumped from the bookshelves. "Everyone needs a little help."

Ivy shut down her computer and grabbed her purse. "I appreciate the company, guys. Really. But I'm doing fine all by my lonesome."

"That's what gets you into trouble."

The masculine voice startled Ivy so badly, she dropped her purse. She turned quickly and saw Prince Duncan standing there.

"I don't suppose anybody in your world ever uses a door or anything, do they?" Ivy pressed her hand to her rapidly beating heart. She didn't kid herself. Part was fear. The rest was excitement. Duncan wore an ivory tunic threaded with gold over black pants. His long hair pulled back from his face accented his cheekbones and eyes.

Ivy glanced around and then looked at the clock. "Listen. I have one more shift to talk to. Then I'll be back at my house. You can meet me there." She heard voices in the hall and winced. "Please."

"At your house?" Duncan repeated.

"Yes!" she snapped. "At my house. Go!" She shooed him with her hands.

Duncan bowed and disappeared.

Ivy gave the paperwork to the officers and locked up her office. She drove home quickly and tried not to think of Duncan. So he was

129

a darkly handsome prince who made her think naughty, naughty thoughts. So she couldn't forget the feel of his mouth or his hands on her body.

"Shit," she muttered. Her best bet was to stay as far away physically as possible. Ivy sighed. And maybe the prince already found his beauty. But if he did, what was he still doing bothering her?

Ivy pulled into her driveway and walked to her front door. The lights were on, and she groaned. She would have the electric bill from hell this month. She unlocked the front door and stepped inside.

Her jaw dropped.

Thousands of tiny crystals lit every inch of her apartment. They sparkled and glowed brightly. Even her threadbare couch looked halfway decent.

Ivy shut the door behind her and slid her purse onto the closest table. Her house was silent. "Hello?" she called out.

Duncan appeared in the kitchen doorway and smiled. "I hope you're hungry."

She blinked twice and looked closely at him. He had a "kiss the chef" apron on, and she laughed aloud. "You cook?" Her tone held disbelief.

He winked. "Yes. And I think it's time you tasted my culinary offerings."

She licked her lips. "Refresh my memory again. Why are you here?"

"I've decided to take you up on your offer." Duncan walked toward her slowly and stopped inches away.

Ivy could actually feel the heat from his body.

"What offer?" Her voice was faint, even to her own ears.

"To be with you." Duncan brushed her brown hair back and kissed her cheek.

She backed up so quickly she almost fell. She held up her hands and shook her head. "Whoa! You haven't thought this through."

"Yes. I have." Duncan approached her again. "Do you ever wonder about love in my world? All those beings falling in love and living happily ever after?" His green eyes darkened as they looked at her. "I want that. And I want you."

Warmth suffused her body at his words. But then reality bit her on the ass. Ivy shook her head. "You're not thinking this through. I'm a means to an end. And even that's iffy."

"Why do you sell yourself short?" Duncan reached out and stroked her cheek.

Ivy brushed his hand aside. "Happily ever after doesn't exist. Don't you get that?" She shook her head. "I've had boyfriends who claimed to love me. But they didn't. And neither will you. It's an improbability."

"I don't say these things lightly." Duncan's eyes flashed.

"I know." Ivy held up her hand and tried to smile. "And I don't mean to insult you. But I've seen the females in your world. And you need one of them. Not me."

Duncan growled lowly, and he threw up his hands. "You are the most obstinate woman in two worlds!"

Ivy touched his arm lightly. "Duncan, you don't need to be with me. We've decided to help you anyway."

"You and Rose will come back to my kingdom?" Hope lit in his face.

"Well, Rose, myself, and Adam."

"Adam?" Duncan's eyes narrowed. "Who is this Adam?"

Ivy snorted. "You're a nut. Don't get your tights in a knot. He was at the party. Prince Charming. Remember him?"

"Ah." Duncan smiled. "I remember him. Nice man." He suddenly frowned. "But what is he doing contacting you?"

"Well." Ivy's voice was dry as dust. "Apparently he has houseguests, too."

Duncan laughed aloud. "This is the first time in a long while that my people have come to your world." He looked at Ivy again. His hand stroked her head lightly. "But enough of business this evening. I have come to you. I accept your terms."

"My terms?" Ivy choked out.

He quoted her words back to her. "'And if you truly want to be with me, you'll come to me in my world.'" Duncan bowed low. "And here I am."

"Oh hell." Ivy's hands shook.

Duncan quirked an eyebrow. "Weren't those your words?"

She bit her lip. "Technically, yes."

"Well, technically, I'm at your disposal." Duncan moved closer. "I have something for you."

Ivy's body flushed. Duncan took her hand and pulled her gently to him. "Dinner's ready," he whispered in her ear.

She pulled back and looked into his deep green eyes. "Let's have dinner, then."

* * * *

Duncan somehow whipped up an amazing four-course meal in her kitchen. And Ivy enjoyed every last bite. Her mind raced over the way she would gently break to Duncan the news she would never be anything more to him than help.

Ivy put her napkin down and smiled at Duncan. "Thank you. Dinner was wonderful."

"I've made dessert."

Her eyes widened. "I don't have room, Duncan. Good grief!"

"You'll have room for this." Duncan opened her fridge and took out a glass platter with a beautiful strawberry pie. The whipped topping swirled in striking designs on the sides. And whole strawberries sat on the top.

"It's beautiful," she whispered. She patted her stomach. "But I'm not hungry."

"I am." Duncan's green eyes studied Ivy's face.

"Oh."

He took the platter and stepped out of the kitchen. "Come with me."

Ivy warred with herself for about two minutes before she stood and followed him.

Duncan walked slowly and carefully into Ivy's bedroom. As he set the platter on the nightstand, he turned to her.

He reached out gently and tugged her closer to him.

Ivy tried to calm her breathing as his warm hands closed over her arms. Then he slid them to her back and pressed her tightly against him.

Duncan rained tiny kisses across her face until he reached her mouth. And then he closed the gap with barely a sigh.

Ivy felt as though she were drowning. Duncan's mouth moved gently against hers while his hands traced the contours of her back. Then his hands moved around to her sides and up across her stomach.

She stilled his hands immediately. The roundness of her stomach bothered her, and she didn't want Duncan anywhere near her flabbiness.

Duncan removed his lips from hers and sank down to his knees. He lifted her shirt gently and pressed his lips to her bare belly.

Ivy drew in a sharp breath and threaded her fingers through his hair.

"So beautiful," he murmured. His hot breath fanned against her sensitive skin.

He stood quickly and pulled Ivy's top over her head and tossed it to the floor.

She felt his hands move to her back and unclasp her white silk bra. Duncan gently took it off her shoulders and slid it down her arms. As soon as her breasts were freed, he cupped them and brought one, then the other, to his mouth.

His tongue traced the hardened nipples and sucked gently at the nubs. Ivy's legs shook with desire. She was on fire. For the first time in a long time, she didn't think of her size. She concentrated on Duncan and everything he made her feel.

"Duncan," Ivy sighed.

"Ivy." He lifted his head and lowered his mouth to hers.

Goosebumps broke out over her body at the sensations he caused. Ivy struggled to form a thought but quickly gave it up when Duncan's hands moved to cup her breasts. He stroked her softly while his mouth teased hers.

Her hands shook as she touched his silky brown hair. When he lifted his head, Ivy swore she could see eternity in his eyes.

Duncan moved her to the bed and had her sit down. She watched while he took a strawberry off the top of the cake and took a bite of it. He moved closer and rubbed the berry slowly across her lips. Then he ducked his head and sucked gently everywhere the berry touched.

Ivy's breath hitched in her throat. Before she could say a word, Duncan moved the strawberry down and made small circles around her right breast. She watched him lower his head and trace the sticky trail with his tongue.

Heat slammed through her with a fierceness she couldn't grasp. Ivy moaned loudly as Duncan's mouth moved over her breasts. Her hands fisted in her comforter.

He took his tunic off and threw it on the floor. Then he moved back and gently parted her legs and situated himself between them.

"Duncan," she whispered.

"Shhh." He took his finger and swiped a bit of topping. Then he started at Ivy's neck and traced a path to her belly button. After Duncan made the path, he stood and gently pushed Ivy back on the bed. Then he covered her body with his own.

Ivy shook with suppressed need. She had never felt anything remotely close to what she felt now. No man set her body on fire with a simple touch. But Duncan did things to her she never experienced.

She lay flat on her back while Duncan dipped his head and traced the topping trail with his tongue. Ivy arched up against him. She wanted more. Needed more. Her hands moved up and traced the muscles of his chest and stomach. He was perfection.

Duncan moved to undo her pants and slid them off her body. Then he stood and removed his own. Ivy watched him lower himself again, and she ached to have him inside her.

136

His hands traced over her bare skin. Ivy's body tightened under his skillful touch. And when his hand dipped below the waistband of her panties, Ivy dug her fingernails into his arm.

"So beautiful," he murmured against her neck. Duncan slid one finger lower and parted her legs.

Ivy cried out at the sensations. Then he slowly stroked her silky flesh while he bit gently on her neck. The ache spread until she thought she would die. And when she thought she couldn't stand another minute, her body shattered against his hand over and over again.

She clutched his body while she arched up to him. Her breath trembled in her throat. Ivy lay back slowly and closed her eyes.

Duncan slid her panties off gradually, and she opened her eyes to look at him. He stood on the side of the bed and parted her legs gently. And when he saw that she watched him, he slid his entire length into her.

Ivy shook as she felt her body tighten and welcome him. She wasn't done. Not by a long shot.

He pulled Ivy's legs around his waist and thrust gently against her. He bent down and took her nipple into his mouth.

The combined sensations Duncan aroused left Ivy awash in desire. She clutched at Duncan's hair while his body moved into hers over and over again. Then he stood once more and moved his hand between her legs to stroke her delicate flesh.

Ivy threw her head back and arched her hips up to meet his thrusts. His fingers moved skillfully, and she cried out as the first wave washed over her.

Duncan moved quicker, and Ivy came with a cry. He growled in satisfaction at the feel of her body and shuddered against her as he joined her in the ultimate pleasure.

She tried to open her eyes and focus them, but it was too much effort. She felt Duncan shift positions and sink down on the bed beside her. He stroked her hair gently and kissed her forehead.

"I've got to go."

Of all the sentences ever spoken after having sex, this one irritated Ivy the most. But she bit down on the hurt and actually smiled. "Okay."

"But I'll be back tomorrow."

"Okay." Ivy turned her back to him and attempted to pretend he wasn't there. She could hear him dress in the dark. And then a slight breeze broke over her body. And she knew he was gone.

"What did you expect?" she asked aloud. Ivy stared into the darkness. It wasn't as if she could knock having sex with a prince. And God knows, her body still hummed with pleasure. Not a bad way to spend an evening. "Just a perk," she murmured to herself. The thought didn't comfort her much. But she would live. She always did.

* * * *

Ivy woke at six thirty the next morning. She actually grew used to it. She glanced around her room and didn't see anything like birds or mice. Even the strawberry cake from last night was gone. Maybe that was a good sign.

She swung her legs over the side of the bed and pulled her hair back into a ponytail. Breakfast would be a good start. She was damn near starving. *All that sex. Hell of an appetite stimulator.*

Ivy walked into her kitchen and opened the freezer. Maybe some frozen waffles or something. A bit of syrup. And a caffeinated beverage of some sort was in order. She pulled out a couple of waffles and slid them into her toaster. She snagged a can of diet cola out of the fridge and stood there.

It was Wednesday. Middle of the week. And only two more days until she and her merry crew left to help out the land of make-believe. She would plan out a couple of things at work. Wednesdays were usually fairly slow.

"Will you need help?" A soft voice broke the silence.

Ivy screamed and looked around but didn't see anything. She held up her hands. "Okay. I don't do badly when I can actually see you. But when you're invisible, it's a little freaky."

"Down here, lady."

Ivy squinted and peered at where the voice seemed to come from. She shook her head. "I'm sorry. Still not seeing you."

"It's okay." She heard a sigh. "I really didn't expect you to. I'm a little vertically challenged."

She bit her lip to keep from laughing and turned her head. "Okay." Her waffles popped, and she put them on a plate. Then she doused them with syrup. Ivy sat at the table and looked in the voice's general direction. "Do you need anything?"

"No, lady. But thank you. Will you need help?"

"Who, me?" Ivy's voice showed surprise. "I'm fine, thanks." She finished her waffles and stood. "Make yourself at home." She cleaned up a bit and dressed for work.

* * * *

When Ivy arrived at work, there were people everywhere. They milled in the waiting area outside her office and took up every bit of available space. Many cried. Some wrung their hands. Despair permeated the air. She frowned and punched the code to open her door. *What the hell was going on?*

Ivy slid her purse into her desk drawer and looked around. Nothing seemed amiss. Then why did she feel as though something very bad were about to happen?

Her fears confirmed when Missy walked into the office looking like death warmed over. Her usual tight ponytail extremely skewed. No make-up. And she wore her civilian clothes.

"What's going on?" Ivy motioned to the commotion in the hallway. "And what the hell is wrong with you?"

"It's bad." Missy took a deep breath. "The police chief is sick. Very sick. And so is half the force. But that's not the worst part."

Dread crept over Ivy's skin, leaving it clammy and cold. "What?"

"The children." Missy's voice broke. "Most of the children are gone."

Chapter 7

Ivy's stomach dropped to the floor. "What do you mean?"

Missy's hands shook. "When these parents went to wake up their children for school, they were gone. Gone!" She bit her lip.

"It's okay." Ivy's mind raced. It had to be connected to the problems already out there. "Listen." She took Missy by the shoulders. "I have to go. I'm sorry."

"You can't!" Missy's voice wavered. "I can't process these people by myself!"

"I'm sorry." Ivy's voice hardened. "But I have something to take care of that won't wait."

Missy's blue eyes welled and spilled over. "You can't leave!" Tears slid down her cheeks.

"You can do this." Ivy tried to smile but couldn't. "And I promise I'll do everything I can to help when I get back." *If I get back*, she added silently.

She left Missy standing there and felt like an absolute shit. But her mind raced as she drove home. It would be too long to wait until this weekend. They needed to take action now. Because there were innocent children involved.

Nausea bubbled in her stomach. *Children.* Whoever upped the stakes would be very, very sorry. Ivy clenched her teeth. She would make sure of it.

* * * *

Ivy phoned Adam as soon as she reached her house. She didn't explain anything. She only told him to be at her house in fifteen minutes. Then she called Rose. Rose tried to ask questions, but Ivy cut her off with an abrupt, "I'll explain when you get here."

Her pulse raced with fear and adrenaline. Ivy changed clothes into a comfortable pant cotton set and paced her living room floor.

Someone knocked on her front door, and she swung it open forcefully. Adam stood there in blue jeans and a yellow button-down shirt. He pushed his glasses back up and frowned. "Where's the fire?"

Ivy held up her hand. "One minute. We're waiting on Rose."

He nodded and stepped inside.

Two minutes later, Ivy opened the door for Rose. She ushered her sister inside and patted Little Brown Bear on his head.

"Here's the deal." Ivy took a deep breath. "Things have gone downhill rapidly. We can't wait till this weekend. We can't wait another damn minute."

Rose paled considerably. "What happened?" She clutched the bear tighter on her hip.

The two looked at Ivy with fear clearly written on their faces.

"The police chief is sick. Along with half the department. But that's not the worst part." An image of Missy's face flashed in Ivy's mind, and she stiffened her backbone. "Most of the children are missing."

"Children?" Rose repeated. Her hand trembled as she brought it up to her mouth. "Who would take children?"

Ivy threw up her hands. "Who would kill a king? Who would try to decimate a kingdom?" She looked hard at the two people in front of her. "Now's the time. I'm going. Neither of you has to come along. Someone upped the stakes. And I don't want you to feel obligated."

Adam scowled. "Don't try to scare me off. I'm coming." He lengthened his stance as if he gained strength from his words.

"I'm coming." Rose kissed Little Brown Bear's head. She looked at her sister. "We stand a better chance together anyway."

Ivy moved closer to Rose. "Are you sure?" she whispered. "What about your health?"

"I'll be fine." Her blue eyes met Ivy's brown ones. "How can we go wrong helping a pair of princes?"

"I don't know." Rose glanced around her home and then back at her guests. "Are you ready to go?"

"Yes." Adam nodded.

"Yes." Rose looked at the bear. "You can stay at my house, Bear. Until it's safe."

"No." His high-pitched voice showed panic. "I go with you."

She smiled and kissed his ear. "As you wish."

Ivy grabbed the box on her living room table and opened the lid. "One carriage to go." She pushed the black button, and they waited.

* * * *

All three riders sat comfortably in the plush carriage while the scenery rolled by at an alarming rate. Rose played with Bear's ears while she stared off into space. Adam took a notebook and scribbled in it.

Ivy braced herself for the oncoming conflict. *Who would take the children? Make the police sick? It had to be connected.* It seemed like the poison from the fairy tale world spilled over into hers with barely a pause.

The carriage came to a smooth stop, and the coachman opened the door. Rose stepped out first, followed by Ivy. Adam climbed out last, and Ivy heard his breath catch.

"Nothing like your first look at the castle." She patted his arm and laughed.

Adam's neck craned to look at every nook and cranny. "It's beautiful." The words were softly spoken and filled with awe.

"C'mon." Ivy pulled him to the front door. "It's time to get to work."

She started to knock on the front door when it was flung open.

"What in the hell are you doing here?" Duncan's eyes raked over the group.

"Well that's a fine greeting." Ivy pushed past him and tried not to think of him in any terms but friendly ones. "We've come to help."

"What happened to this weekend?" Duncan's eyes narrowed. "What are you not telling me?"

"All in good time." Ivy blew out a breath. "Listen. We need to be here. To stay here. So put us up in a room or three and simmer. We can explain everything at dinner. Okay?"

Duncan glanced at all three and snapped his fingers. A maid appeared immediately. "Please escort our guests to their rooms. You two," he pointed at Ivy and Rose, "will have the same rooms as before. Little Brown Bear can have a small bed placed by Rose's. Adam will stay in the east wing with Eric and I."

Ivy smiled. "Thank you."

"Don't thank me yet." Duncan looked at Ivy, and her smile faded. "You and I are scheduled for a meeting in the den."

"Wait a minute!" Rose started to protest when Ivy shook her head.

"Let him rail at me. We're overdue."

Rose looked over her shoulder the entire time the maid led them away. When she turned the corner, Ivy glanced up at Duncan. He was furious.

He led her into the den and slammed the doors behind them. The windows rattled.

"What in the hell were you thinking? Traveling here unprotected?" He turned to her and grabbed her upper arms. His emerald eyes blazed. "You're going to be the death of me."

"Let go," Ivy snarled up at him.

His hands immediately dropped, and he turned around. "You don't know the risks you take."

"Is that why I have fairy tale babysitters everywhere I go?" Ivy moved in front of him. She forced him to look at her. "I came here to assist. So I'm a little ahead of schedule. It couldn't be helped." Ivy sighed. "It appears your kingdom's problems have spilled over into my world."

"Tell me," Duncan commanded.

"When I went to work today, I found out that more than half our police force is seriously ill."

"Oh my God." Duncan walked over and poured himself some amber liquid and drank it quickly. He turned to her and held out his hand. "I'm so sorry."

Ivy grimaced. "That's not the worst part, Duncan." She braced herself for his reaction. "Most of the children are missing now, too."

Duncan's eyes widened, and his grip tightened on his drink. He hurled it toward the fireplace and growled low in his throat. "Children?" he repeated.

"Yes." Ivy had never seen anyone so furious in her life.

"I need to speak with Eric," Duncan muttered and nodded to himself. He looked up and pierced her with his eyes. "You and your group make yourself comfortable. But do not leave the castle."

"Duncan." Ivy laid her hand on his arm and squeezed gently. "Calm yourself. We'll figure something out."

He nodded abruptly and left the room.

Ivy glanced around and noted the wood furnishings and brass that decorated the room. She walked over to a sconce and traced the intricate design on the base. It looked like a mass of entwined fairy wings. Her hand moved down to the shelf below the light, and she admired the intricately carved knobs on it. The top row was Little Bo Peep. The rest of the rows were sheep.

She looked around the room and noted every item spoke of the fairy tale world. But more than this world hung in the balance now.

    * * * *

Ivy took the stairs slowly and glanced around at more of the furnishings. Every time she came, something new jumped out at her. Curtains with gossamer tiebacks and feathery bottoms. Sculptures of wood folk. Her hands traced over several of the items.

She stopped at the top of the stairs and looked left. Her room would be ready for her. Then she looked to the right. But she needed to see someone. And the rest of the evening could wait.

She walked down the silent hallway to the ornate door and stopped in front of it. Ivy rapped softly on it and waited.

The door swung open, and the maid bobbed when she saw Ivy.

"I would like to see King Cedric please."

"Let her in, Tala."

Ivy kept her face blank though the king's frail voice plucked at her heart. She walked inside the room and approached. King Cedric reclined on the bed and looked even older than he had before.

She smiled softly and curtsied. "Your highness."

148

"Come here, child." The king patted the side of his bed softly. "I'm glad you've returned."

Ivy sank down gently on the side of the bed and took the king's hand in hers. "I would like to ask you a few questions, your highness."

His green eyes seemed to sharpen. He nodded slowly. "Ask what you will."

"When did you become ill?"

"About three months ago." He sighed. "I thought it was simply a cold at first. I felt as though I had a fever. Then my bones ached. And I began to age." He touched his gray hair and snorted in disgust. "You don't know how it tries my ego to have you gaze at me in this condition."

Her lips twitched. "That must be a hardship."

Cedric chuckled weakly. "You have no idea."

"Do you have any idea who would do this to you?"

"Not really, child. I have enemies, but I doubt any of them would do this." He looked up at her. "Mutual animosity but no outright hatred."

"What about Rupert?"

The door swung open, and Eric stormed inside. His blue eyes cut into Ivy. "I think it would be best if you left the king alone."

"Eric!" Cedric admonished. "I love the company of a beautiful woman. And I appreciate Ivy's visit."

"Father." Eric strode over to the side of the bed and shook his head. "You need to rest. All these distractions can't be good for you."

"I am the King, Eric." Cedric's eyes focused on his son. "And Ivy is welcome to visit me at any time."

"Yes, Father." Eric looked down at Ivy. "But I need to speak with her. Can you excuse us, please?"

Ivy patted Cedric's hand and stood. "I'll come back, your highness. I promise."

Eric escorted Ivy out of the room and waited until his father's door shut. He took her by the arm and forcefully escorted her downstairs. When they reached the bottom, he spun her around.

"Why are you exciting him?" His blue eyes blazed in his face.

"I know you're worried about him." Ivy tried to soothe him with her voice. "But I'm here for a reason. I only have the king's best interest at heart."

"Then leave him be," Eric demanded. He turned on his heel and strode away from her.

Ivy blew out a breath and trudged back up the stairs to her room.

"Charming family," she muttered. When she reached her room, she swung the door open and stepped inside. It was as beautiful as before. But thoughts preoccupied Ivy's mind. She scowled and walked toward the mirror. "Anything you want to share?" She waited, but nothing happened.

"Figures."

"Magic mirrors are temperamental."

Ivy didn't even shriek. Beings came and went with barely a whisper in the rooms. She turned and looked back at her doorway.

It was the woman the mirror showed her before. Dark, black hair accented a creamy complexion. Rose-red lips parted in a smile. And the woman's figure accented slight curves in all the right places. Even the plain blue pantsuit couldn't disguise the woman's elegance.

"Funny you should say that." Ivy studied the other woman. "Because you were the last thing I saw in this mirror."

"Really?" The woman moved forward with a small smile. She stood in front of the mirror beside Ivy and cocked her head to the right. "That's fascinating."

Ivy refused to study the two of them side by side. She turned away and walked to the foot of the bed. "And to what do I owe the pleasure of your company?"

"Duncan asked me to come."

Jealousy reared its ugly head. And Ivy tried hard not to let it roar. "Really?" she said casually. "How nice."

"I'm Colleen." She extended her hand, and Ivy took it reluctantly. "You don't like me, do you?" The woman's blue eyes examined Ivy.

"It doesn't matter who I like or don't. I'm only here to help." Ivy pointed to the door. "I'm tired and would like to rest before dinner. Thanks for coming by."

151

"The mermaid made you mad, didn't she?"

The sudden turn in conversation left Ivy with her mouth open. "What?" she managed.

"I sent the mermaid to help. But the Merpeople are a little abrupt. No finesse. I'm sorry if she offended you."

"You sent her?" Ivy counted to ten before she responded to the woman's nod. "And why did you do that?"

"I thought it was a nice gesture." Colleen sighed. "Mother says I shouldn't butt into other people's lives."

Ivy studied the woman again. "Snow White?"

"Yes." The woman sank to the bed. "It's rather hard when your mother is fairy tale royalty. Everybody expects a certain something. And I'm afraid I wasn't born with it. So I felt like you and I were kindred spirits." Her blue eyes pleaded with Ivy's. "Don't you feel as though you don't belong sometimes?"

Ivy sat down. "Yes. I do. And I appreciate the offer. Though I was somewhat less appreciative at the time."

Colleen grimaced. "I'm so sorry. Won't happen again." She held out her hand. "Friends?"

Ivy pushed the jealousy aside with a great deal of effort. "Friends."

* * * *

When Colleen left, Ivy lay down on the bed and tried to reason through everything that happened in this kingdom. And the one thing she was sure of was that Rupert knew more than he told them.

152

And the fact he could be the perpetrator quickly followed that. *Why didn't Duncan simply bring him in?*

She sighed and stood. Not a whole lot of good in mentally reviewing the information herself. She glanced at the clock and noticed it was almost six. Ivy opened the wardrobe and thumbed through the clothes. They were absolutely gorgeous. Dresses of the softest silk. Pantsuits that shimmered even in the soft light of her room. And shoes of every description to match the clothes.

Ivy braced herself against the side of the wardrobe and looked at everything before her. She wasn't out to impress anyone. And she didn't care for dresses, usually. They tended to bunch at the wrong spots. And she'd be damned if she wore pantyhose. Tools of the devil.

Ivy frowned and shut the doors. "Could I possibly have clothes that fit my personality along with my size?" She counted to ten and then opened the doors again. A smile danced on her face. *Perfection.*

* * * *

Rose knocked on her door at six thirty, and Ivy opened it with a smile. She hugged her sister and patted Little Brown Bear's head. "You two are lovely this evening."

Rose glanced at Ivy's clothes and couldn't hide the grimace. "Ivy. Do you do this type of thing on purpose, or what?"

Ivy looked down at her comfortable peach sweat suit. "I asked for something my style." She patted the smooth fabric. "I like it." She looked at her sister who wore a long, flowing sapphire gown. Rose's blonde hair brushed against her shoulders, and she wore make-up. Even Bear had a blue pant set fitted to him. "You two look amazing."

"I've never been to the castle before." Bear squirmed with excitement.

They shut their bedroom doors and walked down the stairs. They met Duncan at the bottom. He bowed low.

"Ladies. Bear. I'm pleased to see you this evening. Adam is already at the table. Eric won't be joining us this evening."

"I need to speak with you later." Ivy met Duncan's eyes. She fought the blush that crept into her cheeks. She'd be damned if she thought of jumping his luscious bones every time she saw him. Easier said than done.

Duncan wore a crimson tunic edged in gold. The fabric molded to his muscular arms and tapered to his trim waist. The gold pants he wore left little to Ivy's overactive imagination. She shifted her gaze to the dining room. "Shall we?"

Duncan escorted them into the large dining room, and Adam rose from his seat. He also wore native clothing. It was an emerald suit shot through with silver threads. He looked handsome, if a bit nervous.

Ivy walked over to him and hugged him. "How are you feeling?"

"Overwhelmed." They parted, and Adam looked into Ivy's eyes. "Does that fade?"

"Nope." She laughed and sat down beside him.

Duncan frowned at the seating arrangement, and Ivy smiled at Rose. "Rose, you and Bear can sit beside Duncan. He and I can discuss matters later."

"Rest assured we will." Duncan pulled Rose's seat back and scooted her to the table. He put down a special chair in the regular one for Bear. Then he rang a bell.

The two doors opened instantly, and food flooded the table. Hams, steaks, vegetables, platters of fruit, and desserts of every description were stacked side by side. When the doors shut again, Ivy turned to Duncan.

"There are four adults and one bear eating. Why all this food and fanfare? Is some of this going to go to waste?"

"The food and fanfare are a tradition. And nothing here goes to waste." Duncan lifted his wineglass.

Wine automatically filled the guests' cups. He smiled at each in turn. "To our quest. May our hands be steady and our hearts strong as we undertake this adventure."

They all held their glasses up. When everyone drank, Duncan motioned to the table. "We don't make this amount of food usually.

But this is a special occasion. The rest of this food will be given to staff and residents."

Ivy filled her plate and glanced around. Rose and Adam seemed to take it all in stride. She ate slowly. The tastes were amazing. Everything seemed richer somehow. Deeper.

Adam closed his eyes in bliss after a bite. Ivy nudged him and snickered. "That good, huh?"

"Leave me alone, woman." He opened one eye and looked at her. "This is manna for a confirmed bachelor. I've officially stumbled across culinary bliss." He closed his eye again.

Duncan cleared his throat. "Eat well, my friends. For tomorrow, we begin."

Adam finished his bite and looked at Duncan. "I would appreciate access to the library, Duncan. And I need supplies for notes."

"Done."

"Bear and I would like to interview residents." Rose smiled at Duncan.

"You better let her." Ivy pointed her fork at her sister. "She's good with people. We don't really want to let me loose on the general population."

"I have no objection." Duncan's green eyes moved to Ivy. "I have another project for you." He looked back at Rose. "But you must agree not to cross over the bridge. It isn't safe for a mortal."

"We'll behave." Rose smiled at Bear. "No worries."

156

They finished dinner, and Duncan stood quickly. "Please forgive my abruptness. But I need to speak with Ivy alone." He looked at Adam. "Everything you need will be furnished for you in the library." Then he smiled at Rose. "You have free reign in my kingdom, little one. Go with my blessing."

He walked over and helped Ivy up from her chair. His hand tightened on her arm, and she scowled.

Before she could utter a word, he maneuvered her out of the room and into the den. Duncan shut the doors with a forceful shove. He turned to her with barely restrained anger.

"Why must you spit on me at every opportunity?" He shook his head. "I don't understand you." Duncan sighed. "Am I that repulsive?"

"Repulsive?" Ivy's eyes widened. "Hardly. I simply think it would be a better idea if you and I kept this relationship on a strictly professional basis."

"Professional?" Duncan's eyes showed his disbelief.

"Sure." Ivy shrugged her shoulders and moved away from him. "A simple partnership based on mutual need."

"There's a mutual need between us, Ivy. And it's not professional at all." Duncan's voice lowered as he moved next to her again. "I need you."

She extricated herself quickly. "Listen." Ivy held up her hand. "When this is all said and done, you can ply me with flowers and make promises and all that crap. But for now, don't."

157

"As you wish." Duncan sighed. "Is that all you had to tell me?"

"No." Ivy brushed her brown hair back from her face and squared off with Duncan. "I pissed your brother off earlier. And I'll likely do it again."

"What happened?" Duncan sat on the corner of the desk.

"I went to see your father. I wanted to know if he remembered anything in particular about when he became sick. If any of my questions might trigger a memory." Ivy paced the floor. "Eric found me and became upset. He told me to leave your father alone." She looked at Duncan. "I can understand why he's upset. But I won't quit visiting King Cedric. Period."

"I'll talk with him. Eric has always been a bit emotional."

Ivy nodded. "I get that. But I also have something else to ask you."

"Yes?"

"Did you send me flowers?"

Duncan shook his head. "I'm sorry to say I didn't. Remiss of me."

"That's what I thought. Especially when they exploded."

Ivy wasn't ready for the swiftness of Duncan's actions. He moved off the desk so quickly he was a blur. Then she found herself looking into his worried face.

"Are you okay?"

"I'm fine." Ivy fought the urge to bury herself next to Duncan's golden skin. "Fine," she repeated.

"How long ago?"

She sat down on the nearest couch. "After the first visit. They were there before. But they exploded afterwards. I put them in the trash because there wasn't a note." Ivy attempted a smile. "Made quite a mess."

"Listen to me." Duncan sat beside her and took her hand in his. "Do not accept anything from anyone. Understand me?"

Ivy tried to make light of the situation. "You mean like old hags bearing apples?"

"Ivy…" Duncan began.

"Don't." She stood and looked at the clock. "It's my bedtime. We can discuss the ins and outs tomorrow. We're running out of time. And I refuse to be defeated. There's more at stake than any of us can afford to lose." Ivy stood on tiptoe and kissed Duncan's cheek. "Sleep well." She turned and left the room.

Ivy followed the stairs up to her room and stepped inside. She shut the door behind her and studied her surroundings. Not a horrible way to live while she battled the bad guys. She stripped her sweat suit off and opened one of the dresser drawers.

There were hundreds of negligees. Ivy ran her hands across the soft fabric and inhaled the flowery fragrance that rose from them. She looked around and then lifted one up. It was lilac. The soft fabric flowed from a sweetheart neckline to a billowing waist. Absolutely beautiful.

Ivy pulled it over her head and slid it down her body. She ran her hands down the sides and smiled. A dark purple bow tied right below her breasts. Ivy tied it and walked to the mirror.

"Not half bad," she murmured. Certainly not anywhere near Colleen's beauty. But passable. Ivy stuck out her tongue at herself. Then she turned and climbed into the magnificent bed.

She fell asleep minutes later.

* * * *

"She's beautiful," the male whispered. "You were right to bring in the pretty lingerie."

"I know." The female preened in the dark. "It takes one female to know another. And this one still has a long way to go before she knows herself. But that's why we're here."

"She angered Prince Duncan."

"She pricked his pride." The female sighed. "And she still fights what she feels. It's hard to see yourself as the lesser one."

"Do we stand a chance?" The male's voice showed a hint of panic.

"Be well, my love. There is always hope."

Chapter 8

Ivy woke to the sound of a knock on her door. She glanced at the clock on the nightstand. It read six thirty.

"What is it with these people?" Ivy rolled out of bed and threw open the door.

Duncan stood there in casual tan slacks and a white shirt. His jaw dropped suddenly, and she scowled.

"Yes? Can I help you?" Ivy sighed. "Listen. I know we have to start early. No problem. But if you could manage a word or two, that would be awesome." She pulled her brown hair back and looked for a ponytail holder. "Damn."

Duncan extended his closed hand toward her. Then he turned it over and opened it. A beautiful gold circle lay in the palm of his hand.

"Thanks." Ivy pulled her hair up and studied him. "Have we reached the speaking part of our program?"

"You look lovely this morning." Duncan's eyes traveled from her face to her toes.

The slow realization of her state of undress sank in. She glanced down at herself and then back up at Duncan. Her body flushed hotly.

"I'm sorry." Ivy was afraid to turn around. The negligee not only dropped low in the front, it rode high in the back. She crab-walked over to the nearest dresser and pulled a shirt out quickly. She hurriedly threw it over her head and walked back to the door.

"I've seen your parts before, Ivy." Duncan's green eyes danced with mischief. "And I like them."

"Shush!" Ivy rolled her eyes. "Too early to flirt. I need something with caffeine. And to put on some decent clothes." She paused to look at him closely. "Why are you here?"

Duncan glanced at the clock on the wall. "I thought it best if we started early. Everyone is eager to begin."

"Everybody's already down there?" Ivy glanced around frantically. "Shit!" She grabbed a pair of shorts out of a drawer and slid them on. She slid her fingers through her hair quickly and put it back up. "Okay." Ivy looked up at Duncan. "You going to tell me the next time you're going to spring an early wake-up call on me?"

His green eyes gleamed. "Not a chance."

* * * *

Ivy looked at the crew of misfits at the small table. Amazing how adversity brought people together. She sat down next to Adam and made a plate of sausage and eggs. A maid brought in a cup of soda, and Ivy thanked her profusely.

Rose waited until Ivy finished eating. "Better?"

"Much." Ivy glanced at Adam. He wrote furiously in one of his notebooks. She stilled his hand with her own. "You have a game plan, don't you?"

"Yes." Adam glanced around at the other people at the table. "First, I want to research other healing plants or animals. Maybe we can figure out how to cure the king through other means." His brown

162

eyes shined intelligently behind his glass frames. He pushed them up without a thought and continued. "Then I'll see if I can find some type of potion or elixir that slows down aging."

He looked at Duncan. "Don't you have an apothecary or chemist of some sort? A friendly wizard or two? Anything of the sort?"

"No." Duncan shook his head. "We employed an apothecary over two decades ago. But he left us suddenly. Our father chose not to seek out another one."

"Why did he leave?" Ivy frowned. "Did something happen?"

"I don't know." Duncan shrugged. "We were never told. And I didn't ask. Eric might know. The apothecary trained Eric and Rupert for quite some time."

"Rupert?" Rose leaned forward. Her hair shone in the early morning light. It brushed forward with her motion. "You used to be close?"

Duncan nodded slowly, as if reluctant to answer. "We were as brothers for a long time. And then things changed."

Rose put her hand on Duncan's. "I know it might be hard. But I think we need to know what happened."

Duncan grimaced and looked into the faces at his table. "Rupert's father worked for mine for a long time. We played together since we were young boys. We took our lessons together. We were inseparable."

"Until?" Ivy prodded.

163

"Until we were practicing sword fighting, and I accidentally cut him." Duncan sighed. "Things had been disintegrating between us for a while. Rupert talked about being a charity case for the castle. He grew bitter. Resentful." Duncan pounded his fist on the table. "Things changed so quickly. I tried to approach him a couple different times, but he didn't want to talk with me."

"And you simply gave up?" Ivy shook her head. "Doesn't sound like the Duncan I know."

"My attention was, ah, elsewhere at the time." Duncan ducked his head sheepishly.

Adam chuckled. "I bet." He patted Duncan's shoulder. "Go on."

"He was so enraged that day. Sloppy. I tried to talk him out of the match, but he refused." Duncan's eyes dimmed in remembrance. "I didn't mean to cut him. It almost felt like someone pushed me. Because normally I would feint back. But this time I surged forward."

"His face," Rose murmured. "That's the cut on the side of his face."

"It was awful." Duncan's jaw tightened. "I told him the apothecary could fix it. Make him good as new. But he refused." He shook his head. "The stubborn bastard said he never was part of the royal family, and now everyone would know it. It was one of the last times I talked to him. He moved out less than a month later."

"And his father?" Rose asked.

"His father died not long after Rupert moved out. He was a good man."

Ivy shook her head. "So much anger and sadness here. Who would have thought?"

Adam nodded his head. "But we'll figure things out. I have no doubt." He stood and pushed back from the table. "I'll be in the library."

Ivy watched his slim figure disappear down the hall. She turned to Rose. "Are you going to be interviewing today?"

"Yes." Rose picked up Bear and put him on her hip. "We have a busy day ahead." She bent to kiss Ivy's cheek. "Don't torture him too much," she whispered. Rose left with a brief nod to Duncan and Ivy.

Ivy sipped her drink and pushed her plate back. "What do you have planned for me?"

"You stick with me."

She arched an eyebrow. "Oh, really?"

"Yes. Really." Duncan stood and helped her up from her chair. "I think we need to take this issue to a higher authority."

"Okay." Ivy nodded her head. "Who do you have in mind?"

"The Brothers Grimm."

* * * *

Duncan ordered a carriage and waited for it to arrive. He escorted Ivy to the front gates and smiled at her stunned expression. "A little too much to handle, my lady?"

"Um, maybe." Ivy shook her head back and forth. "I'm floored."

"Well." Duncan looked at the sky. "I tried the Three Fates first. Threatened to suspend their soothsaying license. But they simply cackled and called my bluff. Old hags," he murmured.

"What can you do?" Ivy chuckled. She looked over at Duncan. He peered at her with complex eyes and too many questions. She turned her head away.

"We're talking about the real Brothers Grimm, right?"

"Creators of fairy tales and spinners of stories?" Duncan laughed. "Yes."

The carriage pulled up, and Duncan helped Ivy into it. If his hands lingered a little longer than they should, she didn't say anything. They settled against the cushions, and Duncan put his hands on his lap. "The Brothers Grimm are incredible men. But mortals seem to think that they were, themselves, mortal. In fact, they were not."

"Not mortal?" Ivy's adrenaline kicked in, and she sat forward. "You're kidding!"

"Not a bit." Duncan grinned and showed perfect, white teeth.

"Tell me more."

"The Brothers are immortal bards. They helped create this landscape. This life. Their words shaped worlds."

"Wow." Ivy sat back and looked down at her plain shorts and T-shirt. "I wish you would have brought this up sooner. I may have changed into something a little more suitable."

Duncan's eyes changed colors for the tiniest fraction of a second, and Ivy paused. "What is it you're doing?"

"What?" He shifted his head and showed her his emerald eyes.

"There are times when I could have sworn I've seen your eyes change colors. What are you doing?"

"Looking at you."

"Hmph." Ivy sat back and crossed her arms over her stomach. "Likely story." She watched the countryside fly by the window. "Why haven't you consulted the Brothers before?"

"I hate to bother them." Duncan splayed his hands out on his knees. "It took long enough for some semblance of order to come about. I hate to have to run to them when things begin to disintegrate again. And besides," he pointed out the window, "they tend to move houses a bit."

Ivy frowned. "What do you mean?"

"I mean that their house shifts on a daily basis. One day it will be in the east. The next will be the north. One never knows where they reside. And they prefer it that way."

She looked in disgust at Duncan. "I suppose you're not going to ask for directions, are you?"

He chuckled. "No need, dear Ivy. The horses know which way to go. You needn't look so peeved."

167

"Uh huh. Some things are obviously the same all over."

"I know how to take direction." Duncan moved over beside her. "I'd like to prove it."

Ivy's heart raced in her chest as she stared at the beautiful face inches from hers. *Why did he have to be so damn good-looking? A prince, for Pete's sake!* She looked at him blankly and pointed to the seat across from her.

"Take your lusciousness and sit over there."

He touched his chest. "You wound me."

Ivy snickered. "Sorry about that. Does that mean you're going to move?"

Duncan gave a deep sigh and sat back on the seat across from her. He looked out the window and then up at the sky. "It looks dark outside. That doesn't make any sense."

Ivy peered out the other window and felt a large raindrop hit her forehead. "Hell!" She ducked back inside. Her brown eyes blinked. "What's going on?"

"I don't know." Duncan rapped on the roof of the carriage. It didn't slow a bit. He growled and swung the door to the carriage open.

Ivy's jaw dropped open as he climbed up the side of the carriage to the top. She watched out the window as lightning streaked across the sky, and thunder boomed loudly. The carriage rocked wildly back and forth. She clutched the chair underneath her and prayed Duncan would be okay. *Reckless ass.*

The carriage slowed, and Ivy forced herself to breathe evenly again. She waited for a complete stop before she poked her head out the door. Duncan sat where the coachman was supposed to be. He clutched the reins in his hand and glared at the land around him.

"Not funny!" he yelled. "We could have been seriously hurt. And you've scared the hell out of Ivy." His long brown hair dripped with water on both sides of his face. Duncan looked like an ancient warrior from ages past. His emerald eyes shot sparks.

"I'm okay." Ivy stepped out of the carriage and looked around. The black sky rumbled ominously, and lightning forked across the sky. "What happened?"

"Get back inside the carriage."

Ivy stiffened. "I will not."

Duncan swung his head around and glared down at her. "Get inside the carriage," he said through clenched teeth.

She lengthened her stance and put her hands on her hips. "I don't think so."

"Damn it, Ivy," he growled. Duncan hopped down and stood in front of her. "You have no sense of self-preservation." He motioned around. "We're in the middle of nowhere. I thought the Brothers might be playing a joke. They have a rather twisted sense of humor. But they would have popped out of somewhere by now. And I don't see a soul."

Ivy glanced in each direction. Duncan wasn't kidding. Nowhere would be a good name for this place. Trees surrounded them. And she couldn't tell how the hell they got where they were at.

"Where's the coachman?" Ivy motioned to the top of the carriage.

"I have no idea." Duncan sighed. "I didn't pay any attention when I climbed into the carriage."

"For being a well-rounded, intelligent individual…you don't pay attention to quite a few things."

Duncan narrowed his eyes. "Forgive me if I'm a bit preoccupied saving my kingdom."

Ivy held up her hands. "I'm sorry. Uncalled for."

Duncan held out his hand. "Come on. I don't want to stay out in the open."

Ivy slid her hand into his, and they walked toward the closest copse of trees. She glanced around once and thought she saw someone but quickly realized her eyes played tricks on her. They stopped a couple of feet in. Ivy looked up at Duncan. "I don't suppose you have a cell phone in those pants?"

"I have a lot of things in my pants, dearest Ivy. But no, a cell phone isn't one of them. But we don't need one."

She watched him close his eyes briefly. A frown marred his features. He opened his eyes quickly. "Son of a bitch."

"That would be highly bad, wouldn't it?" Ivy sighed. She cocked her head to the side. "How about we start back down the path?"

Duncan put his hands on his hips with impatience. "This is bloody ridiculous!"

"C'mon." Ivy tugged at his arm. "Let's go." She yanked a little harder, and he followed her, grumbling.

Ivy closed her eyes and pointed. "We go that way."

Duncan shot her a look. "Fine. But you stay close. I don't want you out of my sight. Out of my reach, really." He tucked her arm into his.

She chuckled. "C'mon, studmuffin." A rumble of thunder broke across the sky, and she shivered suddenly. "How often do you have thunderstorms?"

"Rarely." His green eyes fairly glowed in the dark. "Someone doesn't want us talking to the Brothers."

* * * *

Ivy watched the landscape as they walked for what felt like hours. Her feet screamed in her tennis shoes while Duncan only seemed pissed off at the inconvenience of it all. Every once in a while, he would stop and close his eyes again.

"Telepathy out?" Ivy asked.

"Yes," he growled. "I can't believe this. A day wasted." He shook his hands at the sky. "I will not stand for this again."

171

Ivy bit her lip. "When we fix this, you can send us back on the day the children disappeared, can't you?"

"Ivy, I could send you back on the evening before. Twenty-four hours either side of when you left. Now we need to concentrate on finding a way home."

They trudged onward as the sky rumbled ominously. There was no break in the clouds. No flowers. Nothing. It seemed as if they were in the mouth of some great beast. Ivy kicked at a couple of rocks in the road while her brain attempted to sort out the facts.

There was still so much she didn't understand. She only hoped Adam and Rose were doing better than she and Duncan.

They came upon a fork in the road and stopped. Duncan turned to Ivy and raised his eyebrow. "You have an opinion?"

She shivered in the cool air. "That I want to get the hell out of here, yes."

"Which direction, woman?"

Ivy cocked her head to the side. "I can always tell you're impatient when you call me 'woman'. Funny that." She pulled her hair down and redid it while she tried to sort out her thoughts. If they chose the wrong one, they may not make it home that evening. And apparently, they were off the grid. Ivy took a deep breath and pointed to the right. "That one."

"As you wish." Duncan put her arm in his again, and they walked quickly down the path. Ivy grimaced as a light rain began to fall. She rolled her eyes and mentally wondered what else could go

172

wrong. She didn't dare speak it because there really was no telling what might happen.

Duncan waved his arm around them, and a small bubble appeared. It kept out most of the rain, and Ivy looked up at him gratefully.

"If ever I get lost in no man's land again, you can keep my company. Nice bubble, by the way."

"Thanks." Duncan's voice was grim. "But I think you and I need to talk about the possibility of not making it home this evening."

"Okay." Ivy glanced around and noticed their surroundings hadn't changed much. It was still dark and grim as before. "We could do that."

He stopped in his tracks and looked at Ivy. "I am really sorry I've brought you into this mess known as my life." Duncan's voice softened. "And I hope you can forgive me."

Ivy's heart melted at his words. "Nothing to forgive, Duncan. We have to work together to protect our worlds. And if I can help, then I will." She refused to look at him too long because being reasonable was the last thing she wanted to do.

Duncan moved closer. "I didn't want to leave the other night."

"You didn't?" Ivy's voice became breathless, and she fought for control.

"No. I didn't." His hand reached out to stroke her damp cheek.

"You were rather abrupt."

"That's because you're a means to an end, mortal. And he's not afraid to use you if he can."

* * * *

Ivy whirled around and willed herself not to shrink back against Duncan. Rupert stood there and watched them both. His shaggy hair clung to the hard angles of his face and accented the paleness. The scar shone brightly against his skin. He rolled his eyes and grimaced.

"You were smoother in your younger days, Duncan. What's the matter? Don't feel like breaking out the big magic for the mortal?"

Duncan snarled and moved forward. "Shut your mouth, Rupert."

Ivy put her hand on Duncan's arm. "Please don't."

"Yeah, Duncan." Rupert's dark eyes shone hatefully in his face. "Please, don't. I'd hate to have to give you the beating you deserved all those years ago." He glanced around. "Lose your way to the castle again?"

Ivy stepped forward. "We were looking for the Brothers Grimm. Our carriage became lost. Do you know anything about that?"

Rupert threw back his head and laughed. "You amuse me, mortal. And if I said 'yes'? What then?"

"Do you?" Ivy repeated.

"No. I do not." His eyes darkened perceptibly. "But I've heard the Brothers keep to themselves these days."

She nodded. "I see. Then why do you end up in the damndest places, Rupert? Always lurking. Waiting."

Rupert moved forward, and Ivy stiffened her backbone. The man's size intimidated the hell out of her, but she wouldn't show it. She wouldn't give him the satisfaction.

"There is more at stake, mortal, than a few human brats and a dying king." He shot a glance at Duncan and turned his back to them. "Follow this path back to the bridge."

Ivy opened her mouth to ask another question when Rupert disappeared.

"I don't like him," she said.

"Not many do." Duncan spun Ivy around. "And it's not wise to anger a man who can make you feel pain the likes of which you can't conceive."

She shook her head. "Did you hear him?" she asked.

"I did." Duncan nodded.

"What he said." Ivy looked back down the path where Rupert disappeared. "He knows the children are missing."

* * * *

By the time Duncan and Ivy made it to the bridge, they were both cold and irritable. Ivy scowled at Duncan every time he suggested that she stay home tomorrow. She finally had enough.

"Listen here." Ivy stopped in her tracks and put her hands on her hips. She shoved her sopping wet bangs out of her face and glared at the prince in front of her. "I've been through a lot of things you will never know about. I'm not some sniveling idiot who gives up at the first sign of trouble. I knew what I was signing on for when I started this trip. So shut the hell up and quit trying to give me an out. Because I'm not taking it!"

She stomped over the bridge and started up the lane. Ivy was furious. The rain practically steamed off her skin. And she was in no mood for some royal idiot to give her directions.

"Ivy!"

She kept walking.

"Damn it, Ivy!" Duncan ran in front of her and stopped right in her way. "I didn't mean to insult you." He sighed. "I'm worried about you. We're in uncharted territory. I think I can protect you, but today showed me that I couldn't. I don't want anything to happen to you." His green eyes softened. "How am I going to woo you with flowers and crap after this is over?"

Ivy told herself not to laugh. After the day she had, not much was funny. But Duncan's last words were truly hilarious. "Flowers and crap, huh?"

He nodded.

"I'll tell you what." Ivy threaded her fingers through his. "We need some type of deal. You let me approach this the way I want, and I let you do the same. And if they're going in the same direction, great. But if they're not, we won't argue about it."

"I don't want you hurt." Duncan's voice brooked no argument.

Ivy pushed on anyway. "I will not actively seek out ways to harm myself. Okay?"

He turned and cupped her cheek. "That's not reassuring."

"It's all I have," she murmured. Ivy looked deeply into Duncan's eyes and saw the tiny gold flecks that surrounded his emerald orbs. Even his eyeballs were perfect. She felt him bring her closer, and she closed her eyes.

A sharp tug on her pant leg startled her. Little Brown Bear peered up at her worriedly. "We wondered where've you been."

Ivy stepped back, perplexed, when Rose launched herself into her arms. She hugged Ivy's neck tightly until Ivy thought she might lose consciousness.

"Rose!" She tried to pry herself loose.

Her sister moved back and brushed the tears from her eyes. "We found a coachman unconscious, and Eric couldn't track you and Duncan. When Bear and I came back from lunch, there was still no word." Rose's blue eyes moistened again. "I was worried sick!"

"I'm so sorry." Ivy hugged Rose. "We're fine. Just a bit lost." She grimaced as her clothes squished against her skin. "And wet."

A carriage arrived within minutes, and they all climbed aboard. Ivy refused to look at Duncan. Her willingness to let him do whatever he pleased with her irritated her pride. Why couldn't he be

177

all helpless and awestruck at her femininity? The thought tickled her so much, she found herself chuckling.

The other passengers stared at her, and she waved her hand. "I'm tired. That's all there is to it." Ivy bit her lip and looked out the window.

When they arrived at the castle, Eric hurried out to meet them, and he embraced Duncan.

"I've been worried, Duncan. You were gone, and I couldn't find you."

"No worries, brother." Duncan forced a smile to his face. "We're home now. But I'd like to speak with you after dinner."

"Of course." Eric moved past his brother and held out his arm. "Fair Rose, would you like to sit with me this evening at dinner?"

She blushed prettily and stared up at him. "Yes, thank you." She scooped up Bear and put him on her hip.

Ivy watched the trio walk into the castle. "Are you going to ask your brother to keep an eye out and that sort of thing?"

"Whoever did this may target him next. I need him to be careful." Duncan brushed Ivy's wet hair out of her face. "And you need a hot bath. As do I." He put his arm around her shoulder and ushered her inside. "I'll see to both."

* * * *

Ivy let the maid lead her down a long hallway toward a large, oak door. The maid swung it open and guided her inside.

"The bath will run itself, lady." The maid bobbed and curtsied. She put towels on the stool by the bath. They were a luxurious cream color with the royal insignia on them.

Ivy trailed her hand over them and fairly sighed. Beat the hell out of her towels at home.

The maid left and shut the door behind her.

Ivy looked around once and then stripped out of her wet clothes. They splashed onto the mosaic tile floors, and she grimaced. It would feel so good to be warm again. She stuck a toe into the water, and smiled. The tub was huge. It appeared more like a hot tub than anything else. At least eight people could have fit inside.

The maid wasn't kidding. The water and bubbles moved steadily up the side of the tub and stopped a mere inch from the top. Ivy stepped into the water and sank down with a sigh. The warmth of the water worked to soothe her tight muscles and ease away the tension.

She closed her eyes and lay her head back against the side of the tub. What she wouldn't give to stay right here for an hour or two. But she knew Duncan wanted to have another meeting of the minds. Ivy certainly hoped Adam had a more productive day than she did.

"Penny for your thoughts."

Ivy's eyes flew open in disbelief at the voice. She stared angrily at the man in front of her. "You are an absolute piece of work, you know that?"

Duncan stood right outside the tub with a small towel wrapped around his waist. Ivy told herself to pay no attention to the rippling muscles and taut body. She didn't need to linger on the small path of hair that extended from his chest to beneath the towel. She held onto her anger with both hands and refused to be swayed by his masculine beauty.

"I suppose you think you're just going to drop that towel and join me?" Ivy motioned with her bubbly hand. "Just step right in and share this tub with me?"

"I didn't peg you as a selfish woman, Ivy."

"Selfish?" she sputtered. "You blazing, arrogant ass!" Ivy's eyes narrowed dangerously. "You step one foot into this tub with me, and I promise you will find it anything but relaxing."

"Promise?" Duncan casually dropped the towel, and Ivy swallowed convulsively. She watched as he stepped into the tub and sank up to his chest. He watched her lazily with a smile on his face. "See? Harmless. I'll stay on my side. You stay on yours." His emerald eyes sparkled. "Unless you'd like me to scrub your back."

Ivy held up her hand. "Perish the thought." She moved as far away as possible from him and tried to forget the sexiest man she'd ever seen was naked in the same tub. She shut her eyes quickly. Memories of their last intimate encounter played across her mind. And she cursed her weakness. Duncan's hands on her. His mouth on her. Moving against her. Inside her.

Ivy's eyes popped open, and she stared at him. "Why did you sleep with me?"

He slowly moved closer and sat a couple feet away from her. "Because I find you incredibly attractive, Ivy Daniels. Because you have a beauty that is rare to find. And I wanted a taste of it for myself."

She flushed at his words. "Do you still find me attractive?"

Duncan's eyes lit at her words. "Very." His silky voice dropped lower. "And I'd love another taste."

Ivy breathed slowly in and out. It did little good. How often would she have this opportunity again? To be with someone so incredible? She made her decision in a split second.

"Show me," she murmured.

Duncan didn't pause as he moved forward and captured her mouth with his own. His hands tangled in her wet hair as he brought their bodies flush together.

Ivy's heart raced, and her body tightened in arousal. Duncan's slick skin pressed against hers was the stuff of fantasies. Her legs twined around his, and she pressed her hands to his back. His hard body strained against hers while his mouth devoured hers.

Duncan's hand moved to her breast and then trailed across Ivy's body until he reached her hip. He clutched her tightly against him, and she shuddered in need.

Ivy fought to keep her balance as sensations flooded every inch of her body. She wanted Duncan with a fierceness that scared her.

181

He lifted his head and looked at her through lowered lids. "I like you like this." His mouth nipped at her throat. "Wet. Wanting."

She felt him move her higher in the water, and she looked down at him. "What are you doing?" Ivy struggled a bit before Duncan's hands stilled her.

"Plans," he murmured.

"Plans?" she squeaked. Duncan set her ass on the side of the tub and moved up to her knees. He winked at her and kissed one, then the other. Ivy threaded her fingers through his long, dark hair.

She tried to relax but felt exposed. The air wasn't cool, and neither was her blood. But she tried once more to sink back into the bubbles.

"Ivy." Duncan stilled her body again. He grasped her hips and moved forward between her legs. His head rested against her chest for a mere moment before he took her nipple into his mouth and sucked gently. His tongue swirled around the nub, and Ivy moaned low in her throat.

Duncan's hot mouth against her wet, bare skin left her wanting more. His hands moved up her back and grasped her shoulders. He pulled gently, and Ivy let her head fall back in abandon. Duncan's mouth moved against her bare skin, licking and sucking.

Ivy lost all thought at his sweet ministrations. She felt wanton. Worldly. Duncan's mouth left her body for a moment, and she sighed softly. But then she felt him move between her legs and settle his mouth firmly against her hot flesh.

He moved his hands up and gently pushed her down against the side of the tub, never letting his mouth leave her.

She trembled at the first touch of his tongue on her sensitive skin. Duncan's hands gripped her ass tightly while he stroked her folds. And then his tongue moved up and swirled around her swollen nub.

Ivy moved her hand down and clutched his hair in her fist while she arched her hips up to meet his questing tongue. She trembled as the sensations built quickly inside her.

"Duncan," she moaned.

He quickened his pace, and Ivy lost control as the first orgasm slammed through her. She shook uncontrollably and cried out.

Before she could regain her wits, Duncan moved her down into the water again. He slid inside her without pause, and Ivy wrapped her legs around him. Her body still in the aftershocks of her pleasure when he started to move.

Duncan stirred against her slowly at first. He shifted so their bodies touched at every inch. The muscles in his arms bunched against her as he fought to control himself.

Ivy traced up his arm and gently cupped his face. "I won't break, Duncan. And I want to feel all of you. Now."

"Ivy," his voice strained, "I'm barely hanging on."

"Then don't." She bucked her hips against him. "Let go."

Duncan shuddered and wrapped his arms tightly around Ivy's body. He surged into her over and over again. The water lapped against their bodies as he moved.

Ivy scraped her nails lightly on Duncan's back as she felt her body tighten again. She nipped his ear lightly and fairly purred.

Duncan groaned low in his throat. Ivy could feel the first wave break, and she thrust her hips up. He lost control then. They trembled against each other, breathing harshly.

"Good intentions," Duncan mumbled.

"Hmm?" Ivy looked at him through lowered lids. She didn't have the strength to open her eyes the entire way.

"I had good intentions."

Ivy chuckled wryly. "You had the best intentions." She shifted slightly and felt Duncan move away from her.

He shook his head, as if clearing the cobwebs. "We were supposed to talk a bit."

"Your body and mine just had a conversation." She looked at Duncan.

"Not what I meant." Duncan's emerald eyes roved over her body slowly. "You look good wet."

She blushed and held up her hand. "Thanks. But don't get any more ideas. I need something to eat."

"We still need to talk."

Ivy took the words and nodded. "Okay. But later. I'd like a little rest before we launch into another lengthy conversation about you running the kingdom and having all the good ideas. And me just being the token mortal who should do exactly what you say."

Duncan looked indignant. "I am not like that."

"Yes." Ivy nodded again. "You are."

* * * *

They dressed slowly and opened the door to the corridor. Ivy watched a young maid run toward them with fear on her face. She turned to say something to Duncan, but he already started down the hall.

"What is it?" Duncan demanded.

"The king, your highness." The maid wrung her hands as tears streamed down her face.

Ivy watched as Duncan's skin seemed to pale considerably.

"What has happened to my father?" he yelled.

"We can't wake him, your highness. He's slipped into a coma."

Chapter 9

Ivy had to run to keep up with Duncan. His long legs ate up the floor with no pause. When he reached his father's room, he threw open the door and hurried to the king's bedside.

If the king was pale before, he now appeared bloodless. Duncan sank down on the bed and lifted his father's hand and put it in his own. "Have you told my brother?" He looked up at the maid.

She bobbed her head. "We have sent word, your highness."

Duncan stroked his father's hand and smoothed back his white hair. "I will find a cure, Father. I swear it. I will not let you die."

"Oh my God!" Eric's stood in the doorway and looked at his father. He walked over and put his hand on Duncan's shoulder. Duncan looked up gratefully.

"We must find a cure, Eric."

Ivy slipped out the door so the brothers could talk in peace. She walked downstairs and asked a servant about directions to the library. When she was sure she wouldn't become lost, she took off for the room.

The castle was a maze of twist and turns. It felt like she was going in circles until she happened upon the library. The door was half-open, and Ivy glanced inside. She watched in amazement as Adam and Colleen worked side by side.

Ivy cleared her throat and pushed the door open. She walked inside and smiled down at the two.

"Any progress?"

Adam looked up and shook his head. "Negligible." He glanced over at Colleen and smiled. "But I have help."

"I noticed that." Ivy wriggled her eyebrows. Adam blushed bright red. He pushed his glasses up on his face and pretended to read something.

"I didn't know you wore glasses, Colleen."

Colleen smiled. "My mother hates them." She touched the black-framed glasses with the tips of her fingers. "She offered to correct my eyes, but I told her I was fine."

"I think the glasses are lovely." Adam smiled softly.

Ivy cleared her throat again. "I hate to rain on this parade, but I have bad news. And I want it kept strictly between us."

Colleen's head jerked up. "What?"

"The king has slipped into a coma."

The pen Colleen wrote with slipped from her hand, and she turned to Adam. He awkwardly put his arm around her while she cried.

Ivy winced. It would be better if the whole kingdom remained unaware of the king's condition. But they were running out of time.

"Listen. I'm going to have Cook deliver dinner to Duncan and Eric with their father. But I would like for the rest of us to meet in the dining room and discuss plans. Okay?"

"Okay." Adam tried to smile but couldn't quite manage it. He looked at the books scattered on the table in front of him. "Have Cook bring me a plate, too, please. I'll be in here until further notice. I think this is where I will be most useful."

Colleen dried her eyes. "Me, too." She stiffened her backbone and picked her pen up. She leaned over and quickly gave Adam a peck on the cheek. "Thank you."

"No problem." Adam fumbled for a minute before he picked up his pen, too.

187

Ivy left them in the library and started toward the dining room. Rose and Bear would be in there waiting. When she opened the door, she was shocked to find Eric at the table, talking to Rose.

"Prince Eric," Ivy said. "I was going to have Cook deliver a tray to you and your brother upstairs."

Rose jerked her head up, and Ivy could see the tears that flowed from her sister's eyes. Eric handed her a handkerchief and looked at Ivy.

"My brother needed the time to be alone with the king. And I hope to go back to my lab after dinner. I need to find the correct potion to help this situation." His blue eyes dimmed. "I hope you don't mind that I told your sister the news." He patted her back gently.

"Not at all." Ivy moved around to Rose and kissed the top of her head. "We're all working on it, hon. And I know we'll figure it out."

Rose nodded, not trusting herself to speak. She picked up Little Brown Bear and hugged him tightly.

Eric stood abruptly. "Have Cook send the tray down to my lab. She can use the dumbwaiter." He sighed. "I have work to do."

Ivy sat down beside her sister and tried to think of any words to help the situation, but she couldn't.

Rose dried her eyes and set Bear back down in his chair. "Are we the only ones eating in here?"

"Adam and Colleen are eating in the library."

"Colleen?" Rose frowned. "Who is that?"

Ivy chuckled. "Snow White's daughter. And she is drop-dead gorgeous." She rolled her eyes. "And apparently she was the one to send the mermaid to me."

"Ah. Did she say why?"

Ivy grimaced. "Something about me being a little rough around the edges."

Rose bit her lip. "I must meet her."

"Behave." Ivy shook her finger at her sister.

The servants brought dinner in, and Ivy made her plate. Rose made a plate for Bear and one for herself.

"Do we know what we're doing?" Rose motioned with her fork. "Do we have a chance of stopping this?"

"Yes, we do." Ivy took a drink of her soda and looked at her sister. "We're close to something. I can feel it. Because our roadblocks keep growing. Someone feels threatened. And my money is still on Rupert."

Bear opened his mouth, but Rose cut him off. "I don't know why you think it's Rupert. He hasn't done anything to you."

"Right." Ivy rolled her eyes. "Besides threaten my life at every opportunity. He's latent violence in a fairy tale form. What am I missing?"

"Maybe he's lonely."

"Sister, your heart is soft. And that makes it easily manipulated."

189

Rose shrugged. "But your heart is hard. What does that make it?"

"Unobtainable." Ivy took another bite of meat and shrugged.

"There's something different about you." Rose stared. "And I can't quite put my finger on it."

Ivy blushed before she could stop herself. And then cursed silently as Rose's mouth dropped open.

"You didn't!"

Ivy shot a look at Bear and shook her head. "Not now."

"Later." Rose promised. "You and I are overdue for a talk."

"We need to discuss what we're going to do over the next couple of days. I don't know how much longer we have."

"Agreed. Bear and I visited quite a few residents. But none of them remember anything that helped."

"Well, Duncan and I got lost. So I know we didn't do anything for anybody." Ivy rubbed her temple with her fingers. "And I don't know if he's going to want to do anything tomorrow. I may go look around for myself."

They finished eating and walked upstairs together. Rose tucked Bear into bed and made her way over to Ivy's room.

Ivy changed into a yellow short set and waited for the inquisition. She didn't have to wait long.

"Did you have sex with Duncan?"

Ivy's jaw dropped. "Good God! Do you think we could ease into it or something?" She fanned her face while her sister laughed.

190

"I'll take that as a yes." Rose sat down on the bed and patted the spot next to her. "Tell your little sister all about it."

Ivy walked over and sat down. "This is not really a discussion I thought I would be having with you."

"Familial privilege." Rose waited patiently.

Ivy sighed. "The earth moved, the heavens opened up, and the angels sang."

"Wow!" Rose's blue eyes widened. "The angels never sang for me."

"Well, they were in full chorus mode."

Rose shook her head. "Then what happened?"

"Which time?"

"What?" Rose shouted. "There were times? Plural?"

"Simmer, woman." Ivy grimaced. "Just twice."

"Tell. All."

"Well. After the first time, he rolled over and told me he had to leave."

Rose glared. "Does he have a head full of rocks? Is there no etiquette in the world?"

Ivy laughed. "Thanks for that. I thought I was some needy mortal. But I began to see that Duncan was actually inconsiderate. It was as if he didn't have any idea of what to say or do. So he left."

"Typical." Rose snorted.

"The second time was earlier this evening." Ivy's eyes closed in remembrance. Then they popped open. "Right before he was told his father was in a coma."

"Ouch." Rose winced. She patted Ivy's arm. "I'm sorry, sis. Seems like the timing has been off."

"Yeah." Ivy cocked her head to the side. "Now tell me about you and Prince Eric."

Rose snickered and patted her blonde hair. "Nothing to tell, sis. He and I are friends in a fight."

"Uh huh. And that's why you watch his ass every time he leaves a room."

"Oh my God!" Rose held her hands up to her burning face. "Do I really?"

"Yep."

"Well, hell. They could be less attractive."

"They could be," Ivy agreed. "But it's nice to have perks."

* * * *

They talked for another hour before Rose wandered back to her own room. Ivy lay there in the dark and thought about what she would do tomorrow. She didn't want to waste any time. And who knew how much they had left?

Adam and Colleen would research more. Rose would interview residents. And she didn't want to bother Duncan.

Ivy punched her pillow and rolled over in the dark. *Duncan.* Her handsome prince come to life. He was perfect. Thoughtful.

Handsome. Intelligent. She sighed. And her body would never forget the times they spent together.

Who was she kidding? She was smart. Thoughtful on occasion. Ivy rolled over and chuckled. But she wasn't princess material. She didn't know which fork to use. Or how to wave. Or any of the millions of things that some women were born knowing. She wasn't a size zero. And her hair didn't fall in flowing waves down her back.

Rose would have a better chance with Eric than she would with Duncan. And maybe that would work out for the best.

Ivy's heart lurched in her chest. She put her hand over her chest and pressed hard. The ache would go away eventually. She didn't belong here.

* * * *

Ivy woke up with a start. She strained to hear in the darkness. Someone or something was in her room.

"Be easy, Ivy." Duncan's voice floated over to her from the corner.

"Hell, Duncan!" Ivy sat up. "Turn on a light so I can see you."

She heard him shift in the dark as he stood. His shadowy form emerged near her. Duncan sank onto the bed.

Ivy moved forward and hugged him tightly. "I'm so sorry about your father."

He held onto her and stroked her hair. "Thank you."

"Have you slept? Eaten?"

"A little of both." He sighed. "We have to hurry, Ivy."

193

"I know." She pulled him down beside her. "Sleep. We'll start again in the morning."

Duncan lay down beside her, and she shifted to be closer to him. She heard his breathing eventually even out, but she stayed awake. There had to be something she wasn't seeing.

* * * *

When Duncan woke at six thirty, Ivy was propped up on her elbows watching him. He opened those amazing eyes and looked up at her. "Morning, Beauty."

She grimaced. "Morning, Duncan."

He reached down and brought her hand to his lips. "Don't look so irritated with me. I only speak what I see."

"Uh huh." Ivy took her hand back and got out of bed. She pulled her hair up and looked back at Duncan. "What are you doing today?"

"Traveling." He stood quickly. "I will go and see if there are others with ideas to help. Do you want to come along?"

"No." Ivy quickly shook her head. She had plans. But she didn't think Duncan would like them. "You go ahead. I'll find something to occupy my time."

"As you wish." He walked over to her and pulled her hair back down. He ran his fingers through it and brought it up to his face. "Why do you always bind your hair, Ivy?"

"Easier." She shrugged uncomfortably.

"But not nearly as accessible." Duncan kissed her head softly and strode from the room.

Ivy stumbled to the bed and sat down. She snatched up the pillow Duncan used and pressed it to her face. She inhaled deeply and then pulled back. Ivy sighed and put the pillow as close to hers as humanly possible. She dressed and walked downstairs.

* * * *

"Why does she fight her feelings?" the male asked.

The female rolled her eyes. "How long did it take for you to convince me that you were the one for me?"

The male sighed. "A small eternity."

She slapped her hands on her tiny knees and laughed. "There you go. Now let the mortal have some time. Love isn't some prize at the end of a race. It's a journey of two hearts."

"Her heart needs a handicap," he snipped.

The female sighed this time. "It already has one."

* * * *

Ivy checked in the library before she went to breakfast. Adam and Colleen were so close it appeared they could be using the same pair of glasses. She didn't say anything to either of them. She simply shut the door again and walked to the dining room.

Everyone else had been and gone. Duncan ordered a basket to take with him. He left a note for Ivy that explained he would be home for dinner. She tucked the note into her pocket and made a plate. Rose was up at the crack of dawn, raring to go. She and Bear would already be well into their resident interviews.

Ivy sighed. She knew Rose loved this place as much as she did. But their priorities couldn't be normal. There were children involved. An ailing king. And a malevolent presence that would stop at nothing to harm everyone.

She pushed her eggs around and took a couple of bites of sausage. She wasn't that hungry today. Her internal clock kept ticking. And Ivy knew there wasn't much time left.

After she drank her soda, she sent a message to Cook and asked to have a basket made for her. She would be out all day, also. And she didn't plan on coming back until she had some answers.

While Cook prepared the basket, Ivy walked upstairs and knocked on the king's door. Tala opened it and ushered Ivy inside.

Ivy walked slowly over to the king and sat on the edge of his bed. She picked up his hand and slowly stroked it. He appeared so delicate. And it broke her heart to know that his sons were trying their best to save him. But they didn't know if they could.

Everyone felt helpless. The look on Duncan's face when he was told his father slipped into a coma. Ivy felt a tear slip down her cheek and fall on the king's hand.

"Your highness." She leaned in closer and whispered in his ear. "We'll find a cure. Keep fighting, Cedric. You are a strong man. Don't give up hope." Ivy kissed his cheek and stood. She nodded at Tala and left the room.

The wicker basket waited on the front table for her. Ivy hooked her arm through it and walked out the front door. The sun shone

196

down brightly, and the birds still sang. She put on a pair of sunglasses and started down the path.

Ivy tried not to look like an overeager tourist. But it was hard. There were trees with lollipops hanging from them. A row of flowers so large, she could stand in the shade of their petals. And the houses stretched for miles on her left side. There were houses shaped like umbrellas. Big, brown boxes. And several geometric shapes that she didn't have a clue what to call them.

She had to stop and study the rather large shoe that seemed to be alive. There were children hanging on every eyelet and bit of lace. Ivy bit her lip to keep from laughing at the poor, harangued woman who shook her fist and threatened their lives. They would settle down for a minute. And then all hell would break loose again. Apparently, it wasn't time for the woman to whip them all soundly.

Ivy stopped for a moment and reached down to touch the velvety grass. It grew in thick waves along the side of the road. She glanced around to see if anyone watched her. Then she slid her shoes off and stepped into the softness.

"Oh, that's lovely." She sighed.

"Like that, do you?" a small voice asked.

Ivy frowned and peered around. "Hello?"

"Down here, lady."

She leaned down and squinted. A small ladybug sat on the edge of a blade of grass. He tipped his hat to her.

"We have the best grass in all the kingdom, we do. Thanks to Prince Eric. He can make anything grow."

Ivy nodded. "I've seen the lab." She flexed her toes. "And now I've seen the results." She cocked her head to the side. "Does it taste good?"

The ladybug grabbed his stomach and laughed. He wiped his eye, still chuckling. "Have a taste, lady."

Ivy broke off a small blade and put it on the tip of her tongue. Her eyes widened. "You have chocolate grass?"

The ladybug shook his head, and his antenna flew side to side. "No, lady. It tastes as you wish it."

"Wow. Has he been given a medal or anything?" Ivy bent down and broke off a larger blade of grass. She savored the sweet taste with a smile. "I can see this is another perk to living here."

"We have a beautiful home, my lady." He turned his head to look at the castle. "But we still have our problems." The ladybug studied her face again. "How is King Cedric?"

"Still ill, I'm afraid." Ivy sighed. "We need to find what ails him. And then we can cure him."

The ladybug tipped his hat. "My best, my lady. Always my best." He flew off.

Ivy stepped back onto the road and slid her shoes on. She bent down and quickly plucked one more blade of grass. She sucked on it while she walked on.

* * * *

It was quite a trek from the castle to the bridge. Ivy couldn't believe her luck at not seeing Rose. There really was no telling where her sister was. But at least she had a knowledgeable guide in Little Brown Bear.

Ivy stopped before she crossed the bridge and looked down into the bubbling, blue water. The fish were gone. Fish that could perhaps save the king. Ivy stood upright and peered into the darkness on the other side. And plants that could be useful, too.

She had been put off long enough. Today was the day for answers. And Ivy was in no mood to take anything less. She held her head up and crossed the bridge.

Immediately, the mist swirled around her feet, and she looked down. It wasn't an entirely pleasant feeling to not know what she walked upon.

Ivy took off down the main path with sure feet. She had paid attention the last time they came this way. Getting back might be another story. But at least she could get to where she needed to go.

The thorns grew closer together and hung over the road the further she walked. And the air seemed to close in on her. Vibrant, green vines snaked over her head and through the brambles. The sun didn't shine on her. It was damp. Moldy.

Ivy tucked her basket closer and kept walking. She paused once when she thought she heard a wolf howl. And once again when she heard a small hiss. Snakes scared the hell out of her. And crossing one's path wasn't on her agenda. Not now. Not ever.

The path forked, and she immediately took the one to the right and walked on. The thorns tugged at her now. Small scratches on her bare arms as she struggled through. This wasn't an easy route. Certainly not a friendly one.

Ivy's breath hitched in her throat, but she remained resolute. The path narrowed once again, and she cursed under her breath. It seemed almost as if the plants tried to block her path. But she wouldn't be denied.

Ivy came out in the clearing with sweat dripping from her face and a ragged tear in her blue T-shirt. She set the basket down and put her hands on her knees. When she had her breath back, she walked up the stairs and knocked on the door.

The door swung open quickly. "Did you forget something?" Rupert frowned as he looked down at Ivy.

"Avon calling." She grinned up at him. "I can see you were expecting someone else. Now, isn't that interesting?"

Rupert scowled. "Are you insane? Did you come here unattended?"

Ivy nodded. "I'm in charge of my faculties, thank you very much. And I remembered the path from last time." She glanced behind her. "I didn't pass anyone." She swung back around. "So who was here?"

"You try my patience," he growled.

Ivy brushed past him and walked inside. "Then we're even. Because you have yet to answer any questions I've asked."

"Who are you to ask me anything?" Rupert slammed the door shut and turned to her. "A mere mortal? Unattended?" He put his rather large hand in her face. "I could crush your skull with barely a pause."

"Skull-crushing is overrated." Ivy sidestepped him and walked to the couch. She sat down and patted the basket. "I have food from Cook."

Rupert glanced at the basket and then at Ivy. "Prince Duncan doesn't know you're here, does he?"

A small sliver of fear inched up her backbone, but she kept her voice even. "No. He does not."

Rupert threw back his head and roared with laughter. His greasy, black locks swayed back and forth in merriment. The windows shook in the small cottage, and the floor rumbled.

"That amuses you?" Ivy asked, coolly.

He nodded. "More than you know. That the great Prince Duncan cannot handle a mere mortal. Times have changed."

"Yes. They have." Ivy looked up at Rupert. "And not for the better. We still need to find the fish and plants that could possibly help heal the king."

Rupert shrugged. "It matters not to me."

"I think you lie."

His eyes narrowed dangerously, and his fists clenched by his sides. "What did you say?"

Ivy stood. "You lie. You are either lying about the healing items, or you are lying about the king. But you are most certainly lying."

Rupert walked over and glared down into her face. "Just because you let Duncan between your legs doesn't give you the right to talk to me in that manner. Do I make myself clear?"

Ivy clenched her teeth. "Yes." Her brown eyes shot sparks.

He nodded slowly. "Not everything is gained by force. And I think you have yet to learn that." Rupert paused and motioned to the basket. "What did you bring to bribe me?"

She lifted the basket and held it out in front of her. "Beef pastries. Cheesecake. And some vegetable Cook covers with cheese. I have yet to figure out what it is."

"Ah." Rupert smiled and took the basket. "I may let you live."

Ivy blinked. "There was some doubt?"

He put the basket down on the nearest table and looked at her. "It is not customary here to barge into another person's home and be a nuisance. It's become a habit with you."

"Listen to me." Ivy put her hands on her hips. "I don't give a damn if you like me or not. I don't give a damn if I'm the biggest pain in the ass you've ever come across. There are children's lives at stake here. And that takes precedence. So if I have to knock on every damn door on this side of the bridge, I will."

"You risk your life."

"Gladly."

Rupert sighed. "You need to be home before it's dark. And I won't be escorting you anywhere. I have things of my own to oversee."

"Then you won't help?" Ivy clenched her fists.

"Go home." Rupert pointed toward the door. "Take the path across from my door. Not leading to it. You'll arrive at the bridge in less time." He motioned to her torn shirt. "With less scratches."

"Who were you expecting to come back?" Ivy studied Rupert's face.

It grew stony and hard. "None of your business, Princess."

"What are you planning, Rupert? What have you been sneaking into the woods to gather at night?"

His face showed shock before he could stop himself. Then he growled low in his throat. "Get out. And do not come back." Rupert grabbed her arm and forced her to the porch. He slammed the door loudly.

Ivy looked around. Not even the damn bugs chirped here. She rubbed her arms and stepped toward the path Rupert pointed out. Well, she succeeded in pissing him off. That was about it. But she also knew he had a secret. Now she simply had to figure out what it was.

* * * *

The road back was less rocky and thorny, but it was still a major pain. It dipped in several areas, and there were loose rocks all over it. Ivy slipped at least twice and skinned her elbow. The big oaf probably hoped she would fall and break her neck.

"Ass," she muttered.

It felt like she had been walking for miles when she finally came across the bridge. The sun was already low in the sky on the other side. She shook her head. She would never figure out this whole temporal anomaly.

Ivy walked over the bridge and crossed. She rubbed her sore elbow and cursed Rupert again. Just as she started up the road, a large black carriage rumbled up. The door flung open, and Duncan stepped out. He took one look at her and hit the side of the door.

"If I weren't so happy you are alive, I'd kill you myself."

Chapter 10

Ivy glared at him. "I've barely been gone two hours. Simmer."

"You've been gone nine!" Duncan yelled.

She blinked. "Nine?"

"Get in the carriage," he ordered. "We'll talk about this at home." She started to climb inside when he grabbed her hand. "And you'll need another hot bath."

Ivy flushed and took her hand back. "Alone. Thank you very much." She climbed inside and sat down. She crossed her arms over her stomach and looked out the window.

Duncan shut the door and sat across from her. He tapped the side of the carriage, and they rolled toward the castle.

"Did you have any luck today?" Ivy asked.

"No." Duncan's eyes flashed. "And I would say you didn't either." He moved to sit by her before she could stop him. "Look at your arms." She winced when he touched her elbow. "So much for you staying out of trouble."

"Got to have a hobby." She moved her arm and looked outside. Ivy frowned. "How can it be nine hours later?"

Duncan took her chin and moved her head to look at him. "Where exactly were you?"

"Over the bridge and through the woods?" She tried for a light tone.

"Ivy!" He grabbed her shoulders and looked her in the eye. "It's not funny. Not in the least. What in the hell were you thinking?"

She scowled. "I was thinking that Sir Rupert of the Black House knows more than he's telling." She looked away. "Don't know why he has to be such an ass," she mumbled.

"You're under house arrest." Duncan moved back to his seat and looked at her smugly.

Ivy glared at him. "I'd like to see you enforce that."

Duncan put his hands on his knees and moved forward. "I'm not a violent man. But sometimes you tempt me, Ivy Daniels." He sat back again. "It won't be hard at all to enforce. In fact," he said as they rolled up to the gates, "it's as good as done."

"What do you mean?" Ivy panicked.

He opened the door and stepped out. Ivy followed him distrustfully. Duncan opened the front door and walked inside. Ivy followed.

And when he turned to shut the door behind him, he smiled. "It's done. You are no longer permitted outside this castle. No door here will let you out."

Ivy tried to count to ten but got no further than five. She yanked the door open behind her and tried to walk through it. It was as if she ran into a solid wall. She could see through it, but she couldn't pass.

"You lowlife son of a bitch," she bit out. "I come here to try and help. And you pen me up like a piece of cattle."

Duncan nodded. "I'll do whatever it takes to make sure you're safe."

Ivy turned on her heel. "Screw you. And don't think I won't find a way around your door trick, either." She snarled once more and walked up the stairs. *Arrogant bastard.* Her mind raced with possibilities of how to get out of the castle. And she didn't see Rose rush toward her.

"Ivy!" Rose hugged her tightly, and Ivy winced. "Where have you been?" She held a tissue up to her nose and blew softly.

Guilt flooded through Ivy. "I'm sorry, hon. It's hard to keep track of time here. I thought it had only been a couple of hours."

"Duncan was furious." Rose shook her head. "I've never seen him so angry. And no one knew where you were."

Ivy patted Rose's shoulder. "I was eating chocolate and admiring the scenery." She cocked her head to the side. "And now Prince Pain in the Ass has decided I'm under house arrest."

Rose's mouth dropped open. "You're kidding!"

"Wish that I were." Ivy snorted. "And he'll wish he'd never done it." She pulled her brown hair out of the holder and ran her fingers through it. "I'm for a hot bath. And then I think I'll just have Cook send up a tray." She winced. "I'm sorry you were worried."

Rose hugged her again. "I'm simply glad you're safe." She pulled back and sneezed.

"Bless you." Ivy frowned. "Are you feeling okay?"

"I think I'm getting a cold." Rose wiped her nose with a smile. "But I can assure you that I won't break out in hysterics or anything of the sort."

"You take it easy. I think I'll have Cook send some chicken noodle soup up later to you. How's that?"

"Great." Rose sniffled again. "I think I'll go lay down for a bit."

Ivy watched her walk away. She hoped Rose was right. The last thing they needed right now was hysterics. And her sister with a cold wasn't a good thing.

* * * *

Ivy found the large bathroom again and opened the door. She almost sighed in relief. Her arms ached, and she needed to soak in something hot and lovely. She stripped out of her clothes in record time and slid up to her neck in bubbles. Her mind began to wander, and she told herself not to think of Duncan. Not his body. Not his hands. And most certainly not his mouth.

If he thought he could keep her in this castle while everyone else was out doing his or her part, then he was sadly mistaken. She would find a way around his stupid magic gate and be free to help the way she wanted.

Ivy sank lower. She could feel the weight of the world on her shoulders right now. As far as being any help, she felt absolutely useless. She hadn't found any of the healing items. The children were nowhere to be seen.

"Shit," she muttered.

Her body only mildly ached as she climbed out of the tub. Ivy ran her hands over the scrapes and was amazed to find them all gone. She rushed over to the mirror and looked at her arms. Where there had been scrapes and scratches before, now there were none.

Ivy threw an ivory robe on and slid some slippers on her bare feet. She hurried downstairs, not caring about her manner of dress. Her wet hair clung to her face as she rushed to Duncan's room.

Ivy knocked impatiently, and Duncan opened the door. He arched an eyebrow and looked down at her.

"You've changed your mind about the bath?" His tone was polite.

"No. Look!" Ivy pulled up the sleeves of the robe and showed Duncan her elbow. "The scrape is gone. I think the bathtub has healing properties. Perhaps we can put the king in there and let him soak for a bit."

Duncan's face fell. "We've tried it, Ivy. The bath does not heal all. Just the minor bumps and bruises."

"Oh." Ivy sighed. "I'm sorry." She turned to go when Duncan reached out and stopped her.

"Do you understand why I can't have you running about the kingdom?" His green eyes studied her.

"No." She crossed her arms. "I thought that was why I was here. And now, come to find out, that my comings and goings are subject to your whims. I think it's ridiculous."

"There is plenty for you to do here." Duncan ran his hands through his long hair. "Adam and Colleen will need help. And there are other resources in the castle you can use."

"You want to keep me here for my own good." Ivy's eyes flashed. "Or at least that's what you're trying to peddle to me. But I don't buy it."

"Exasperating woman." Duncan shook his head. "Buy it or no, you won't leave the castle." He nodded once and shut his door again.

Ivy looked at the closed door and balled her hands into fists. Her temper built quickly, and she scowled. Prince Duncan was in for a rather large surprise if he honestly thought he could keep her locked up here.

She stomped back to her room and shut the door. Ivy thumbed through her closet and found a yellow pajama set. She changed clothes and sat on the edge of her bed. She picked up the pillow Duncan slept on and held it to her nose again.

"I'm ate up," she muttered. "Sniffing a pillow. I need to figure out how in the hell to get out of this castle."

Ivy put the pillow down and grabbed a piece of paper. Time to get to work.

* * * *

She woke up at six thirty the next morning. It almost wasn't a hardship. She was beginning to get used to it. *How sick was that?*

Ivy swung her legs over the side of the bed and quickly changed into jeans and a light green T-shirt. She pulled her hair up and

210

knocked on Rose's door. When she received no response, she opened it slightly. No Rose. She frowned and left her room. Her sister probably already left so Ivy wouldn't be tortured with the fact that she couldn't.

A smile flitted on her face. That wasn't going to last much longer. Ivy hadn't stayed up last night past midnight twiddling her thumbs. She had a game plan.

She walked to the library first and opened the door. No one was inside. Ivy frowned and shut the door. She caught the first servant she could find.

"Where is everyone?"

"Prince Duncan is traveling, lady. Your sister and Little Brown Bear left half an hour ago. Prince Eric is in his lab. And Sir Adam and Lady Colleen left earlier."

"Thanks." Ivy smiled and watched the woman leave. The smile slid off her face. She walked into the dining room and ate a quick breakfast. All she had time for this morning was a couple of pieces of toast. Her mission for the first half of the day was finding an exit. Then she would settle down in the library and do some research of her own.

Ivy finished her food and walked back to the front door. She opened it and tried to step through. Didn't happen. She thought as much. Then she methodically moved from door to door. There were at least a dozen on the first floor. Ivy tried each and every one. She fought down her temper and told herself it was as she expected.

211

Then she had a brilliant idea. Ivy raced back into the library and threw open the windows in there. She climbed up on the ledge and tried to ease herself down on the other side. Another wall. She threw her hands up. *Fine!* She would spend the rest of the day doing research.

Ivy skimmed the titles in the library and found a book about potions. She pulled the jade book out and touched the silvery pages. The book itself was beautiful. A slight flowery smell rose from the pages. Ivy ducked her head and inhaled. How she loved this place!

She settled herself on the couch and opened the first page.

"Hello!" A cheery face erupted from the first page.

Ivy jerked but didn't drop the book. It was a small miracle. "Hello," she said.

"Is this your first reading of *Potent Potions*?"

"Yes." Ivy smiled down at the face. "Are you a table of contents or something of the sort?"

"You could say that." The face smiled back. "Can I help you find anything?"

"I'm looking for something to help cure the king." Ivy bit her lip. "Do you have anything in here?"

"I'm sorry, lady." The face saddened. "Many people have already looked through me. And I haven't been helpful. Let me suggest alternate reading." He named off three more books.

Ivy thanked him and put the book back. *Well, that saved a lot of time. Nothing like a book that could tell you what it was about.* She sighed and shook her head. Now to move onto the next.

She read the three other books and didn't find anything. And not all of them featured a helpful being in the front. Ivy shut the last book and put it back. She glanced up and saw there were at least two rows she couldn't reach without a ladder.

"Damn," she muttered. Ivy looked around and found a single chair she could move over to the books. She dragged it over and stood on it. Then she reached on tiptoe so she could reach the spines. Her hand brushed against a rather large one, and she pulled it out with a groan.

The book was one heavy piece of work. It was at least four inches thick and covered with dust. The binding and cover may have once been red or brown. But now they were a dusty gray that cracked and groaned as she handled it. The pages were a faded gold that flaked in her hands.

Ivy opened the cover slowly.

"Get out!" it screamed.

Her arms pinwheeled as she tumbled from the chair and landed hard on the floor. The book hit the floor with a smack, and she bit back her scream.

There was no friendly face in this book. It had been a fierce skull with glowing red eyes. The skull was a faded ivory color with dark spots along the sides. The jaws snapped at her hand as it yelled.

Ivy moved her right arm and winced as the pain shot through her elbow. "Son of a bitch," she muttered. "If it's not one damn thing, it's the next." She stood slowly and eyed the malevolent book. The last thing she wanted was to touch the book again, but she made herself approach it.

Her foot shot out and flipped the cover open.

"Get out!" it screamed again.

"No!" Ivy yelled back. "I will not! You hateful thing."

Red eyes glared at her. "You are not of this kingdom. Put me back." His maw stretched threateningly. "I can hurt you, mortal."

She took a calming breath. "Please. I need to find something to help the king. I'm sorry to disturb you. But I simply need to know what you have inside."

The red eyes narrowed. "Nothing to help you. Only potions that harm. Not heal."

Ivy sighed. "Okay. Thanks." She started to kick the cover closed when his voice stopped her.

"Leave me out, mortal. I may be able to help."

She glanced at him. "Are you sure?"

The skull grimaced. "I've had my own company long enough. Perhaps I will be useful in other ways.'"

Ivy smiled. "I would appreciate it, sir." She eyed him carefully. "Can I pick you up and put you on the table?"

He smirked. "Scared?"

"Hell yes," she admitted.

The skull laughed. It was a creaky sound. Like chalk on a chalkboard. But at least he was amused. "Pick me up, mortal."

Ivy bent and slowly lifted him. She placed him on the table gingerly. "My name is Ivy."

"I am Jack."

"Pleased to meet you." She glanced back at the bookshelves. "Any books that you can think of to help?"

"The top shelf is a little hostile. And you won't find any answers there."

Ivy arched her eyebrow. "Thanks for the warning." She grimaced as she moved her arm. "I think I sprained something."

"Didn't you think about perhaps asking one of the princes for help?" The skull rolled his eyes.

She put her hands on her hips. "Prince Duncan is traveling. Prince Eric is brewing up something in his lab. So I decided to try and help as best I can." Ivy sighed. "And I'm under house arrest."

Jack's eyes widened, and then he let out a blast of laughter. "I may like you after all, mortal. Ivy," he corrected himself. His red eyes glanced around. "Now let's get started."

* * * *

Ivy glanced at the clock. It was nearly six. Her back ached, and her arm throbbed. But she had written at least five pages of notes. Jack helped tremendously. When he wasn't heckling her. Somehow, between directing her to the right books, he found time to make fun of her heritage, her accent, and her method of taking notes. The afternoon was anything but boring.

She rubbed her eyes and yawned. "It's almost dinner time." She glanced down at Jack. "What would you like me to do with you?"

He studied her intently. "Can you do me a favor, Ivy?"

"Maybe." She was cautious.

He chuckled. "Nothing that will get either of us into trouble. So don't worry."

"Okay. What?"

"Can you please direct one of the maids to dust us?" He grimaced. "I hate to be seen in this condition."

"There's a lot of pride in this kingdom." Ivy smiled. "I'll dust you myself. How's that?"

His bony jaws stretched into a smile. "Excellent. And I'll help you out once more. Deal?"

Ivy nodded. "Sure. If you're not too tired."

"Ivy." He blinked. "This is not about the king. At least not directly. But I know how to circumvent your house arrest. What do you say?"

She clapped her hands together. "Let me just dust you off. Then we'll talk." She cleaned the cover carefully and removed all the dust. "Better?" she asked.

"Much." Jack's voice was full of satisfaction. He looked up at her. "The answer to your dilemma is not an easy one. Are you afraid of heights?"

216

Fear skittered along her nerves. "Mildly," she admitted.

"If you climb out a second story window and drop to the ground, at least two feet above it, then you'll be free. But it must be at least two feet. Do you understand?"

"Yes." Ivy smiled. "I appreciate the help." She waited for a minute. "Does it bother you to have the cover closed?"

His mouth moved to smile before he caught himself. "I'm like a turtle in a shell, woman. So no. It doesn't bother me. But I appreciate the concern." He glanced at the shelves. "Can you put me back without harming yourself?"

"Can you let me without screaming at me?" Ivy retorted.

"Possibly."

Ivy moved to close the cover when the library door opened. Duncan strode in and studied the scene before him.

Papers and books covered every inch of the large, oak desk. He glanced at Ivy and then down at the book before her. His eyebrows shot up as he looked over at the bookshelves.

"Tell me how in the hell you reached the forbidden section without a ladder."

Ivy calmed looked at him. "Funny story."

"I bet," he bit out. Duncan shook his head. "Can't even leave you alone in the library, for Pete's sake!" He walked closer and looked at the books. "Hello, Jack."

"Prince Duncan." The skull looked up at Ivy. "I haven't got all day, mortal. Put me the hell back now!" he shouted.

217

Ivy jumped and picked him up. She started to take him over to the bookshelf when he winked at her. "Remember what I said."

She narrowed her eyes. "I will get you back," she promised.

Jack snickered. "So you say…"

Ivy snapped the cover shut when she heard Duncan approach her. He snatched the book out of her hands and glared at her. "If you think for one minute I'm letting you climb back up there, you're out of your mind."

"Then do it yourself." She spun on her heel and gathered her notes up from the desk. "Have you seen Adam and Colleen?"

Duncan shook his head. "I've only arrived home. But they told me they had a lead on another plant that might be used for healing."

"What?" Ivy yelled. She pushed her brown hair back with a scowl. "And you decide to keep this information to yourself?"

"The last thing I need is you haranguing them."

Ivy blinked slowly. "Excuse me?"

Duncan waved his hand, and Jack slid back where he came from on the bookshelf. "I didn't want you taking off after them and making the situation more uncomfortable than it already is. So I sent them out extra early."

"I see." Ivy put her papers in a pile and shoved the books into stacks. She grabbed her notes and walked toward the door.

He reached out to grab her arm, but she pulled it back.

"Don't," she snarled. "You don't have the option of me being good enough to screw but not good enough to help."

"Ivy." Duncan's voice floated over to her. But she kept walking.

* * * *

Ivy checked in on Rose as soon as she reached her room. She slid her notes onto the nearest table and opened the adjoining door. Rose lay peacefully in bed with Little Brown Bear tucked beside her. A large box of tissues lay on the nightstand, and Ivy could see that Rose's nose was red. She sighed and shut the door. Maybe Adam and Colleen found something.

She brushed her hair and pulled it back up. Jack's advice echoed in her head. Ivy stood and walked over to her window and opened it. She bit her lip and looked down. That was a hell of a lot of distance between here and there. She shut the window and tried to forget she didn't even like to climb on ladders.

Fifteen minutes later, Ivy walked downstairs and into the dining room. Duncan sat at the head of the table while Adam and Colleen both sat on his left. Ivy glanced at the chair beside him but opted to skip one before she sat. She ignored the look he shot her way.

"What did you two find out?"

Adam's face grew grim. "There is supposed to be a Brandis root that will help heal. But we can't find the exact geographical location. The book was vague as to directions and such." He smiled at Colleen. "But Miss Colleen here narrowed it down to two locations. We checked one out today. And tomorrow we will look for the other one."

"Excellent." Ivy snatched her goblet up and drank deeply. The caffeine was exactly what her weary brain needed. She put it down and tapped the table. "Do you need any help?"

Adam shot a look to Duncan, and Ivy narrowed her eyes. "Adam." He looked back at her. "I'm not asking if it's okay with Duncan. I'm asking you if you need help."

He shook his head. "Truthfully, no. Colleen navigates, and I take notes. We found a recipe for the potion yesterday. Now all we need is the root." He glanced around. "Where's Rose?"

"She's sleeping. And she's feeling under the weather right now. A slight cold, I think." Ivy motioned to one of the servers. "Could you please have Cook prepare chicken noodle soup for my sister?"

"Gladly, lady." The server bobbed and disappeared into the kitchen.

"Have you had any luck, Duncan?" Adam pushed his glasses up and waited for an answer.

"None." His voice was weary. "I have searched and questioned to no avail."

Ivy winced as she bumped her arm on the edge of the table.

Duncan frowned. "The bathtub is at your disposal."

"Quit trying to shove me into the tub," she snapped.

Colleen bit back a laugh and took a sip of her drink.

Ivy shook her head. "He thinks it's the exact thing for whatever my problem is." She smirked. "And if I could drown him in it, he'd probably be right."

Colleen choked on her drink, and Adam patted her back. She sputtered and dabbed her mouth. Her blue eyes were wide in shock. "You would drown the prince?"

"Probably not." Ivy shrugged. "But it gets me to sleep at night."

"You're just angry that you are not allowed outside." Duncan said it calmly though his eyes shot sparks.

"You think?" Ivy slammed her hands on the table. "I'm not here to be your pet mortal. I'm here to help."

"Ah, yes," Duncan derided. "That's why you fell on your ass while trying to access the forbidden section of the library."

Colleen and Adam's mouths fell open as they watched the conversation.

"At least my ass was doing something. Instead of being chained like a dog on a leash."

"Doing something?" Duncan stood up and glared down at her. "You're constantly doing something! I can't get you to stop doing something! You need to slow down before you get hurt. But you can't even do that here!"

Ivy shook with fury. She stood slowly and nodded to Colleen and Adam. "I'll take my tray in my room. I appreciate the update you've given me." She turned on her heel and walked out the door. She hadn't even reached the stairs when Duncan ran in front of her and stopped.

"Damn it, Ivy!" His muscle worked in his jaw. "You infuriate me without even trying. Why is that?"

221

"Because you're an overbearing ass who always has to have his own way?" she asked sweetly.

Before she could even blink, Duncan pulled her against his hard body and kissed her. But it wasn't a soft kiss meant to woo her. It was a dangerous kiss. A kiss that warned her that Duncan was almost at his wits' end. It both excited and infuriated her. Ivy squirmed in his arms, but he wouldn't let up. And then the kiss changed into something else entirely.

His mouth moved against hers with a knowing that brought a flush to Ivy's entire body. Her breasts peaked against his hard chest while her legs trembled beneath her. It was a kiss that told her he knew exactly how to pleasure her. And could. And it touched parts of Ivy that she shut off long ago.

She broke away and stumbled backwards. Her big brown eyes watched Duncan struggle for composure. He closed his eyes briefly, and when he opened them, he stared at her.

"What do you do to me, Ivy?"

"Nothing." She touched her bruised mouth and looked at Duncan.

"Everything." He brushed past her and up the stairs.

Ivy watched him go with mixed emotions. She looked up the long flight of stairs and didn't know if she would make it or not. All her pent-up emotions were right below the surface, and it scared the hell out of her. Somewhere along the line she lost control of her relationship with Duncan. And that wasn't good for either of them.

She grabbed the banister and sighed. Her body ached. Her mind ached. But she wouldn't go to the tub tonight. Because the last thing she needed was another reminder of what Duncan could do to her.

Ivy climbed slowly and slid her hands along the smooth wood. She was worried. What had she been thinking? That she could just pop in? Demand answers? Put on her super cape and everything would be fine?

"Hell." Ivy ran her hands through her hair and tugged lightly. And now Rose was probably ill. They were no closer to the damn healing items.

The only good news came from the update Adam and Colleen had given her. It had done her heart wonders. Perhaps they were on the right trail. It would be miraculous to have some good news instead of bad piling on top of bad. She clung to the hope with both hands.

Ivy reached the top of the stairs and pushed her door open. Her bed looked so large and forlorn. She sighed and shut the door behind her. And that damn pillow probably still smelled like Duncan. She didn't know whether to laugh or cry.

She opened the adjoining door and peeked in on Rose. Little Brown Bear was nowhere to be seen. And her sister lay curled up on her side. Ivy crept quietly to the other side of the bed to make sure Rose was all right.

She stared down at the woman in the bed but didn't recognize her. Ivy frowned and stepped forward. She glanced back toward her

223

room where the door was still open. And then she realized what the woman was wearing.

Ivy pressed her hand to her mouth and backed up. She swallowed her scream and whimpered a bit. Because the woman in the bed was her sister. But now she looked older than Ivy.

Her blonde hair was finer, and she had lines around her eyes and mouth. The skin on her hands was looser, and Ivy shook with rage and fear.

Ivy hurried out of Rose's room and ran down the hallway. Her heart beat frantically in her chest, and she was afraid she would faint before she got to Duncan. As soon as she came to his door, she pounded on it with all her might.

Duncan opened it a couple of seconds later, and she launched herself at his chest. She trembled in his arms and prayed for strength.

He moved her back and looked down at her. "What's wrong?"

"Rose." The tears she held back before trailed down her face and fell, unheeded, on the floor. "Rose has the same disease as the king."

Chapter 11

Duncan's eyes widened as he looked down at her. "You're certain?"

Ivy nodded her head and fought to keep her voice steady. "I went to check on her since she's been sniffling. And when I looked in on her this evening, she had aged." She clutched his shirt in her hands. "She's still asleep, Duncan. I don't even know if she is aware of what's happened."

Duncan pulled Ivy back against him and hugged her tightly. He kissed the top of her head and promised he would do everything he could for her sister. But she was scared to death. *How long would it be before Rose slipped into a coma? How long do we have to find the cure?*

Ivy followed Duncan as he sent a maid for Eric. He turned back to her and worry etched every line in his face.

"This is unheard of, Ivy. And I'm so sorry that I brought you and your sister into this." He rubbed his hand over his face and sighed. "Maybe Eric can help us with this. At the very least, he can make your sister comfortable."

"I should have paid attention." Ivy looked off into the distance. "She told me she wasn't feeling well. But I assumed she was back to her hypochondriac ways. And now she's gravely ill." She pressed a hand to her stomach. "What have I done?"

"Listen to me!" Duncan grabbed her by the shoulders and made her look at him. "This is not your fault. None of it." He turned away from her when he heard footsteps.

Eric practically ran into them. His blonde hair was mussed, and his hands were stained a bright yellow. He wore a lab coat with several stains on it and brown boots that tracked dirt across the wood floor.

"What's happened?" he demanded.

Ivy swallowed back more tears. "Rose has the same disease as your father. She's aging."

Eric's face mirrored the shock that Ivy felt. He shook his head. "Impossible. I don't understand." He looked at Ivy. "But you are fine?"

"Yes."

"Then how can Rose be ill?" He ran his hands through his hair and scowled. "How is she taking it?"

Tears slid down Ivy's face again. "I don't think she knows."

Eric's face grew grim. "We have to tell her. I can, if you wish."

"No." Ivy shook her head. "I'll do it."

Duncan put his arm around her. "We'll all go."

It was a sad and somber trio that walked back up to the west wing and opened Rose's door. Ivy wiped her tears away and walked slowly toward Rose. She turned on the lamp by the side of the bed and looked at her sister. She took a deep breath and shook Rose's shoulder.

"Rose," she whispered. "Wake up."

Rose shifted and blinked wearily. Her blue eyes were hazy with sleep. "What's wrong, Ivy?" She focused slowly and noticed Eric and Duncan. "Has something happened?" She struggled to sit up.

Ivy took Rose's hand in her own and stroked it softly. "Yes. Something's happened. And I don't want you to worry. We'll fix it. I promise."

"You've lost me." Rose looked around. "Where's Little Brown Bear?"

"I don't know." Ivy tried to smile. "We'll find him in a little bit. But right now, we have to tell you something."

Rose watched her expectantly and frowned. "It's something bad, isn't it? You have that look on your face like the time you told me you broke my favorite porcelain doll."

"Rose. I know you've felt ill this last week."

"Yes." She nodded. "A cold, mostly." She motioned to the tissues by her bed. "But I feel better. Cook keeps sending soup. And my sinuses have cleared."

Duncan moved forward and put his hand on Ivy's shoulder. She looked up gratefully and then at her sister.

"You don't have a cold, hon." Ivy struggled for composure for a minute before she steadied herself. "We think you have the same illness as the king."

Bright blue eyes blinked in shock. "What?" Rose shook her head. "I feel fine. What are you talking about?"

227

Eric stepped forward then. "You look a bit older, love." He knelt by the side of the bed and touched her blonde hair softly. "Just a touch. But we think it's the same disease."

Rose lifted her hand and looked at it. Then she brought it to her face and touched the lines that hadn't been there this morning.

"I'm aging?" Her voice held disbelief and fear. "How can that be?" She looked at Eric and Duncan. "You haven't aged." Rose patted Ivy's hand. "And Ivy hasn't aged. Why me?"

"We don't know." Ivy bent to kiss Rose's forehead. "But we'll find out. We can have Cook send up a tray every day if you wish."

"No." Rose sat up and swung her legs over the side of the bed. "I'm not staying in bed. I'll get around on my own two feet while I can." She glanced up at the mirror on the dresser and then down at Ivy. "Do I look awful?"

"Certainly not. You're still a beauty." Ivy stood also. "You simply look like an older sister instead of a younger one."

Rose shook her finger at her sister. "Don't let this go to your head."

Ivy put her arm around her sister's shoulder, and they walked to the mirror together. Rose appeared to be in her early forties instead of her late twenties. She touched her face again and sighed. "I guess using cosmetics would just be a waste. I don't think even Mary Kay could fix this mess." She looked at Ivy in the mirror. "Don't be so sad, sis. You'll find a cure. I know you will."

Ivy refused to let more tears fall. "Bet on it."

228

* * * *

Ivy stayed with Rose until she fell asleep again. Little Brown Bear was still nowhere to be found, and that worried her. He never left Rose's side. She crept back into her room and opened the huge windows once more. Tomorrow she would try Jack's plan. Because there was no way in hell Duncan would keep her locked up tight in the castle.

She lay down in bed and stared up at the multicolor banners that hung from her ceiling and crisscrossed the room. Guilt crept up on her with vicious talons and ripped at her heart. Rose was here because of her. There was no way around that. And now her sister would remain in danger until a cure could be found.

A soft knock on her door startled her, and she frowned. Ivy stood up and walked over to the door.

"Who is it?"

"Duncan."

Ivy sighed and opened it.

He moved into the room without invitation.

"Come right in," she said sarcastically and shut the door. When she turned to face him, he moved to hold her. Ivy stepped back.

"The last thing I need is a romp right now. Thanks anyway."

"I was offering comfort." Duncan dropped his hands to his sides. "We are all extremely sorry this has happened." He studied her closely. "I know you'll want to stay with your sister as much as possible. But I can engage a nurse of sorts to come in and look after her."

Ivy shoved her hair out of her face and blew out a breath. "First, I will be spending more time with Rose. But I will also still be looking for the cure. This changes nothing. If anything, it's more motivation. I won't stand by and let my sister lapse into a coma." She moved farther away from Duncan. "So engage your nurse." She cocked her head to the side. "Have you seen Little Brown Bear?"

Duncan shook his head. "Not for quite some time." His eyes were puzzled. "He hasn't left Rose's side."

"Exactly." Ivy clapped her hands together. "And don't you find that odd? I'm worried about him. And I know Rose will be, too. Can we send a search party or something?"

"We'll search the castle first," Duncan promised. "And then we'll expand the search. We'll find him."

"I have a couple of questions." Ivy moved a bit closer. "Have you consulted higher authorities and all that? The Fairy Godmother? Mother Goose? Anyone else who can help?"

"We've had conferences." Duncan's mouth tightened. "They don't know a thing. Just the damn poem. And they are as worried as the rest of us."

"Okay." Ivy nodded. "And something else." She watched his handsome face carefully for reactions. "Why wasn't I invited to the mixer at an earlier date? There was some mention of it."

Duncan sat down on the edge of the bed. "The Charmed Committee is in charge of invitations. As soon as Mother Goose made mention of it, I asked them." His emerald eyes pierced hers. "You were apparently having problems in your life at that time."

"Problems?" she prodded. "Could you be more specific?" Ivy sat down next to him. "It is rather spooky that you can peek in and out of my life at will."

"It doesn't really matter." Duncan took Ivy's hands in his and stroked them gently. "It matters that you are here. Now."

"That doesn't answer my question."

"You are the most obstinate female alive," he growled.

Ivy looked at him calmly and waited.

"Fine!" he barked. Duncan stood and paced in front of her. "Apparently you had some personal problems. A boyfriend named Tommy decided to put you in the hospital."

The color drained from Ivy's face. Tommy Puckett was her boyfriend from around ten years ago. He was tall and muscular. Liked to play football. And she thought he was wonderful. But then things disintegrated. And all the good feelings faded.

It started out with fighting. And Ivy couldn't understand why they started. It was as if Tommy looked for the slightest things to fight about. They agreed to work through it. And then Ivy came home from work one day, and he flew into a rage. He gave her a black eye, several bruises, and a broken arm. As soon as she regained consciousness, she called 911 and then Missy. The ambulance took her away, and Missy filed the restraining order on her behalf. She never saw Tommy again.

Ivy fought back the humiliation, but it wasn't easy. She worked long and hard to distance herself from that time. She never stayed with a man who showed the slightest tendency to violence. Her arm healed after a couple of months, but she still remained leery.

Ivy set her jaw and looked up at Duncan. "So your committee just popped in and noticed I had the shit beat out of me. And they, in their infinite wisdom, decided it was a bad time to issue an invitation?"

Duncan sank to his knees in front of her. He softly brushed back her hair. "I'm sorry, Ivy. So sorry. You shouldn't have had to go through that."

She brushed his hands off her knees. "It's called the real world, Duncan. It's where I live. And unpleasant things like that happen all the time. I work in an office where the most hideous crimes are reported. And I have to read every one of them."

Duncan put his hands back on her knees. "We will find a cure, Ivy. And you will see that not everything is as it seems here." He stood. "We'll talk again when this is over." He turned on his heel and strode to the door. Duncan turned around at the last minute. "I'll engage a nurse tomorrow." Then he left.

Ivy sat on her bed and pondered Duncan's words. She didn't blame anyone in this kingdom for the messed-up time of her life. She was a big girl. And bad decisions were a part of the growing process. But to have Duncan know parts of her painful past actually pained her.

"Doesn't matter," she murmured. Ivy tucked herself into her blankets tightly and willed herself to go to sleep. Tomorrow was a big day. And time seemed to be moving quicker and quicker.

* * * *

Ivy woke up at six thirty on the dot. She quickly rolled out of bed and threw on a pair of capris and a yellow T-shirt. She knocked softly on the adjoining door and waited for Rose.

"Come in."

Ivy opened the door and walked inside. Rose was already dressed. She wore powder blue slacks and a white blouse. Her blonde hair was loosely bound on top of her head. And she wore no make-up.

Ivy smothered the shock of seeing her sister in her forties. It wouldn't do either of them any good to dwell on it.

"Well then, sister of mine. Are you ready for breakfast?"

Rose nodded. "Have you seen Bear? I couldn't find him when I woke up."

"No." Ivy took her sister's hand. "Duncan promised to look for him today in the castle. And if we don't find him, then he'll widen the search."

"I'm worried about him." Rose sighed. "He wouldn't just leave."

"We'll find him," Ivy promised. She opened Rose's door and escorted her sister to the stairs.

Rose shot her a look and snorted. "I'm not made of glass, woman."

"Sorry." Ivy winced. "I feel like a failure at this whole thing. I haven't found a cure. I've let you become sick." She threw up her hands. "I need some grass."

"What?" Rose turned her head and looked at her sharply.

"Oh geez!" Ivy threw back her head and laughed. "Enchanted grass. Outside the castle. It tastes like chocolate." She snickered at Rose. "I wasn't advocating drugs. Sorry about that."

"Yeah, well." Her sister shook her head. "If I weren't already old, that would have aged me about a decade." They both looked at each other and laughed until tears streamed from their eyes.

"Oh, God." Ivy wiped her face furiously. "You're killing me."

"I'm not the one talking about needing grass," Rose said primly. She bit her lip to keep from laughing again.

They walked downstairs and into the dining room. Adam and Colleen sat in their same spots while Eric sat beside Duncan. Rose sat next to Eric, and he smiled at her. Ivy moved to the empty seat next to Rose.

Two servants brought in plates of food and placed them on the table. When they left, Duncan tapped his glass.

"We are running out of time. Not only is our king sick, Rose is ill, too."

Adam reached across the table and patted her hand. "How are you feeling?"

"Okay." Rose smiled gratefully and patted her blonde hair. "Ask again when I'm an octogenarian."

"Not funny." Ivy shot her a glance. She looked up at Duncan. "What do you have planned?"

"Adam and Colleen will travel to North Shantro to try and find the Brandis root. It will be a three-day trip. There and back. Provisions and transportation are ready. They leave after breakfast."

"I will be in my lab." Eric smiled at Rose. "Looking for something for my fair Rose."

She blushed, and Ivy rolled her eyes. "Okay, pretty boy. I'll keep that in mind." Her gaze shifted back to Duncan. "And you?"

"I will make a day trip to the elves. They seem to think they may have found something to slow the aging process. And I've already contacted a helper for Rose. She should be here this afternoon."

"Thank you, Duncan." Rose inclined her head.

Ivy waited expectantly. When Duncan said no more, she scowled. "And I'm supposed to twiddle my thumbs? Maybe polish the furniture or something?"

Eric snorted behind his hand, and Duncan frowned.

"Well?" Ivy demanded. "Spit it out."

"Eric and I think you and Rose are targets now. It's safer for you to be here than anywhere."

"Ah. So there it is." Ivy made eye contact with the brothers. "Read my lips, gentlemen. You will not keep me wrapped up in here like a present waiting for Christmas. Know that."

Duncan slammed his hand down on the table, and the plates jumped. "I warn you, Ivy. If you leave this castle, I won't be responsible for what happens to you."

She blinked twice and then smiled slowly. "Fine." She took a sip of her soda. "Besides. You've already closed off the exits, haven't you? Then I suppose you have nothing to worry about."

* * * *

Everyone filled their plates with sausage, bacon, pancakes, eggs, and some type of bread that Ivy would love to be able to eat every day. It was light and fluffy. But a dark blue color. She wrapped one in a napkin and saved it for later.

As soon as breakfast ended, Adam and Colleen hugged everyone and left. Ivy watched from the window and vowed to make sure they weren't the only ones leaving that day.

Eric bowed low and kissed Rose's hand. "I'm at your disposal, Rose."

"Thank you, Eric." Her lips twitched.

Duncan patted his brother's back. "I suppose I won't see you for a couple of days?"

"I'll be busy." Eric looked at Rose and smiled. "Some things take priority."

Duncan nodded. "I'll send trays down periodically."

They watched Eric trot off.

"Your helper should be here in approximately three hours." Duncan leaned in and kissed Rose's cheek. "Try not to give her too hard a time."

"I promise." She held up her hand. "Has there been any luck finding Bear?"

"None, so far." Duncan waved his hand, and a scroll appeared. "Apparently only a fourth of the castle is complete. So he may still be here." He made a motion, and the scroll disappeared.

"Handy," Ivy muttered.

Rose glanced at one then the other. "I'll be in my room, reading." She turned and walked up the stairs.

Ivy waited until Rose was out of earshot. "When are you leaving?"

"Soon." Duncan moved closer until his breath fanned against Ivy's face. "But don't think I don't know what you're planning. I can see the wheels turning. You would do well to remember what I said, Ivy."

She shivered and looked deeply into his eyes. He was the stuff of dreams. Girlhood fantasies. And womanly passions. Too bad he was so damn bossy and arrogant.

"I heard every word." She turned to go when he snatched her back and pressed his lips quickly to hers.

"Don't do anything foolish, woman."

Ivy nipped his lip and laughed lightly. "Who me?"

* * * *

Ivy watched Duncan leave and waited a full half an hour before she attempted her escape. To tell the truth, she was scared shitless. But what choice did she have? She knotted together the sheets and strips from the room. They were sturdy to say the least. She swung on a couple of them before she decided to inflict her mass upon them.

The entire time she knotted them, she said a little prayer. *They will hold. They won't break.* And several variations on the first two.

Ivy opened her window and looked down with butterflies in the pit of her stomach. She really was mental. There could be no other explanation. It was at least twenty to twenty-five feet from her window to the ground. And Jack's words echoed in her head. *At least two feet.* Two feet or she may as well just lie in bed and eat bonbons. Ivy sighed.

"Shit," she muttered. "Now or never."

Ivy hefted a backpack on with supplies inside. There was rope. A flashlight. A change of clothes. And some food she saved from breakfast.

She tied the sheets to her rail and flung the rest over the side. They billowed down the side of the castle like a multicolored flag. Ivy flung her leg over the silver railing and clutched the colorful sheet tightly in her hand.

"Don't look down," she whispered. "Just a little wall scaling today. No big deal." Ivy gripped the sheets firmly and scooted down,

238

inch by inch. She had to be careful not to let herself go too far too fast. She was afraid she'd bounce off the castle like some human ball. The thought did nothing to ease her fear.

Her whole body wrapped tightly around the sheets, and Ivy swore as her hands began to burn a bit. The pressure of keeping her body weight aloft wore on her. She had no experience with rappelling. So she inched down like a worm fighting for its life.

Ivy glanced down and blanched. Her hands trembled, but she steadied them through sheer willpower.

"Damn man," she muttered. "Bossy." She inched down some more. "Arrogant." Another few inches.

By the time she reached "egotistical", she was close enough to the ground to jump. Or at least she hoped. Her ass still hurt from yesterday and her fall in the library. And her elbow wasn't particularly happy with her either. She would be a mass of bruises before her adventure was said and done.

"Okay." Ivy took a deep breath. *What is the worst that can happen anyway?* She let go of the silky sheets, bent her knees, and tried to cushion her fall.

She rolled to the side and onto her backpack. Pain shot through her elbow, and Ivy cursed through clenched teeth. But at least she was on the ground. She pumped her fists in the air.

"Woo!" Ivy did a little dance of victory. She landed on the east side of the main road. It wouldn't take much for her to stay just this side of the major road. She would be careful and be back to the castle before Duncan. He didn't physically scare her in the slightest, but she didn't know what he had up his magical sleeve.

Ivy swung her backpack up and kept to the side road. There were several houses that caught her attention, but she told herself she couldn't stop and stare. Even when she passed a house of straw, wood, and then brick. She couldn't, however, escape the laughter. What would her friends say if they could see her now?

She looked down with a grin at the green, velvety grass. Ivy bent to pick some up and put a couple of blades in her mouth. Greenery never tasted so good.

"I thought you were under house arrest."

Ivy bit back a shriek and whirled around. Rupert stood there, propped against a tree, staring at her.

His black hair hung in ropes on the side of his head. And his dark eyes took her in with a look of cold contempt. He wore the stained clothes she first saw him in and the same type of boots Eric wore the other night.

"I've managed a reprieve." Ivy raised her head haughtily. She sighed. "Never mind all that. I need to speak with you."

Rupert turned his back to her. "I don't think so, mortal." He walked back toward the woods.

"Wait!" she shouted. Ivy took off after him at a trot.

He wound through the outer layer of the woods without pause. And then he disappeared down one of the three trails.

Ivy paused for a second and bit her lip. Wasn't it a bad thing for her to be walking in the woods in a fairy tale kingdom? Following a man, who in all likelihood was out to get them all? Ivy glanced around. "Nothing ventured, nothing gained," she muttered. Her hands clutched the backpack tightly as she started down the same path she saw Rupert take.

There were no brambles, but the path was rocky. And Ivy slowed down so she wouldn't fall and break her neck. Which was probably what the giant asshole wanted her to do. She stopped a second and bent over with her hands on her knees. Her breath whistled in and out of her tired lungs.

"You're the same as Duncan!" she yelled. "Arrogant ass!"

The low growl startled her, and she looked up quickly.

Rupert strode over to her and sneered down at her. "That mouth of yours does you no good, mortal." He reached down and forcefully straightened her body.

Ivy forced herself to meet his angry eyes. "I have bigger worries than you, giant."

Rupert's eyes widened, and then he threw back his head and roared with laughter. "Giant, eh?" He set Ivy back down and shook his head. "That would be a great word to describe your mouth."

"How do you know so much about what goes on? I wonder." Ivy studied Rupert with cool, brown eyes. "You knew about the children. You knew about the house arrest. And I have to wonder

241

what else you know." She ticked off each item with a different finger. "Do you wish to harm me? Or help me?"

"I have no business with you, mortal. You're like an irritating bug which flies about my head. One that I will soon be rid of, I'm sure."

"Like my sister?" Ivy clenched her fists at her side. "If I find out for one second that you've harmed Rose in any way, I will make you pay. And that's not an idle threat in the least."

Rupert studied her. "You think your threats bother me?" He snorted derisively. "And why would I do anything to the puny one?"

Ivy steadied herself. "She ages." Her eyes dropped momentarily. "She ages as the king does." She lifted her head defiantly. "And I will not fail her."

His eyes narrowed. "Don't you think it's time to leave this world then? Rid yourself of these troubles?" Rupert cocked his head to the side, and his hair swung close to her head. He leaned down into her face. "Why don't you just leave?"

"Because the thought of you doing the happy dance sickens me." Ivy put her hands on her hips. "I followed you for answers. Answers you choose not to give me every time we meet. And my suspicion grows."

Rupert's face showed no emotion. "I have business to tend to, and you will not dog my steps."

"Then answer me, damn it!" Ivy was so furious, she thought her head would explode. *What was it about these damn supercilious men? Who in the hell did they think they were?*

She poked her fingers in his chest. "You." Poke. "Are the most irritating man here." Poke. "Except for Duncan." Poke.

Rupert lifted his hand, but Ivy didn't budge. "I have no answers for you, mortal. Now leave my sight. Before I decide to make you into a nice hedge." He pointed at a squirrel, and she watched the furry mammal transform before her very eyes. His tail lengthened and stiffened. It snaked into the ground. His arms and legs became limbs, and his head changed shape and became velvety, brown leaves. The tree grew to around ten feet tall and then stopped.

When Ivy turned back to look at Rupert, he was gone.

"Shit." She moved forward and reached out trembling hands to stroke the smooth bark. Tears slid down her cheek when she thought of the life the squirrel lost.

"Don't cry, child."

Ivy looked behind her and saw the Fairy Godmother. She slid toward Ivy and patted her shoulder comfortingly. "He hasn't harmed the squirrel. Only changed its shape."

"He's cruel and hateful!" Ivy cried. "And I think he has something to do with King Cedric's illness." She sighed. "And Rose's."

"I've heard your sister has taken ill." The woman's blue eyes were kind. "And you won't find the answers in the woods, dear. Go

243

back to the main road. Seek answers from those who don't mind the questions."

"Is that going to help?" Ivy braced herself. "Duncan has questioned everyone. Rose questioned everyone. And now we're stuck at an impasse. And I don't care for it." She looked into the kind godmother's face. "There are children at stake."

The godmother winced. "Please, Ivy. Have a bit of patience."

"No." She spoke the word flatly. "I will not. Screw a bunch of that." She shrugged off the Fairy Godmother and picked up the backpack. "I have work to do. Float back to wherever you came from." Ivy hefted the backpack and turned. She glanced back toward the woman. "Thanks for the advice."

* * * *

She took the middle path and started down it. Hopefully every damn trail ended up somewhere by the main road. This entire world began to tick her off. *Why did it have to be so hard? Why couldn't Rose just come over here and marry a prince and make everything better?*

"Some kind of fairy tale world." She snorted and rolled her eyes.

"And you think your world is wonderful?" a deep voice asked.

She squealed and looked to her right. "Hell in a handbasket!" she snarled.

Three bears stood before her with wide smiles. They bowed in turn. "We've never seen a mortal. And Baby Bear became so insistent." Mama Bear patted her child.

Ivy put a hand to her rapidly beating heart. "Could someone, perhaps anyone, clear their throat before speaking here?"

Papa Bear laughed heartily. "You're a bit high-strung, woman."

"Ivy." She sighed. "May as well call me by my given name."

"Ivy," he repeated. "Lovely name." Papa Bear turned back to his child. "Give it to her, son. Maybe it will help."

Baby Bear moved forward shyly and held out his hand. He turned it over, and Ivy saw a small pendant with the bears engraved on it.

"For luck," he said.

Ivy took the pendant from his hand and looked gratefully at the family. "Thank you. I do appreciate the help." She glanced around. "Could you show me the right path out of here?" Ivy glanced up and noticed the day seemed to slip away from her. "I'm running out of time."

Papa Bear nodded. "Take this road." He pointed to the right fork in front of her. "It will take you where you need to be." He bowed low. "Don't give up hope, lady. It has sustained us for longer than I can remember." They turned as one and walked down another path.

Ivy ran her thumb over the pendant in her hand. It was no bigger than a quarter, but it was heavy. She tucked it into her backpack and took the path Papa Bear pointed out.

* * * *

Ivy made her way back to a side road and paused for a bite of blue bread and something to drink. She realized she only had perhaps three or four hours to finish up outside the castle. The sun moved quickly across the sky. She tucked her provisions back in the backpack and turned to follow the road.

There were several citizens out and about in their yards or gardens. Ivy started at the first house and asked a few questions. The large, white rabbit couldn't help her, but he gave her a small pendant with three carrots engraved on it. It was brass and shined beautifully in the sunlight.

Ivy thanked him and moved to the next house. A beautiful woman in flowing jade robes couldn't help, either. But she handed Ivy a pair of earrings with green stones that glowed.

All along the path, Ivy found those who couldn't help but who gifted her with prized possessions and well wishes.

Her heart and backpack were heavy as she walked steadily back to the castle. Maybe one or two of the items she carried could help slow down the aging process. She marveled at the kindness and generosity of some of the inhabitants of this world. Ivy had no doubt they would have given her anything she desired in their possession. The thought humbled her.

Ivy glanced at the sun and congratulated herself on making it back before Duncan. She swung her backpack off her shoulder and turned the knob on the front door. But her pleasure faded at the look on Duncan's face as she opened it.

She licked her lips and took a second to form an excuse. But she shouldn't have bothered.

Duncan calmly took her backpack and put it inside the door. Then he moved forward and swung Ivy over his shoulder and started up the stairs.

"Wait!" she yelled. Ivy pounded her fists on his hard back. But he didn't yield. In fact, he sped up. They took the stairs two at a time.

Ivy tried to keep her wits about her even as the stairs sped by. Her head spun, and she finally gave up pounding on Duncan. Because he didn't seem to appreciate her efforts.

Duncan finally put her down in the large bathroom with the magical tub. He moved his hand out, and the door automatically shut.

Ivy heard the lock click, and she felt her pulse quicken. To say that he was furious would be putting it mildly. There was no expression whatsoever on his face, and that scared the hell out of her.

She put her hands up. "Listen. I know you're mad. But I'm okay. See?" She tried to smile at him.

Duncan growled low in his throat and muttered something. The next thing Ivy knew, she was naked. A second after that, she was up to her neck in the magical waters of the tub. Ivy sputtered as she received a mouthful of bubbles.

"Are you insane?" she shrieked. She tried to rise but couldn't move from the water. Ivy narrowed her eyes. "If you even think about joining me in this tub, I swear to you you'll regret it."

Duncan calmly looked at her and began to disrobe. Ivy struggled in the water, but it did no good. She watched as Duncan's nude body slid into the water next to her. He tugged her closer and settled her between his knees.

Ivy tried to turn around, but he forced her to face forward as he wet her hair and worked soap through it. She kept her back stiff while he massaged her scalp and rinsed her hair. Then he picked up a soapy sponge and started washing her neck.

"Say something," she muttered.

Duncan remained quiet while his hands moved over her body and didn't leave an inch untouched. Ivy refused to admit she enjoyed every second of it. Strong-arm tactics just pissed her off. And Duncan seemed to have a knack for it. But his hands stroking her body lit a fire she couldn't quite defuse.

Ivy leaned back against him as he washed her arms and breasts. He moved lower, and she tried to hold on to her anger. She had to be mad, didn't she? Never mind the fact her elbow already felt better. And more than likely all the bruises on her ass would be gone. It was the principle.

"The principle," she murmured.

"Hmmm?" Duncan moved the sponge up her inner thigh. "Did you say something?"

Ivy shook her head. She could feel Duncan's muscled chest under her back, and she reveled in the fact she could lean on his strength. Even if only for a minute.

"I'm sorry I made you mad." Ivy held her breath as she waited for Duncan to respond.

"Ivy." He nipped her neck. "It was either kill you or heal you." His voice grew gruff. "You had a bruise on your elbow the size of a grapefruit. There are twigs in your hair. And you're walking with a slight limp."

"You should see my ass," she muttered.

"Oh, I will." Duncan's silky voice held a promise. "It's on my to-do list."

Warmth suffused Ivy's body. For a day that started out with a threat of pain, the end more than made up for it. Duncan turned her around and settled her legs on either side of his waist. His mouth dipped to her breasts and sucked gently while she arched her hips against him.

"Duncan."

"Ivy." She felt him smile against her skin. "You're addictive."

She chuckled.

"And infuriating."

Ivy opened her eyes and peered down at him. "And your point is?"

249

Duncan slid his hands up her legs and cupped her ass. "My point is that you consistently disregard my rules for your safety. You seem to think that I simply like to hear the sound of my own voice. But I put these rules into place so you won't be hurt." He closed his eyes, as if in pain. "The guard found your sheets dangling out of the window and notified me." He opened his emerald eyes, and she could see the worry.

"Do you know what that's like? To know you would rather risk your life than listen to me?"

"Let me help, Duncan." Ivy wound her arms around his neck. "It's why you've brought me here. It's what I need to do."

"You are a guest here." His tone brooked no argument. "You are under the rules and regulations of this kingdom. Since you choose not to abide by them, I have no choice." Duncan paused for a second. "Ivy Daniels, you're under arrest."

Chapter 12

Ivy blinked slowly. Then she eased away from Duncan with a puzzled look on her face. "Did you just say I was under arrest?"

He crossed his arms over his broad chest and nodded. "I did."

"You're going to put me in jail?" Ivy glanced around for an escape route.

"No." Duncan sighed. "But if you leave this castle again, you will be forcefully detained. Do you understand?"

"Perfectly." Ivy eased out of the tub and put a robe on. She pulled her hair back and looked down at the prince in the tub. "The next time you decide to have a mixer and invite mortals to your world to help save it, leave me off the guest list." She turned on her heel and left the room.

Ivy's blood boiled at Duncan's words. *What gave him the right? Here, Ivy. Come to my world. Let's have great sex. But you can only do as I say. Oh, and help me save the kingdom.*

"Asshole," she muttered.

She stomped to her room and changed into some comfortable clothes. Then she opened the adjoining door to check in on Rose. Ivy crept closer to the bed and fought back the shock. Rose aged nearly two decades in one day. Even the king hadn't aged that fast. Ivy looked around for the help Duncan promised, but she couldn't find any.

Her heart sank. They were trapped here. Ivy walked back to her room and shut the door behind her. She wouldn't sneak out of the castle again. But she and Duncan had a lot to talk about tomorrow.

Ivy glanced on the bed and noted that someone brought her backpack upstairs for her. She sat on the bed and unpacked her treasures. There were pendants, charms, and jewelry of every sort.

Tomorrow. Tomorrow she would confront Duncan for the last time. And she would make sure he either helped her or stayed the hell out of her way.

Ivy put all the items back in the backpack and lay back on the bed. Duncan's scent rose from the pillow beneath her head and tickled her nose. She scowled. How could one man who absolutely infuriated her mean so much? Ivy thumped the pillow and threw it on the floor.

The last thing she needed was another distraction.

* * * *

Breakfast the next morning was a somber affair. Ivy found herself eating alone, and she didn't care for it a bit. Duncan left a note stating he needed to check in on Rose's helper because she didn't make it yesterday. And he was worried.

Adam and Colleen were still gone and wouldn't be back until late tomorrow. Little Brown Bear was still missing. And her sister still rapidly aged.

Ivy rubbed her temples and sipped her soda. The children's disappearance played heavily in her mind. *What would it be like to wake up and have a child missing?* Her stomach lurched. She slammed her hands on the table and stood up.

"Enough." Ivy turned and left the dining room. She made a right and followed a hallway until it ended. Then she started opening doors.

It was amazing the things she hadn't seen here. There were rooms of such breadth that she couldn't fathom them ending. There were works of art that glittered and gleamed. An entire room consisted of items from Mother Goose rhymes. A crook for sheep. A large clock that showed tiny prints running up it. A horn. A rusty pail. A candlestick. A bare cupboard. An oven. A cradle.

Ivy's head spun. Little snippets of rhymes filtered through her head while her hands brushed over the revered objects.

She closed the door quietly behind her and opened the next. There were golden treasures displayed on every gleaming piece of wooden furniture. Large, gold lamps and gold coins sparkled in the sun. There were scales and necklaces. Bracelets. Mirrors. Ivy shook her head and moved on.

The next room boasted sapphire gems. They adorned candlesticks. Treasure boxes. Knives. Ivy moved on. The following room was rubies. And the one after that was emeralds. Her head spun as she opened each new door to a vast treasure.

Ivy's heart pounded in her chest when she came to the end of the hall. She leaned against the wall and told herself she could handle this. But it was hard. Her ratty, reliable couch never seemed so far away.

She pushed herself away from the wall and started down the next hallway.

* * * *

Ivy found another library of sorts and was buried in a potions book when Eric flung open the door with a wild look on his face. His normally calm blonde hair flew about his head almost as if it had a life of its own. There were stains all over his royal clothing, and his hands were covered with bruises and cuts.

She stood up quickly and hurried over to him. "Are you okay?"

"No." He shook his head furiously back and forth. "There's something you have to see, Ivy. You won't believe it." Eric grabbed her hand in his and practically pulled her along with him.

"Wait, Eric!" Ivy tried to slow down. "Don't you think you should notify Duncan?"

He looked back impatiently. "I have! Now hurry up! Your sister's life depends on it!"

Ivy broke into a run as Eric opened the door to his lab. She followed him down into the darkness and waited impatiently for him to open the lab door.

He swung the door open and waited until Ivy stepped inside.

* * * *

Ivy turned back to the door, and Eric slammed it shut. He smiled then and motioned inside. "Have a look."

254

She spun around and frowned. His worktable was a mess. There were shattered glasses and liquid spilled down the sides of the table. A dark green puddle oozed from the center and off the backside. There were broken chairs and pieces of wood scattered about the floor.

"Okay." Ivy put her hands on her hips. "What are you supposed to show me? I don't get it."

Eric patted her back gently. "I'm showing you everything, Ivy. Everything. I think it's important that you know exactly why you're here." He waved his hand.

She gasped at the sight before her.

Duncan and Rupert hung from crimson cuffs on the wall. They stood on a narrow ledge that supported their weight. They were both battered and bruised. One of Rupert's eyes was completely swollen shut. They attempted to talk, but Ivy couldn't hear a thing. Their mouths moved, but no sound came forth.

She moved toward them quickly.

"Don't!" Eric commanded. "If you care to live for another day, you won't take another step."

She spun and glared at him. "You lowlife son of a bitch." Ivy bared her teeth and clenched her fists. "You've done this. Who in the hell do you think you are?"

"I am Prince Eric. Rightful heir to this kingdom. And the only true ruler this kingdom will ever need." His blue eyes blazed with madness. "And the rest of you are expendable pieces of flesh."

255

"You are a psychotic piece of shit!" Ivy snatched a long, wooden rod off the table and brandished at Eric. "Let them down. Now."

He laughed at her then. "Mortal, you have no more power in this room than that spider." Eric flicked his hand toward the wall, and Ivy watched as the bug burst into flame.

She gasped.

Eric turned back to her. "I dare you," he said casually.

Ivy gathered her wits. "What do you want?"

He cocked his head to the side. "I want world peace." He paused and smiled. "My world peace."

"Why would you want to kill your own father? Is this about power?"

"Power?" Eric rolled his eyes. "You mortals are simpleminded." He sneered at her. "Stupid creatures."

"Get to your point." Ivy glared at him.

"You killed my mother."

"What?" Ivy wasn't she sure she heard him correctly. She saw Duncan slightly move out of the corner of her eye. But she didn't glance at him. She needed to focus on Eric.

"Those parties for mortals." Eric spat on the floor in front of Ivy. "And King Cedric invited my mother to attend." He paced in front of the table. "She didn't want to go. I know she couldn't have. But she did. Because it was her duty. It was expected." Eric slammed his fist on the table. "And you germ-infested vermin killed her!" He

256

moved to within inches of Ivy's face. "You made her sick. She died because of you."

"I killed no one." Ivy held up her hands. "I would never harm any of you."

"Liar." Eric spun on his heel and walked back to the table. "You are all liars." He picked up a vial and shattered it against the wall. His blonde hair moved wildly around his head. Sweat poured off his face. "This kingdom doesn't need mortals. And I've tried to tell everyone that. But they cling to the old ways. And those are killing us."

He sneered at her. "You and your kind have no right to be here. And that's what I tried to get through Rupert's head." Eric shot a glance at the battered man. "But he and I just don't seem to agree on much of anything anymore." He walked over and looked up. "We used to be as brothers. Both interested in magic. Eager pupils of the alchemist. But I felt his interest wane one summer when he turned sixteen. Some little chit aroused his interest. And so I took matters into my own hands. Literally."

Eric smiled up at Rupert. "You thought it was Duncan, didn't you? The one you caught your love interest with. But it wasn't." He laughed evilly. "A small lock of my brother's hair, and I was in. So to speak."

Ivy watched Rupert's eyes widen, and he struggled fruitlessly against his bonds.

"I drive a mean wedge, don't I?" Eric licked his lips and winked. "And she was so eager." He smiled at Ivy. "But that wasn't the only gift I've given Rupert. He seems to have a habit of making poor decisions." He sighed. "Can you believe this great hulk actually fell for a mortal?" He snorted in laughter. "That he wanted to be with her? And she, alas, with him."

Ivy grimaced and looked up at Rupert. Pain was clearly written across his injured features.

Eric patted the man's feet. "Don't worry. I've taken care of everything. It hurt when she didn't remember you, didn't it? And there was pain when she refused to see you." He sighed. "It took a powerful potion. I believe I've successfully killed every feeling she ever had or ever will have for you. I've murdered them all." He chuckled ruefully. "So all those late-night excursions into the forest are for naught. Because you can't undo what I've done."

Ivy glanced up once more. "You were trying to reverse the damage. To make her remember what she felt." She spun around and stood between Eric and Rupert. "Is that what you do? Destroy what you don't understand?"

Eric shrugged. "I'm righting a wrong, mortal. Do you honestly believe you can do anything to stop me?"

"Why are you poisoning your own father?"

Eric shook his head sadly. "He's lost his way." The sadness gave way to fierce anger. "King Cedric, mighty ruler, actually thought he could replace my mother. Replace her!" He clenched his teeth. "So I had to get rid of the wicked stepmother, too."

Fear raced along Ivy's nerves. She was in over her head. A magical madman paced in front of her, telling her of atrocities he committed. And the help she desperately needed was strung up on the wall behind her. Her heart broke to see Duncan trussed up. And she felt slightly ill when she realized that Rupert only tried to recover a lost love. He didn't harm anyone. He may not have been the most social creature, but he never deserved her malice.

"What did you do?" Ivy strove to keep herself steady.

"Why," Eric's blue eyes widened in merriment, "I blew her right out of her shoes."

Duncan's feet rattled against the board. But Ivy never looked up. "What do you mean?"

"Our dearest stepmother didn't belong here. She liked mortals. Accepted them. And so I sent her exactly where she needed to be. To your world as a mortal." Eric turned and looked at Ivy. "Amazing, really. I had never tried the spell before. It was quite powerful. Here one minute." Eric snapped his fingers. "Gone the next." He shrugged. "I'm sure she's happy somewhere as the wife of a mortal man. Bearing mortal children."

He ran his hands through his hair, but it flew right back up. "The only sacred thing in this kingdom, and everybody here wants to piss it away!" Eric's blue eyes blazed at Ivy. "And then we're forced to endure you and your sister as guests. And the puny male, Adam Stott."

He swept some of the vials off the wooden table. They fell with a loud crash to the floor. "It's an abomination of everything we hold dear. What we love. And I won't sacrifice it for anyone."

Ivy moved forward. "You've poisoned your father and my sister. You've taken every healing item that can help. You have stolen mortal children. You have lied, cheated, and stolen the entire time. Where's the dignity in that?" She slammed her own fist on the table. "You are a manipulative piece of shit with no idea of how to be a king. You are no ruler."

"Ivy, Ivy, Ivy." Eric shook his head sadly. "Such dreams and delusions of grandeur. Did you really think you stood a chance here? To save a kingdom? To reverse my plans? A mere mortal against a powerful magician?" He snorted in disgust. "And just because my brother felt the need to try you out, it doesn't ensure you privileges."

Eric swept his arm wide and two wooden panels disappeared. Ivy gasped and moved forward. One wall held a large tank with luminescent green and blue fish. The other wall held plants with blood red centers and glistening white leaves. She tentatively reached out and stroked the fish tank.

"They're beautiful." The fish swam up to the glass and looked at her with small, buggy eyes. Their gills moved, and their tails waved in unison. She walked over to the plants and traced a leaf with shaking fingers. They were smooth with blue veins streaking

260

through them. The veins fed into the core of the flower where the blood red center pulsed.

Ivy turned and looked at Eric. "How can you take hope from these people? How can you justify harming so many for your own selfish needs?"

Eric's blue eyes glared at her. "I don't have to justify shit to you, mortal." He looked up at Duncan and Rupert. "These two have been a thorn in my side long enough. Unfortunately I don't have it in me to kill them. Though it might be easier," he muttered. "So I plan on sending Duncan to live with those he holds dear." Eric pointed at Ivy. "You damn mortals." He looked at Rupert. "But this one is harder. He has magic deep in his veins. And I'm not quite sure I can vanquish all of that."

"You will let your father die?" Ivy's voice held disbelief. "You will banish those who oppose you?" She growled deep in her throat. "You won't get away with it."

He shrugged. "But I will." Eric held up his hands as if showing Ivy a picture. "I can see it now. A huge battle occurs. Duncan and Rupert vanish. I will, of course, be wounded." He placed his hand over his chest. "King Cedric will die. And all the mortals shall be expelled. These damn mortal mixers will be prohibited."

"What else have you done?" Ivy swept her hair back from her face and looked around. "What else have you twisted for your perverted means?"

Eric threw back his head and laughed. "Perverted means?" He snorted. "I have sealed the Brothers Grimm in their own house. I have taken mortal children. I have maneuvered every situation to my favor. That, you mortal bitch, is what I've done."

Ivy's hands hooked into claws.

Eric snapped his fingers. "I almost forgot." His blue eyes studied her face intently. "You were supposed to be here years ago. There were oracles and signs that heralded a new age in this kingdom. But I didn't want that. Not until I deemed it time."

Her eyes narrowed, and she felt panic build. "What did you do?"

Eric shrugged. "I put a little bug in your boyfriend's ear, mortal. He seemed to respond appropriately. You were in the hospital, were you not?"

Duncan's body jerked against his restraints.

"I was." Ivy stared at Eric stonily. "And why did you think it was me, Eric? What was I going to do to alter your little world?"

"Don't piss me off," he warned. "Right now, you are merely alive for my amusement. And I bore quickly."

"I'm serious." Ivy's brown eyes peered closely into Eric's stern face. "Why me? Why not Rose? Why not some other mortal?"

Eric stared at her, and Ivy saw his eyes change color for a flicker of a second. She stifled her gasp.

"Because you are the one, mortal. There is something in you that speaks to the prophecy. And I won't have it." Eric tapped his fingers against the wooden table. "So I'll have to kill you both just to make sure. Just a little insurance. Collateral damage, so to speak."

He winked at Ivy and waved his hand again.

She turned and noticed a cage that she couldn't see a minute ago. She ran to it quickly. Her fear fairly choked her. Rose lay on a small cot inside. And she was at least eighty years old now. Her skin almost transparent, and her hair so fine it looked like spun silk. Her body trembled under the narrow blanket that lay on top of her.

Ivy spun around and bared her teeth. "You vindictive son of a bitch!" She snatched a large, wooden stake off the floor. "I'll kill you myself."

Eric chortled. "Sure you will." He motioned to the door on the cage, and it opened creakily. "But I think first you'll join your sister while I check on what you've been doing."

She felt herself pushed to the door. Ivy struggled, but it didn't help.

"Shoo!" Eric commanded.

Ivy fell to her knees inside the doorway and looked up to see it close behind her. The cold metal clanged against itself. She hurried over to Rose and stroked her cold cheek. Her sister was dying before her very eyes.

Eric glanced up at the wall with the two men suspended on it. He smiled and waved his hand.

"What do you have to say, Duncan? Any last words of wisdom as the ruler of this kingdom? You know. Before I start working on your nonexistence here."

Duncan coughed a couple of times before he spoke. "Let the women go. You can erase their memories. Let them start anew. Erase all the magic. I don't care. But let them live."

Eric rolled his eyes and sighed. "Is that it?"

"You're a sorry piece of work, Eric," Rupert snarled. "You and I have unfinished business. And don't think you'll escape this life without tending to it." He struggled some more, but the cuffs wouldn't budge.

"You know as well as I, Rupert, that it will take someone stronger than you to free yourself." He laughed. "And as far as any business between you and I, we have none."

Eric glanced at Duncan. "And for the mortals..." He paused for a second. "They need to die. Because I really don't want a poor decision now biting me in the ass ten years from now." He patted his brother's leg. "Forward thinking, you know."

Duncan shook his head in disbelief. "What's happened to you? How have you become such a monster?"

Eric bowed low. "I am merely a product of my surroundings. Mother's tragedy changed me, Duncan. And I began to see my calling." He motioned to the cage, which contained Ivy and Rose. "They are pestilence. And Rupert here seems to have a problem with immunization." He shot a look at the big man. "Seems our burly, ill-tempered brethren may be getting sweet on another mortal." Eric's blue eyes narrowed to slits. "A certain fair-haired maiden."

Ivy's head shot up, and her heart raced. *Rose*. Her sister's words echoed in her head. *Maybe Rupert was lonely*. And leave it to her softhearted sister to try and fill the gap.

"Where is Little Brown Bear?" Ivy asked.

Eric frowned. "Another resident fraternizing with the enemy." His face cleared. "But not a worry anymore. He's tucked in tight with his favorite mortal."

Ivy rummaged around in the covers and pulled Bear out with a cry. He was still as death. His once lively eyes now dull and lifeless.

"What have you done to him?"

"He's comatose, too." Eric slapped his knee and laughed. "After all, if it's good enough for the king, it's good enough for a lowly bear."

Ivy put the bear down slowly beside her sister and walked over to the door of the cage. "I will stop you."

"You won't leave that cage. Really *is* appropriate, isn't it?" Eric started to hum while he mixed up a blue and green liquid.

Ivy looked over at the wall and made eye contact with Duncan. His emerald eyes shone fiercely in his face.

She turned back to Eric. "Did you send me exploding flowers, too?"

"Yes." He didn't even bother to turn back around. "Thought you might be injured a bit. Put a damper on your visits here." He

265

shrugged. "Poor timing." Eric turned back to her once more. "It really is a shame. You have such a pure heart." He grinned evilly. "It'll look lovely on my table over here."

"Eric!" Duncan struggled once more. "We can work a way out of this situation. You don't need to harm anyone. You don't need to take matters into your hands like this."

Eric picked up Ivy's backpack off the floor. "I've meant to look in this but haven't had the time." He looked back at her. "Anything of value in here?"

She ignored the question. "Where are the children? What have you done with them?"

"Ah. The children." Eric brushed his blonde hair back and took a sip of one of the drinks on his table. "They are here, also." He pointed to the long hallway behind the cage.

Ivy watched it light up in sections. And she caught her breath. The children, still in their nightclothes, lay side by side on the ground. Still as death.

"What have you done to them?" she demanded.

"They are asleep, mortal. I have no wish to harm them. They were simply a means to an end." He rubbed his eye and squinted at her. "They'll be returned with no memory of this and no harm whatsoever."

Ivy's trembling hands fell from the bars. At least the children would be safe. Now if she could figure out something for the rest of them.

"What about Adam?"

Eric sighed. "He'll be returned as well. No real harm done. Of course, he won't be able to see Colleen. That's one beauty I may claim for myself." He waved his hand and a sturdy, wooden chair appeared. Eric sank into it. "Your male mortal seems to think he stands a chance with the royal beauty. But I beg to differ."

"You will ruin all our lives through your selfishness." Ivy stood at the cage door and glared at Eric. "I pity you."

Eric slammed the chair back as he stood. "Pity me?" he roared. "You? Pity me?" He clenched his teeth and cocked his hand back. "Save your pity for yourself, mortal. Because I plan to kill your sister before you." He lowered his hand slowly. "And I may leave the remnant of the memory in there for a couple of days." Eric grinned. "Just because I can."

"Stop it, Eric!" Duncan glared down at his brother. "You have a chance to stop this. To quit harming people."

"My lines of destiny were drawn long ago." Eric sat back down. "About the time my mother was murdered by a mortal."

"She was my mother, too!" Duncan took a deep breath. "You don't have to go through this alone. I can help. We can all help."

Eric waved his hand around. "Whatever. Save your strength, Duncan. Right now I can't decide what I want to do first. Kill the mortal women or alter you two." He shook his head. "Decisions, decisions."

Rupert threw back his head and howled, "You will not succeed!"

Eric chuckled. "Sit and watch." He hefted Ivy's backpack onto the table and unzipped it. "I'll have to return all these charms to their proper owners." He turned to glare at Ivy. "You should never have been allowed to touch any of them."

"They were given in faith," Ivy reminded him. "In hope and trust." She shook her head. "Don't you think the givers will know something has gone terribly wrong?"

"There are ways." Eric dipped his hand into the bag and withdrew the three bears' pendant first. "I can return these things without too many questions."

Ivy looked around desperately. She felt her time slipping away at a rapid rate of speed. She glanced down at her sister and then up at Duncan and Rupert. Her heart shifted in her chest, and she put her hand up to cover it.

"Fear not, child," a voice whispered softly in her ear. "We are here to help. Have faith. Have hope. Say you believe."

Ivy blew out a soft breath and closed her eyes. "I believe," she whispered.

She felt herself being pushed slightly aside. And then her whole being grew somehow. And Ivy was filled with the most brilliant light she had ever seen. A million children's voices filled her head. Bits and pieces of rhymes filtered through her subconscious and warmed her.

268

"Let us speak, mortal. Let us help you."

Ivy nodded. And then the light completely took her body over.

Eric must have sensed a change in the room because he looked up instantly at Ivy. Fear lit quickly in his blue eyes as they widened.

"Impossible," he muttered. He stood up with a jerk and held up his hands. "Impossible."

"Why, Prince Eric?" The words poured from Ivy's mouth like honey.

"You're not real." Eric looked at the glowing woman in the cage. Her hair billowed about her head as if it had energy of its own. And her eyes glowed like two opals with shifting colors of blue, pink, and gold. Light seemed to erupt from every pore of her body, and she floated at least six inches off the ground.

Duncan's breath whooshed out of his body as he looked at Ivy. And Rupert seemed so startled that he couldn't speak.

"I am real, Prince Eric. You, yourself, have brought me here." The woman held out her hands.

"No!" Eric looked around in panic.

"Yes." She smiled genially and looked at the children. "They sleep. And so they dream. Such dreams." She sighed. "So simple and innocent." Her eyes shone brightly as she turned back to Eric. "You know who I am, child. Who we are."

"No." Eric shook his head vehemently back and forth.

"I am the hopes and wishes of the children and the dreamers." She spread her arms wide. "They speak to me. They desire the end

269

of this animosity." Her eyes lit on the treasure in the backpack on the table. "Citizens in two worlds called to me." She pointed to the table, and the backpack floated over to her. It hovered just outside the cage door.

Eric moved forward quickly and snatched the bag back. "Go to hell," he said coldly, with a sneer. "You can't prevent anything. I have you locked tight."

The woman blinked slowly and shook her head. She extended her right hand and the door swung open silently. She moved outside the cage and tilted her head to the side. "Why do you hate so fiercely?" Her opal eyes studied him intently.

"Mortals should not be allowed here!" he yelled. "In this world. They destroy. They kill."

She softly sighed. The sound brought goosebumps to Eric's arms. "Mortals help. They create, not destroy. You have misplaced your anger."

"Get out!" Eric held up his hand. "I'll kill you. You have no idea how much power I have running through my body." His hair flew about his head wildly.

"I know you're a child in pain."

"I am no child," he growled. "And I'll be more than happy to prove it to you." His blue eyes blazed. Eric waved his hand, and a ball of fire appeared in it. He threw it toward the glowing woman in front of him. She opened her hand and caught it lightly. He backed up a step and glared.

"Let them go. Let them all go. I can help you. I can make the pain go away." Her melodious voice flowed through the room.

"Ivy." Duncan's voice broke into the conversation.

The woman turned toward him and smiled. "Fear not, Prince. Your mortal is safe. She has let us borrow her for a bit." Her eyes shone brightly. "Such an uncommon beauty she has. Trust. And a love." The woman stopped suddenly. "Ah. I see." She smiled up at Duncan with sparkling multicolored eyes. "Some things are better left for a later date."

She turned back to Eric. "Let them go."

"Make me," he snarled. He moved his hands above his head and brought down a large, silver sword with a serrated edge. The light from the room glinted off the sharp blade. He charged forward with a yell.

"Look out!" Duncan and Rupert struggled against their bonds.

But the lady caught the sword easily in her hand. She gripped it loosely and slid it along her palm. A beautiful, glittery trail clung to the blade and changed it into a flag of shimmery ribbons. They billowed softly.

Eric threw down the sword. "Your piteous magic will not prevail." He spoke a few words in a low undertone, and the room exploded with black creatures that appeared as scorpions. Their pincers as big as human hands. And their stingers rose six inches from their bodies with tips that narrowed dangerously to a sharp point.

271

Duncan and Rupert jerked back against the wall, and their crimson cuffs rattled, as at least half a dozen scorpions moved toward them.

The lady smiled widely. "What lovely creatures." She picked one up and brought it closer to her face. Her fingers stroked their shiny, black backs.

Eric snarled.

Then the lady lightly kissed where her fingers had stroked. There was a loud pop, and the creatures turned into beautiful pink balls of fur.

"Enough!" Eric picked up a yellow vial from the table and held it high. He glared at the men on the wall and looked back at the Lady. "I will be back for you. I am not nearly done." He threw the vial and disappeared in a plume of smoke.

The lady waved her hand, and the men found themselves standing on the floor. Duncan moved toward her, but she held her hand up. "You have business, Prince Duncan." She motioned to Rupert. "The both of you do."

"I can find him," Rupert rumbled fiercely. "And I will."

"Not so fast." The lady motioned to the fish and plants. "Use these. Make the potions. Heal the king and the mortal woman. And don't forget the bear." She chuckled low. "Such a loyal heart." Her eyes glowed intensely. "I have business to attend to."

"Wait!" Duncan held up his hand.

The lady turned and arched her eyebrow. "Time wastes."

272

"This body." He sighed. "Please be careful with it."

She chuckled. "Some things never change." And then she disappeared.

Chapter 13

Ivy felt safe. That was the only thing she was sure of at this point. She was somehow cushioned inside her own body. The feeling was not entirely unpleasant. The voices continued to filter through her, and she smiled. Whatever held her in its grasp was the only thing that could help both worlds.

The lady appeared in a circle made of stones. It was a small clearing in an otherwise wooded area. Tall, black trees rose hundreds of feet in the air. And no bird called. It was dark and still. The air was damp, and mist curled around her feet.

"Come out, Eric." The lady smiled. "We have not finished our business."

"You stupid bitch!" Eric strode out from the trees on the outside of the circle. "I knew you would follow me. Attempt to stop me." He shook his head. "But you can't. Not here. Because this is my magic. And my circle. And whatever I wish to happen to you, will."

"I offer you a chance, Eric. A chance to rectify these mistakes you've made. You've been misguided. Your judgment affected by a tragedy. And no one can fault you for that. There is still time."

"There is no more time!" He glared at the woman in the circle and shook his fist. "I will make sure this never happens to our kingdom again. I'm saving this world." Eric put his hand behind his back and a large orange cylinder appeared. He held it up and sneered at the woman.

"Even now you inhabit the body of a worthless mortal. One who does not even know the true meaning of magic. Or how special this world is. She will destroy us." He threw the cylinder into the circle and watched.

As soon as the cylinder hit the ground, a large explosion rocked the circle. The earth shook, and the trees groaned in sympathy. Huge walls of flames burned inside the circle, and the orange-red flames licked at the sky.

Eric threw up his hands in victory. "It is done." He bowed his head low. "And now I will finish my work at the lab."

"Not so quick, my child."

He watched in disbelief as the lady emerged from the flames, untouched. She turned her back to him for a second and held out her hands. She slowly turned them upside down and pushed them lower. The flames dwindled until not even smoldering ash remained. The lady turned back to Eric.

"Do you honestly believe there is one inch of this kingdom I am not connected to?" Her opal eyes searched his shocked face. "I am the heart of this world. Every unspoken dream. Every wish. They are all part of me." She reached out and touched his feverish face with cool fingertips. "Do you not think I know of your pain? That our hearts did not break with yours when the queen passed?" The lady brushed his hair back from his face gently.

"We all lost a guiding light. But your family suffered an especially monumental loss." Her opal eyes softened. "So much for a young boy to endure."

Eric jerked his head away. "Don't speak of my mother."

"But when you were given a second chance with a stepmother, you rebuffed her. Stripped her of her life and sent her away." The lady shook her head. "You have harmed many in your misguided quest for vengeance." She stood up to her full height and looked intently at the prince. "And now we must right your wrongs. For the path you took affected everyone around you." The lady looked sternly at the prince. "Rupert lost his first true love."

Eric shook his fist at her, and his blue eyes burned brightly. "He should have been my friend. Instead he chose Duncan over me. And then some stupid female who didn't know any magic."

"Duncan lost his mother, too."

"He didn't care," Eric spat out. "All he wanted to do was to step into Father's shoes. Rule the kingdom. He doesn't have a clue what to do."

The lady sighed. "Did it ever once occur to you that you needed a female to help guide you? To soften the edges, so to speak? To help you understand the things a father simply can't?"

"You're trying to trick me." Eric wiped his hands on his stained tunic and frowned. But his blue eyes were puzzled. "It's not going to work."

"I don't need tricks when I have the truth, child." The lady opened her hands, and a crystal sphere appeared. "There are consequences for our actions. And you have disrupted two worlds." She held the sphere up. "Look what you have done."

He peered into the ball, and his eyes widened in shock. "It's a trick! There is no truth to it."

"It is what you have done. And now we must work to undo." The lady folded her hands, and the sphere disappeared.

"Quit lecturing me!" Eric growled. "I did what I had to do."

"I've given you every opportunity, child. To renounce your actions. To show some remorse. And now you are out of time."

Eric lifted his head proudly. "You would kill me?" he challenged.

The lady sighed and held out her hand. "Come here, Prince Eric."

He walked to her against his will as if in a trance. And when he reached the circle of her arms, he stopped.

The lady folded him tightly against her and crooned softly. She rocked him back and forth gently. And a solitary tear slid from her eye. It glistened brightly in the dark cocoon of the trees. And then it dropped onto Eric's head.

A bright light flashed and enveloped the two inside. After a minute, it gradually faded and left the lady standing there. Holding a small baby swaddled tightly. Large, blue eyes stared at her unblinkingly.

"You will be cared for, Prince Eric. And taught that love needn't hurt. You've been given a second chance." She kissed the prince lightly on his cap of blonde hair. "And now we must work to give others the same."

* * * *

The lady appeared in the den of the castle. She glanced toward Duncan and Rupert. They both paced the floor.

As soon as they noticed her, Duncan rushed forward.

"What's happened?" He raked his hand through his long hair with worry clearly written in every line of his face. He glanced down at the baby in her arms. "What's going on?"

The lady looked into his face and made him meet her eyes. "Have you given the king and the mortal woman the potion?"

"Yes!" Duncan said impatiently. "Now answer me!"

The lady's opal eyes flashed. "Tread lightly, Prince. Your sharp tone is neither warranted nor appreciated."

Duncan cocked his head to the side. "Is that you talking or Ivy?"

The lady suddenly laughed. "'Twas me this time, Prince." She placed the infant in his arms. "Your brother has been given another chance. A time to renew himself. To right his wrongs."

Rupert glared at the child. "What have you done?"

The lady patted the giant man on his scarred cheek. "Ease your mind, Rupert. And put those feelings you have dwelled on away. This baby has done nothing to invoke the wounds you carry."

"He took from me." Rupert asked for understanding from the lady. "I've lost," he cleared his throat painfully, "someone who mattered to me."

"I know." The lady's voice was soft. "But your heart is healing. And there has been another who has touched it." She traced the scar on his cheek from top to bottom. Her fingers left a trail of light. And when she lifted her hand, the scar faded completely away.

Rupert touched his cheek in awe.

"There is no need for a constant reminder, Rupert. You know now it wasn't Duncan. That he did not betray either your friendship or your trust."

Duncan still stared down at the infant. "This is Eric?" His voice was raw with emotion.

"Yes." The lady stroked the infant's cheek. "Don't be sad, Duncan. He will still be raised as your brother. And you can shelter him with all the love he felt denied."

"My father…" Duncan trailed off as tears welled in his eyes. "He will wonder what has happened."

The lady shook her head. "He will understand." Her opal eyes flashed up at Duncan. "And you need not shoulder any guilt. I can feel it rolling off of you even now."

Duncan's emerald eyes shone brightly in his face. His jaw clenched against the powerful emotions. "I failed him."

"Would you be so quick to blame Rupert? Or your father? Or your mother?"

The prince's head jerked up. "No!"

"Then why do you find it so easy to blame yourself for something utterly out of your control?" She took a deep breath. "The Brothers Grimm have been uncloaked. Your father and the mortal woman will live. Your brother can now live the life he was meant to have. But there is one thing that needs to be settled. And I will not be the one to tell you what it is."

The lady blinked slowly. "I will send the children back and reverse time. Their parents will not wake up to empty beds and broken hearts."

"What is it?" Rupert moved forward. "What will you not tell us?"

"Soon," she promised. Her head drooped forward, and her hair stilled. The light dimmed around her to a pale glimmer. "Take care of the mortal. Ivy." She smiled slowly. "She will need rest. We've asked much of her." The lady looked up at Duncan.

He hurriedly passed the infant to Rupert as the lady's eyes faded from opal to brown. Then Ivy collapsed in his arms.

* * * *

Ivy shifted under the covers but didn't open her eyes. She was so tired. And her body felt like someone ran it over with a truck and wanted to try a second time for fun. She fought against the urge but finally couldn't help herself. Her eyes popped open, and she looked around.

It was dark. And she peered into the darkness with a puzzled look on her face. Then two bright lights descended onto the blanket pulled over her. Her eyes widened as the pixies stopped just above her chest and bowed.

"You have finally woken up." The male smiled. "And we have much to thank you for."

Ivy looked from one to the other. "Have I missed something?"

"No, child." The female laughed lightly. "We were sent by the Brothers Grimm to watch over you and to help bridge the worlds when the time came." She patted her silvery hair and smoothed her dress. "They will be most pleased."

"They sent us when they felt the darkness." The male shuddered. "We almost didn't make it."

The female patted the male. "It's all right, dearest. Order is restored. And we can arrive home with our heads held high."

Ivy glanced around the room. Duncan sat in a chair by the wall. He held a book in his lap, but he wasn't reading it. He stared toward Ivy.

She looked at the pixies, clearly startled. "What has happened?"

"Just a little time twist, my dear." The female smiled. "We needed the time to speak with you before anyone else."

Ivy nodded. "I know what you want me to do." Her heart lurched in her chest. "They're going to be furious at first."

"We hoped you would remember." The male glanced about uncertainly. "We realize it's a lot to ask. But it might be best coming

281

from you." He sighed. "They will be angry at first. But then they will be relieved."

The female pixie slid her hand into the male's. "The Brothers wait for us. And they are anything but patient."

The pair flew forward and kissed her left cheek. "We hope to see you again, Ivy." They turned and vanished into thin air.

Light flooded the room, and Ivy blinked furiously. The pixies must have dimmed the interior, also.

"Hell," she muttered and threw up her hands.

Duncan rushed forward and gathered her quickly in his strong arms. He kissed her hair and murmured things she couldn't understand. He pulled back and looked into her face.

"Are you okay?"

"I'm fine." She smiled. "Just a little tired." Ivy looked around. "Where is everybody?"

The door swung open, and an enormous man walked inside. He had the body of an oak tree and the commanding presence of royalty. His emerald eyes lit on Ivy, and he beamed at her. He wore a gold tunic and black pants. A gold and diamond crown kept his long, dark hair at bay. He walked quickly over to the bed and dropped to one knee.

"We are at your disposal, dear one."

Ivy blushed and glanced at Duncan. He rolled his eyes. "My father has a gift for melodramatics. Though my sentiment is the same."

King Cedric picked up Ivy's hand and kissed the back of it. "We are eternally grateful, Ivy Daniels." He kept her hand in his. Duncan arched his eyebrow.

Ivy glanced from one to the other and tried to fight back the grin. They were so alike that she was sure they drove each other crazy. King Cedric had regained his former appearance and looked no older than Duncan's elder brother.

She looked from one handsome man to the other and dreaded telling them the news she knew she must. "I have something to tell you both."

The king stood quickly. "After dinner, if you feel up to it. Cook is preparing something special for you." He glanced at his son. "We realize you have things on your mind." He turned on his heel and left the room.

Ivy watched him go and turned back to Duncan. "How is he really doing?"

Duncan sighed. "We had to tell him what Eric had done. And it broke his heart. But when we explained about the second chance, he understood." He shook his head. "I still think it will be very hard for him. Not that he'll show it."

The door slammed open again, and Rose rushed inside. Ivy held out her arms, and her sister flew into them. They clung to each other tightly, and Ivy could feel Rose's tears soak her shirt.

Ivy stroked her sister's silky, blonde hair and sniffled a bit herself. It was so good to see her sister back in proper form.

Rose pulled back and dabbed at her eyes. "How are you?"

Ivy smiled. "Never better, sis. And you?"

"Back to normal. And so is Little Brown Bear." She sighed. "He's been through a lot."

"He's not the only one." Ivy studied Rose. "Why didn't you tell me that you went to visit Rupert?"

Duncan started to stand up when Rose's voice stopped him. "Don't go. I don't mind if you're here." She patted Ivy's hand. "You seemed convinced he would eat you or something. And I didn't want to argue. I thought I had a good guide in Bear. And so I didn't worry much."

"You traipsed all over the other side of the bridge? With just Bear for company?"

"Yes." Rose's blue eyes shone with pride. "I've come a long way, baby."

Ivy snickered. "Tell me about it." She arched an eyebrow. "You and I will discuss this Rupert thing later."

Rose stood up. "I'm going to have Cook make you a tray. And Adam and Colleen are dying to see you." She kissed Ivy's cheek and walked out of the room.

A minute later, Adam and Colleen walked in. Ivy looked at each in turn. And she couldn't help but notice the looks they exchanged.

"What?" she asked.

Adam pulled a chair up to the bed. "We're miserable failures. And we're sorry."

"Huh?" Ivy shook her head back and forth as if to clear it. "What do you mean?"

Colleen grimaced. "He means we've been on a wild goose chase. There is no Brandis root. Eric planned the whole thing to get you alone."

"We're so sorry." Adam's face was chagrined.

"Don't be silly!" Ivy sat up a bit higher and looked them both in the face. "You were doing your level best to help. And we all appreciate it. There is no way you could have known what he planned." She fluffed her blankets. "Honestly. No need to blame yourself."

Adam's lips twitched. "You took that rather well."

Ivy shrugged. "There are some things that really don't seem worth the bother anymore." She glanced from one to the other. "Is there anything else you're not telling me?"

Colleen blushed. "No. Not a thing." She glanced at Adam briefly.

"We've got to go." Adam stood. "But we'll see you when you're up and about." He left the room quickly. Colleen followed.

"Something is not right there." Ivy's brown eyes were puzzled. "I can feel it."

Duncan settled into bed next to her and pulled her tightly to his chest. "They've been bickering. I overheard them in the library."

"Over what?" Ivy tried to pull away a bit, but Duncan wouldn't let her. She settled back against him with a resigned sigh.

"I'm not sure."

Ivy fought the urge to crawl on top of Duncan and lay there like a contented kitten. She shifted and tried to look him in the face. "There are things we need to discuss."

Someone cleared his throat, and Ivy looked up.

Rupert stood in the doorway proudly. "May I come in?"

"Sure." Ivy smiled. "And you were the only one to ask. Everyone else just barged in."

He walked over to the bed and looked down at Ivy. "I owe you an apology and a thanks." His large frame shifted uneasily.

She looked up into his face and realized that when he wasn't threatening her life, he was actually handsome.

"Rupert," she drawled, "I owe you an apology. And I'm sorry it's taken so long to issue it." Ivy reached up and touched his hand. "I've been rude. And I jumped to conclusions." Her brown eyes softened.

He cleared his throat. "I've done the same."

"Truce?"

"Yes." Rupert blew out a breath. "That wasn't as hard as I thought it would be."

Duncan laughed. "You've both done well. Maturity at last."

Ivy scowled at him. "I'd watch out with that whole being sarcastic thing while you're within my reach."

Rupert chuckled. "He'll learn." He bowed slightly and left the room.

She waited until he left to look at Duncan. "Listen. There are some things I need to tell you."

Duncan jumped off the bed so quickly that Ivy didn't see him move. "It can wait a bit," he said. "I have a few things to attend to this afternoon. But I'll see you at dinner." He bent to kiss her cheek and strode swiftly from her bedroom.

Ivy frowned and blew her breath into her palm. She sniffed and shook her head. She may need a breath mint, but that wasn't the reason everyone left her. There was more to it.

She focused her eyes on one of the dark, red strips on the ceiling. Her breathing evened out, and she felt a new awareness spread through her body.

They thought she would leave. Duncan was terrified he would lose her. All his emotions flooded her body and brought tears to her eyes.

Ivy's heart raced. She felt what Duncan felt. For only a brief span of time, but it was powerful. Somehow her part in this changed her. Gave her a gift she previously didn't have. The thought both scared and exhilarated her. She sat up a little straighter, but the weariness suddenly overtook her. Ivy toppled over to the side and slept.

* * * *

She woke up sometime later and found herself surrounded by her friends and family. Ivy held her hand to her head at the slight headache and scowled. "Do you feel the need to babysit me?"

Cedric studied her. "You've been unconscious for two days, Ivy. How are you feeling?"

Rose and Duncan both moved forward.

"I'm fine." Ivy pushed herself up to a sitting position. "But I'm starving. Could you ask Cook to make some of that blue bread? And not to put the pink flower on. I like blue."

Duncan's head swiveled toward her. "What did you say?"

"Blue bread. Blue flower." She rolled her eyes.

He sat on the side of her bed. "Look at me."

Ivy pushed her knowledge of Duncan's feelings down low and met his eyes.

"You're not telling me something." His voice grew concerned. "I'd like to ask you a few questions."

"Sure."

"What book am I reading?"

Ivy bit down on the answer. Even though she hadn't seen it, she knew it was *A History of the Magical World.*

"Don't know," she murmured.

He nodded. "Okay. And what did I have for breakfast?"

Eggs, pancakes, and sausage. Ivy shrugged her shoulders. She glanced over and saw Rose frown.

"And for the final question. And this one's important."

Ivy held herself very still.

"Who gave me Scout for my fifth birthday?"

"His name wasn't Scout. It was Brutus." Ivy clapped her hand over her mouth.

Duncan looked down at her with a satisfied look on his face. And then he peered into her face. "Your eyes change color. It's the most fascinating thing."

Rose blinked. "I thought I saw something. And then it faded."

Cedric looked kindly down at Ivy. "Seems you've gotten more out of the bargain than a simple trip, child." He looked at his son. "Her body needs to adjust. That's why she slept so long. And that's why she needs her rest. As soon as her body acclimates, then she can move about."

Duncan frowned suddenly. "What else do you know?"

"Nothing." Ivy felt panic well up.

"Son." King Cedric touched Duncan's arm. "Let her rest. We can speak with her later."

"I'm staying." Rose glanced up at the two men, as if daring them to say different.

"As you wish."

Ivy watched everyone leave but Rose. She glanced up at her sister gratefully. "I owe you one."

"That you do." Rose smoothed Ivy's hair back. "What didn't you want to tell Duncan?"

"Gee." Ivy grimaced. "Only that I know some of his thoughts."

"I can see where that might cause a problem." Rose tilted her head to the side. "What do you see in me?"

"That you seem to like tall, dark, and sometimes spooky men."

Rose blushed, and Ivy laughed. "I didn't have to look too hard to see that."

"What are we going to do?"

Ivy sighed. "I don't know. It's not like they've asked us to stay or anything. We've done our job. And now they may want us to simply move on and go back to where we came from."

"Adam's unhappy."

It was an understatement. Ivy read his face the minute he stepped into the room. He cared for Colleen. But there was a large impediment in the way. Snow White.

"I'm working on it," Ivy promised. She patted her sister's hand. "And what are you going to do about Bear?"

A tear slid down Rose's cheek. "I don't know. He's like part of the family. But I know he can't live with me forever in our world. It wouldn't be fair to him."

"We'll figure it out." Ivy closed her eyes. "Wake me for dinner. We have lots to discuss." And then she fell asleep.

* * * *

Ivy struggled for a second against the weight on her chest. She moved out from under it and opened her eyes. Duncan lay in bed with her. His dark hair unbound. And his handsome face tilted toward her.

She traced the contours of his perfect face and sighed.

290

"The weight of the world isn't on your shoulders, Ivy." Duncan opened his eyes.

"A bit of it is."

He moved from the bed and came over to her side. "I have something to say. And I want you to hear it."

Anxiety rushed through her body.

Duncan knelt beside the bed and took Ivy's hand in his. "Marry me."

Ivy's mouth dropped open, and he gently lifted her jaw and put it back. If he would have announced that he really was a frog, she couldn't have been more surprised.

"I don't belong here." Ivy motioned to the opulent surroundings. "I'm a fish out of water."

He gazed up at her with his heart in his eyes. "Be my wife, Ivy Daniels. Share my home. Bear my children. Comfort me when I am sad. Laugh with me. Be with me for the rest of my days."

Ivy bit her lip and looked away. "I don't want you to think that you owe me."

"Will you always make things this difficult?" Duncan turned her face back to him. He placed her hand over his heart. "Tell me what you feel, Ivy. Right this minute."

Her trembling fingers lay against the soft fabric of his tunic. But what she felt was entirely different. Love flooded every inch of her body, and she gasped at the powerful emotion. Everything Duncan felt raced through her and left her breathless.

She snatched her hand back and looked at him in wonder.

"Do you see now?" Duncan leaned forward and placed his lips against hers.

Ivy held him as close as possible. She ran her fingers through his long, dark hair and sighed in contentment. As long as Duncan loved her, she could survive in this world. And if she didn't exactly look like everyone else, then she could live with that, too.

"What about Rose? And Bear?"

"They are family, Ivy." Duncan's emerald eyes shone brightly. "They will always have a home here."

"Your father?"

"Already loves you as a daughter."

Ivy moved away with a great deal of effort. "I need to go back to my world tomorrow. I have unfinished business. And then we all need to sit down and talk."

Duncan frowned. "I can do whatever you need me to do." He looked concerned. "You haven't fully healed."

"The very least I can do is say good-bye to my friends."

He opened his mouth again, and Ivy held up her hand. "I can handle it. Send me back on the same day I left."

"Very well." Duncan lay back down on the bed and pulled Ivy closer to him. "I don't suppose your stubbornness will ever abate."

She sighed. "I don't suppose it will."

* * * *

Ivy dressed and went back to her world. She stopped off at her work first and found Missy.

"Is your sister still looking for a job?"

Missy nodded. "Sure. No luck so far. She's a little discouraged right now."

"I'm about to turn in my notice." Ivy ignored Missy's gasp. "And I would suggest that someone get her resume handy." She walked over to her desk, and Missy followed.

"You're not serious!"

"But I am." Ivy cleaned out her drawers and dumped everything in a large box. She glanced around one time. "I'll miss all of you. But I have someplace to be. Someplace that needs me."

"Will you at least write to us?"

"Maybe." Ivy hugged Missy. "But no promises." She picked up her box. "Oh. And tell your sister that a little bit of doughnut in the bottom slot of the copier is a good thing." She waved and walked out the door.

* * * *

Ivy had Duncan move her entire house to one part of the castle so she could pick through her belongings at leisure and incorporate them into the household motif. She changed into a pair of jeans and a yellow T-shirt.

They wouldn't believe what she had to say at first. And that was fine. Because she still had the proof. Her hands shook slightly as she made her way downstairs. It would be incredibly hard to hear.

293

She walked into the dining room and noted everyone was already there. Even Rupert joined them and sat by Rose.

Ivy sank into her seat by Duncan and cleared her throat. "I have something to say. News to share. And I want you to listen carefully."

All eyes turned to her.

"Everyone here knows that Eric sent the king's second wife to the mortal world."

Cedric grimaced, but nodded.

Ivy pulled up every ounce of strength she had. "He also sent her unborn child."

Chapter 14

Pandemonium broke out at the table. Ivy glanced at the king to make sure he didn't pass out. Shock clearly written on every face there.

"How do you know?" Cedric demanded.

Ivy opened her hand and showed everyone the small crystal ball in her hand. She whispered the words, and it grew to fit her palm.

It was as silent as a tomb while she waved her hands over the sphere. And then the mist parted.

"Oh my God!" Cedric leaned forward in his chair and looked at the picture before him.

A young woman with his features hung clothes out on a line to dry. Her clothes were baggy and dirty. The jeans at least two sizes too big. And the white shirt hung on her frame. But her heritage was unmistakable.

"We have to get her." Duncan's breath fanned the side of her face. "That's my sister," he whispered.

Ivy waved her hand and the ball disappeared. "I can tell you what I know. What I was told." She threaded her fingers through Duncan's.

"The girl's name is Fallon. Even though her mother didn't remember the magic, part of her remembered the heritage." Ivy counted the names off on her fingers. "Cedric, Duncan, Eric, and now Fallon."

Cedric drank deeply from his cup but said not a word.

"She is twenty-two. Alone. Poor. Her mother died when she was seventeen." Ivy glanced at Cedric. "I'm so sorry." She sighed. "She's uneducated but bright. No one has ever given her the chance to become more than she is now."

"I will go rescue her." Duncan started to stand when Ivy tugged him back down.

"No one here knows what she has gone through. No one knows what secrets her heart keeps. And no one here can expect to simply snatch the girl up and assume everything will be okay." Her eyes glowed opal for a brief moment. "You will not go off half-cocked and scare the hell out of her."

Ivy looked at Cedric. "She doesn't know she has a living father. Or brothers. Or a magical life. And though she is strong, I believe it would be too large a risk to simply bring her here. We need an ambassador."

Duncan frowned. "I will appoint one this evening."

"No." Ivy shook her head and looked directly at Rose. "I had someone in mind."

Rose's blue eyes widened. "You aren't serious!"

"But I am, sister. You are perfect. And you can ease the transition for her."

"An ambassador?" Rose flushed. "I hardly think I warrant all that."

Rupert winked at her. "You can do it."

Rose's skin reddened further, and Ivy laughed. "Yes. You can. We know it."

Cedric looked over at her. "Please, fair Rose?"

"Okay." She sighed. "But I don't want to let anyone down."

"You won't." Ivy was pleased.

Duncan tapped one of the glasses lightly. "I also have news." He glanced at Ivy and smiled. "We're getting married."

* * * *

The marriage was a grand affair with guests from every corner of the kingdom. Ivy wore the same dress she wore to the "One Enchanted Evening" affair, but a few sizes bigger. Rose was her maid of honor. And Rupert stood up for Duncan.

She couldn't believe how different her life had become. Or how much she could love one man. Ivy watched her husband mingle with the visitors and felt her heart race. *My husband.* Ivy grinned. That title certainly had its perks.

"I see that look on your face." Rose walked over to Ivy and hugged her. "I would say your husband is in for a few surprises later."

Ivy laughed. "Maybe." She looked at her sister. "You look stunning."

Rose wore a powder blue gown with a sweetheart neckline that hugged her every curve. Long, white gloves completed the picture. Her blonde hair was swept up on her head in an elaborate mass of curls with diamonds sprinkled throughout.

Ivy looked through the crowd until she picked out Rupert's tall frame. "Tell me. Anything going on with you two?"

Rose rolled her eyes. "We're friends." Her eyes found him, also. "He's scared to death to fall for another mortal. Like he needed any more issues."

Ivy fought the urge to laugh. Her sister wasn't kidding. "Are you going to be ready this week?"

"To go rescue the lost princess?" Rose grew quiet. "I'm scared I'll fail."

"Listen to me." Ivy looked deeply into her sister's eyes. "You are the only one who can bring her here. I feel it."

Rose laughed shakily. "No pressure, sis."

Duncan strode over and put his arm around his wife. Ivy tilted her head and grinned up at him. He winked at Rose. "She would have usually elbowed me by now. I can see marriage will do wonders for her temperament."

Ivy elbowed him, and Rose laughed. Duncan chuckled and rubbed the sore spot on his chest. He reached out for Rose's hand. "We appreciate what you will do. And I want you to know that we have faith in your quest."

"Thank you," Rose said softly. She kissed Ivy's cheek and faded back into the crowd.

Duncan rubbed Ivy's shoulder. "How are you, wife?"

Ivy's lips twitched. "Fine, husband." She glanced around. "But I think I may have bruised my arm earlier. I probably need to go visit the healing tub. I guess I'll have to wait until our guests leave."

He spun her around and looked down into her mischievous face. "I see." Duncan held his hands up and clapped them loudly. Everyone turned to look at him.

"Please feel free to help yourself to dinner and dancing." He hooked his arm through Ivy's and walked briskly toward the stairs.

Ivy hid her laugh behind a quick cough and willingly started up the stairwell. She waved to everyone and hurried along. It didn't help that Duncan already had his hand on her ass the entire way up the stairs.

They reached the top, and she turned into him. "Can I help you?"

Duncan's emerald eyes gleamed. "I'm here to help you, dear wife."

She laughed. "I'm a big girl. I can do it myself."

He smiled. "You're a Beauty."

Ivy's eyes changed colors for a minute. This time she believed him.

****

Crystal Inman

10/3/25

Revised edition

Crystal Inman is the eccentric, eclectic author of more than two dozen novels. She delights in weaving together Romance, Fantasy, and LGBTQIA+ themes with her own quirky twist. Her first Erotic Romance, *What He Wants*, became her publisher's #1 bestseller for three consecutive years.

A devoted reader from an early age, Crystal grew up devouring Romance, Fairy Tales, and Stephen King—making her, in her own words, their unruly love child.

Keep up with her latest releases, news, and musings at www.inmanbooks.com.

www.ingramcontent.com/pod-product-compliance
Lightning Source LLC
Chambersburg PA
CBHW030424180626
46812CB00005B/2168